PU
TH

Euterpe lay as the Earth lay, ~~been a haven for refugees from Earth,~~
the Ennead. Originally it had ~~been a haven for refugees from Earth,~~
but now it too was dying. The people on Erato, second in the system,
were determined to avoid the same fate; so all behaviour on this bleak
planet was rigidly controlled.

Isaac was an outsider on Erato, the lone survivor of a disaster
elsewhere in the Ennead, and outsiders had a difficult time of it. Still,
by scheming and bribing – by accepting Erato's rules – he had
become steward of an important household. But life remained
precarious, and to his increasing resentment Isaac's survival de-
pended on the goodwill of others. So when the chance came to rescue
a girl from Euterpe, somebody who would be forever in his debt,
Isaac grasped it enthusiastically. But when the girl arrives, Isaac's
dreams of power begin to go awry: she makes an unexpected
friendship, and in doing so evokes long-suppressed ideas from Earth
which threaten everything Isaac and the worthy citizens of Erato
have built up.

This is Jan Mark's third book. A compelling story, written with
great verve, this extraordinary picture of a corrupt and authoritarian
society marks a radical departure from her earlier novels, *Thunder and
Lightnings* (which won the Carnegie Medal in 1976) and *Under the
Autumn Garden*. Both these books and *Hairs in the Palm of the Hand* and
Nothing to be Afraid Of are also published in Puffins.

THE ENNEAD

JAN MARK

PUFFIN BOOKS

Puffin Books, Penguin Books Ltd, Harmondsworth, Middlesex, England
Penguin Books, 625 Madison Avenue, New York, New York 10022, U.S.A.
Penguin Books Australia Ltd, Ringwood, Victoria, Australia
Penguin Books Canada Ltd, 2801 John Street, Markham,
Ontario, Canada L3R 1B4
Penguin Books (N.Z.) Ltd, 182–190 Wairau Road, Auckland 10, New Zealand

—

First published by Kestrel Books 1978
Published in Puffin Books 1981
Reprinted 1983

—

—

Printed and bound in Great Britain by
Cox & Wyman Ltd, Reading
Set in Monotype Baskerville

For Neil

CONTENTS

THE
ENNEAD

Euterpe lay as the Earth lay, third planet in a system of nine that turned about the star Mnemosyne. Between Euterpe and that star were Calliope and Erato, hot and hard; beyond it, Thalia and Urania, red and black, and barren; cool Clio, cold Melpomene, and in the icy distance beyond even human ambition, Terpsichore and Polyhymnia. They had been the Muses, daughters of Memory: they became the Ennead, the group of nine, and Euterpe with her islands and continents and great oceans became the new Heaven and the new Earth.

The colonists, people drowning in a sea of people, came out of the darkness and settled like moths. More and more refugees fled to join them, from the twin evils of famine and filth, and the Colonial Government congratulated itself on having achieved the long-desired melting-pot where race, colour and creed were abandoned in the spirit of pioneering brotherhood.

They paid Euterpe the compliment of turning her into an exact replica of the world they had left, and as the refugees continued to come, regardless of race, colour or creed they turned on each other with a total lack of discrimination and fought to the death for the means to live.

The Government, despairing, vowed that the latest fleet of immigrant ships must be the last and prepared grimly to turn back the next when it should arrive. The ships never did arrive. They awaited them for five years and then gave up in grief, and relief. No one heard from Earth again: they were alone in space.

So they ceased to look homeward and turned their attention to the other planets that might support them. Erato was a rich desert, and her satellite Thamyris, named for the blinded upstart who tried to outsing the gods, a high-speed missile. Calliope was unfriendly, but her small moon Orpheus welcomed them kindly enough. It seemed that man might live again on Orpheus and the first settlers built little huts, then little houses, even little offices for the first administrators. Then some fool built a little factory. Orpheus, after all, gave them so many new things to play with. When the skin between their fingers began to turn grey they blamed the climate, shrugged their aching shoulders and closed their sore eyes.

Meanwhile Clio, fertile and generous, offered almost boundless hope, so Clio became the granary of the Ennead, the dairy, the fish-pond, and maintained by trusted simpletons, policed ferociously, shipped back her produce to starving Euterpe, while Calliope and Erato became quarries, oil-wells, mines. Clio was nourished and nurtured; they were ravaged, a just return for their lack of hospitality.

Orpheus was rendered uninhabitable at a speed that surprised even those who remembered Earth. It seemed to the sick and bewildered settlers that they saw their land through a shattered prism. The yellow sun turned to rust in an indigo sky. The grass grew in a wonderful variety of new colours, and then stopped growing altogether. One year the leaves turned brown in autumn and when they came again in spring they were still brown. They were the last leaves ever to unfurl on Orpheus, but by now there was no one left to see them; except for a feral child with red hair and attenuated limbs who walked among the dead wearing a puzzled scowl, wondering why he had been left behind. He ate whatever he could lay his hands on, first poisoning, then immunizing himself, since there was nobody to tear the tainted food from his fingers. He had always been a recalcitrant child, and he refused to die.

Erik Swenson, the interplanetary pedlar, arrived on Orpheus with a crew of daring men, to see what was left. He came upon the child in a ruined laboratory where he was conscientiously extending the ruin with a crowbar.

'What is your name?' asked Swenson, going down on one knee before the child and looking at its ravelled red hair. 'Where is your mother?'

The child had forgotten how to answer questions but at the sound of that last word he pointed with the crowbar towards a distant hut. Swenson went to see what there was to be seen and then came back to the laboratory.

'You had better come home with me,' said Swenson, weeping, and held out his hand. The child bit him, more from habit than from principle, and followed him to the ship which took off very rapidly. The little satellite was left spinning poisonously alone.

It was time to try again.

Thousands had applied to go to the new planets but the Colonial Government, finally seeing where madness lay, applied the brakes at last. No one might leave Euterpe without the certainty of work and the waiting lists grew longer as the miners came home rich. But by now the prospect of returning to Euterpe had become less and less attractive and some brave men began to establish themselves permanently on the planets. The thought of toxic Orpheus and the tales of its one survivor saved Clio from an early death. Calliope shook off the brave men with earthquakes and volcanoes, but Erato

13

allowed them to stay, and around the mines small communities began to grow up. The inhabitants were determined that they should remain small. They sent home for wives and bred cautiously, dispatching their children to be reared on mild green Clio and await their inheritance.

At night they watched their moon race across the sky in pursuit of Mnemosyne and, looking fearfully back towards dead Orpheus, dying Euterpe, lost Earth, they swore it should never happen again.

PART ONE

ISAAC

1

Isaac danced in the dust and the dust danced with him.

It lay about his ankles and when his feet left the ground it lifted like a white shadow, drifting and sifting round his knees, floating to his shoulders and tumbling in a turbulent dry cloud above the road, after he had passed.

Isaac was celebrating his fifteenth birthday. It might be the last thing that he ever celebrated. He danced in the dust.

Loukides, Sergeant of Colonial Police, looking out of his window, saw the dust storm approaching uphill and recognized the capering figure at the heart of it. The measured tread of staider citizens in heavy boots raised nothing more than flatulent puffs which dissipated in the air. Isaac's chicken-bone ankles could not support boots. He wore instead foot-shaped gloves, laced across the instep with black string.

'Many happy returns,' said Loukides, opening the shutter a little further, to let out his voice without admitting too much dust. Isaac hesitated in mid-spring, but afflicted with perpetual motion, he continued to bounce from foot to foot under the window of the police station.

'I hope so,' said Isaac. 'Very much, I hope so, so-so-so-so-so,' he muttered, in time to the bouncing.

At fifteen, Isaac was legally a man. In Loukides' opinion he would never be anything of the sort, whatever his age.

Isaac blinked back at Loukides who, massively draped in his robes of office, formed a human pyramid, all by himself. Only the apex of the pyramid was visible to Isaac; much shorter and seldom still long enough to stand upright. The dust that settled relentlessly on everything else never had time to settle on Isaac.

'Made any plans, boy?' said Loukides.

The green shadows on Isaac's white face darkened.

'Any plans – I don't – plans? I don't make plans,' he said, his fingers chafing at the window sill. 'Theodore makes plans. I don't.'

'Ah. And what has he planned?' Loukides was interested both privately and professionally. He wanted to know how anyone could make coherent plans that included Isaac and as the Government's legal arm in the township of Epsilon, it would be his duty to remove Isaac if Theodore's plans failed to include him. He was able to remain quite detached on both levels.

'He doesn't tell me – hasn't told me yet,' said Isaac. 'T-t-t-today he tells me.' He was gradually disappearing inside the dust cloud, the upper layers of which were beginning to seep in at the window. Loukides closed the shutters and Isaac turned to continue his ascent of the hill towards Theodore's house.

Theodore was out, having arranged to make conversation with Cameron that afternoon, and Isaac did not expect him back until shortly before supper. The rocky banks of the road gave way, on his left, to the high white walls of the house, cut from the same rock and relieved only by small windows near the roof, with a steel grille before each. Isaac paused, wavering on one leg, and riffled through the collection of ironmongery at his belt, spanners, keys, files and knives, while selecting the spindle that unlocked the front door.

He opened it wide, to indicate that the house was occupied once more, drew the curtain that hung in the doorway to postpone the dust, and stepped into the cool

18

hall. The late spring light of Mnemosyne already held some heat. It was making its last appearance of the day between the pillars of the loggia that flanked the hall, before sinking below the garden wall.

It lay across the carpet of white dust on the marble tiles of the hall and sank into the porous stone of the walls. Once a younger, smaller, happier Isaac would have run down the steps from the porch and skated the length of the hall on one foot, leaving a long, carefree skid in the dust. Now he took a soft broom from the recess by the front door and swept the dust outside, into the garden. It hung about for a while under the loggia, humouring him and then, when he turned his back, followed him indoors again and lay in leisurely flocks about the hall. As the dust settled, the sunlight in its turn settled on the dust.

Isaac had no time to admire the sunshine. He had many things to attend to, chief among them being Theodore's supper, which must be ready when he returned home from Cameron's, and a small explosion under the cold room, which was Isaac's own affair.

He replaced the broom in the recess and tweaked the curtain across to conceal it. The curtain was the thick, heavyweight shroud that had hung there all winter. It would soon be time to take it down and hang in its place the fine light veils of summer that had to be changed and washed every few days. Isaac had the washing of them, and of all the other curtains that hung in every doorway and window. The curtains were there to protect Theodore's lungs. In the doorway to Isaac's own kingdom, the kitchen, the curtain was normally looped back for convenience. Isaac kept one hanging there only to give Theodore the comforting illusion that the dust did not get into the food.

Today he untied the curtain sash and let it fall behind

19

him. He bolted the shutters across the kitchen window and in the secret gloom opened the steel door that led into the cold room. He began at once to cough. The cold room, usually as clean and white as a new tooth, was hazy with agitated dust. Isaac closed the door and crossed the room to the meat rack where three frozen carcasses swayed gently above the trays of fish, poultry and small joints, flown in from Clio by the Intergalactic Freight Company.

Something had happened behind the meat rack. Isaac peered through the dust by the light of his hand lamp, fluttering on the last of its carefully hoarded cells. He knew by the silence that the refrigeration unit was no longer working and the slight rise in temperature told him that the thaw had set in several hours ago; at the twelfth hour, to be precise, since the explosive had been wired to the timer and Isaac himself had fixed the wiring and set the timer. Afternoon blasting at the Omega mine, five kilometres away, began at the eleventh hour. In the unlikely event that anyone in the township had heard or felt Isaac's explosion it would be attributed to an extra powerful charge at Omega. He slid back the panel that covered the refrigeration unit and looked inside.

From floor to ceiling a narrow crack ran up the wall in a series of right angles as it passed between the blocks of stone. It was a discreet-looking injury but it had been sufficient to wrench the motor out of its mountings. Ruptured wires glinted in the lamplight. Isaac avoided them for they were still live, being connected to the generator that was housed in a small outbuilding on the other side of the wall. Theodore never came near the servants' quarters, so only Isaac knew that Theodore's father had been cheated by his builders and that the rear wall of the house, of which this was part, contained a rubble-filled cavity instead of solid stone. He turned the beam of the lamp upwards. The ceiling also showed signs of imminent collapse. Isaac slid the panel back into place and returned to the kitchen to prepare Theodore's supper.

Theodore was coming home. Isaac heard him chuffing through the dust on the road outside. He skipped across the twilit hall and waited, quivering, at the top of the steps, one hand on the curtain, one on the light switch. As Theodore stepped into the porch Isaac threw the switch that illuminated the whole hall. Concealed lights glowed and flickered in every corner as Theodore came in from the windless evening and Isaac punctuated his entrance by closing the door with a conclusive thud. Such small ceremonies gave Theodore great pleasure and Isaac thought that Theodore should have as much pleasure as he could comfortably absorb on this particular evening, and perhaps a little more.

'Cameron? How was Cameron?' said Isaac, removing Theodore's winter cloak and following him with it, dipping and swooping, while the cloak dipped and swooped behind Isaac and a dozen shadows mimed a servile dance on the high ceiling.

Theodore entered the dining hall where Isaac had served his supper on the white marble table. All the furniture in this room was made of stone. There were no trees on the planet Erato and wood was rarer than water. Theodore sat on a marble bench that grew out of the floor, alongside the table.

'Master Cameron to you, Isaac,' he said finally. 'In future, if you have a future, you call him Master Cameron.'

Isaac, hearing that his future might be extended past

midnight, twitched less noticeably. He managed to keep both his feet on the ground for as long as it took Theodore to ingest his soup.

In his inferior position, Isaac was not entitled to use his own surname; in fact he did not have one. Properly he should have addressed Theodore as Master Swenson, but since his adoption ten years previously, by Theodore's father, he had grown up with Theodore; not quite a brother, not quite a servant, always a problem.

Theodore appeared to be reading his thoughts, an unexpected occurrence, for Theodore was not a literary man. Isaac occasionally wondered if he could read at all although he was eleven or twelve years the elder, and head of the Intergalactic Freight Company.

'You call me Master Swenson, from now on,' Theodore continued, as Isaac replaced the alabaster soup bowl with an alabaster plate of meat. There was no clay on the planet. Pottery was rarer than wood. 'Outside the house, of course,' Theodore added. 'Alone we shall go on as before; if you decide to stay, that is.'

If I decide? thought Isaac.

'I have something to show you, after supper,' said Theodore. Isaac withdrew to the kitchen, bearing the soup bowl. He placed it in the sink and glanced in at the cold room. The crack had widened perceptibly.

And I've got something to show you, thought Isaac. He returned to the dining hall, hovering in the doorway to regard his erstwhile brother and perhaps future employer chumbling at his food. Theodore, dwarfed by the steep walls and monstrous furniture, was reduced yet again in the great concave mirror that clung above him where wall curved into ceiling; his father's penultimate bid for social supremacy: totally useless, utterly priceless. Nobody needed a concave mirror, everybody wanted one, so in a way the bid had succeeded, unlike the very last one which had killed old Mr Swenson and almost demolished the house.

Having made his pile in the mines Mr Swenson had initiated the Intergalactic Freight Company to support him in his old age. The intergalactic part of the name was no more than a boast since the haulage ships never ventured outside the system of Mnemosyne, amassing a considerable fortune for their owner by plying from planet to planet, but the name hinted at present expansion, further enormous gains, and the miners poured money into the enterprise as Mr Swenson provided them with all the expensive luxuries that they did not need but had to possess: luxuries that were only expensive because they were brought in by Intergalactic from Clio, Calliope and, sometimes, even Euterpe. Other things that were not luxuries were also expensive, such as food. On a planet with no natural soil the colonists survived on imports, and Mr Swenson first survived, then flourished on the colonists; always reserving the costliest, the least necessary imports for himself. Thus the mirror and the pottery that was too rare to use, and the lawn in the garden that was also the only one of its kind in the township; grown from seed imported from Clio, grown on soil imported from Clio. Theodore had recommenced to import soil against the chance that someone else would start a lawn. It was stockpiled in the city, under guard.

His father's final act of profitable folly had been to bring stone to a planet composed of nothing else. Soon every miner owned marble furniture, alabaster crockery, slate panelling and gravelled terraces. Mr Swenson, growing madder by the million, invented a new type of aerial hoist and tested it by ferrying in a block of red Thalian core stone, quarried at the cost of human life on a planet without atmosphere, and which was intended to stand as a megalith at the end of the Swensons' garden.

The property was built on the highest land in Epsilon and Mr Swenson, who had seen the town grow from the cluster of mine workings that had first borne that name, wished to see it even higher. He had positioned the hoist over the hilltop when the retro-jets failed. He and the hoist had landed resonantly on the other side of the road, neither in working order. The block of Thalian core stone had balanced momentarily on one end and then crashed full length, to land centimetres from the loggia. It still lay there since no one had the heart, or the nerve, to raise it; twelve metres of monument to Mr Swenson who had been dug out of the dust with considerable difficulty and interred elsewhere.

Isaac had sincerely mourned Mr Swenson during the last five years, for the falling stone had effectively smashed his adoptive security. He had lived out that time in accelerating fear of his fifteenth birthday, when his childhood dependence ended and he must make his own way.

Today he was a man, and to stay on Erato a man must be able to support himself. Miners' children, on reaching the age of fifteen, became heirs, a situation that could be regarded as a form of employment. Isaac, nobody's child, faced a perilous tomorrow. He stood in the doorway and watched the guardian of his hopes chewing a warm carrot, brought in at fearful expense from Clio.

Theodore set aside the remains of the carrot. In mining circles it was thought inelegant to eat the core and a ring of them lay discarded round the plate. Isaac earmarked them for his future consumption. Not being a miner he could eat what he pleased, subject to availability. In the menial privacy of the kitchen he ate the same food as Theodore but in larger quantities, since no etiquette required him to leave most of it on the plate. He needed the energy.

Theodore reached for the wine, another of his father's imports. The cellar under the kitchen was stacked with it. Isaac, seeing that the meal was at an end, took away the plates and added the remains of the food to his own meal that was waiting in the hot cupboard beside the stove. Fear had prevented him from eating it earlier.

'Bring another cup,' Theodore called after him. Isaac took down a plastic beaker from the shelf and then replaced it. On the next shelf stood a row of alabaster goblets to match the one that Theodore was using. It was, after all, his birthday.

He drew up a cast-iron stool to the opposite side of the table and crouched on it, both hands wrapped round the wine cup. Theodore had been into the study and fetched a file: the contents were spread out before him on the table. Isaac looked first at the papers where he could see his own name, upside down, and then at Theodore. Even on this most pregnant of occasions Theodore looked as vacant as ever, as if he were merely a Theodore-shaped hole in the air, eked out with incidental matter. Isaac did not like Theodore but he needed him and cursed the arbitrary fate that made someone as intelligent as himself dependent upon someone as stupid as Theodore.

'Father left no will,' Theodore said. 'He didn't expect to die.' He became aware that among the other nervous tics on the face opposite, Isaac was raising his eyebrows. Theodore frowned. 'I mean, he didn't expect to die so soon, so suddenly. Otherwise he would have provided for you. Your finger is in your wine, Isaac. As it was, I inherited everything. You know that.'

Everything. The house, the money, the land, the Intergalactic, the name. He could have left me a name at least, thought Isaac.

'In a way,' said Theodore, smiling, 'I inherited you. You were never formally adopted, you know that. As you were a child when he died I owed you a home. Today you are a child no longer, you are a man, an adult. If we look at the situation legally, you have no right to be on Erato, and if you walk out of this house tomorrow without a job, you'll have no right to stay. You know what we say on Erato – there is no room for a parasite, and a man without a job is a parasite, whether he means to be or not. You know that.'

I know a damn sight more than you do, thought Isaac. I know what's going on under the cold room, for a start.

'Would you work in the mines?' Theodore was not too stupid to be cruel. Two or three times a year the great Government ships from Euterpe unloaded a cargo of desperate immigrants who had travelled two years or more in order to bury themselves in the mines of Erato and earn the living that was no longer a right on their own planet. Diggers. A digger was the lowest form of life until he had earned enough to retire on, when he would call himself a miner and employ other diggers to do his mining for him. When the Epsilon mine was worked out, Theodore's father had bought the land and leased it to his fellow miners who settled there, so that Epsilon mine became Epsilon town. Miners were aristocrats and did not care to recall the days when they too had been diggers.

A digger was, by necessity, a short solid man with hands of iron. Isaac looked down at his own slender flippers trembling round the cup. The lowest form of life was Isaac.

'Not the mines?' said Theodore. 'What do you want to do? Has anyone offered you work?'

'No,' said Isaac, winding his legs round the legs of the

26

stool. 'No one has – has asked me, offered me – I don't want, I thought –'

'To stay here?'

'I ought,' said Isaac. 'Ought to stay here.' The next remark cost him some effort. 'I owe you so much, so much, and there's so much I can do. You don't have any others. Other servants.'

'You aren't a servant,' said Theodore.

Well, you don't pay me, thought Isaac.

'I let you look after the house because I thought you enjoyed it.'

'I do. I do enjoy it.' He took a deep breath to get him over the next bit. 'But it's work. A house doesn't k-k-k-keep itself standing. The fabric, the foundations –' He stopped and saw that some of his fear had crossed the table. Theodore's eyes widened. For all he knew about foundations the house might be floating in the air.

'What's happened?'

Isaac prepared to deliver his *coup*.

'A crack. In the cold room. S-s-s-subsidence. The walls are all rubble inside. Perhaps the blasting. The blasting at Omega has shaken them.'

'Rubble?' said Theodore. 'What are you gibbering about? These walls are solid stone. My father saw them built himself, this whole house.'

'Not the back. He was on a trip to Calliope when they b-b-b-built at the back, and you were in the city.' As he found himself gaining control over the situation Isaac's words came less painfully. 'He was on Calliope and the builders finished without him. I remember. I was alone here with the steward.' The steward who had died when the stone fell and who had never been called to account.

'You mean that you knew? You knew he'd been

cheated and you said nothing?' cried Theodore, scattering documents in sudden frenzy.

'No. No. No!' Isaac sprang up and the wine, still untasted, slopped over his fingers. 'I didn't know then. But ... but when I saw the crack I remembered. That he didn't, tha-a-at he didn't build that wall himself, didn't see it built. I've found a way in. Under the floor. I was right.'

'Show me,' said Theodore, growing calmer. Isaac followed him into the kitchen. He hadn't been in there, so far as Isaac knew, since the house was finished, eight years before. Isaac remembered the youth who had swaggered in front of the fraudulent builders, and the fragile, frightened little boy who spied on them.

'Where's the cold room?' asked Theodore, and Isaac, no less inquisitive now than he had been then, marvelled at a man who knew so little about his own house that he had to ask where the food was kept.

He led the way and Theodore followed, shivering as he passed into the charnel air of the cold room. The three carcases swung in the draught from the opening door. Theodore glanced up and stood away from the rack where they hung by the heels. Isaac ducked under them with a pleasing vision of Theodore strung up to make a fourth. He danced up to the refrigeration unit and opened the panel. Theodore examined the crack.

'There's no rubble, surely. You can see where the crack follows the stones. Only the mortar is damaged, I imagine.'

'I wish – I wish it were,' said Isaac, lying through an honest smile. Isaac had no more control over his smile than he had over his feet. Theodore did not suppose that he was amused.

'This is only part of it,' said Isaac, and tried to breathe slowly in preparation for the long untruth to come, which

28

he had been rehearsing for days, 'When I came home ...
came home this afternoon, I –'

'Where had you been?'

Isaac was ready for this.

'Down to the railway. I had to fetch up some tools.
When I came home, came back, I found the ref-f-f-
frigerator had stopped. I got the hand lamp and looked
in here, I saw the crack, I looked at the floor. There's a
hole down there. Not a cellar, not a cellar at all, like
under the kitchen. Just a great hole, under the floor.'
Isaac knew all about the hole. It had taken him several
days to make the entrance large enough to admit his
narrow body.

Theodore took one look at the gash in the floor of the
recess and retreated as far as he could without leaving the
room.

'What are we standing on, then?'

'Holes,' said Isaac, skipping about as if the better to
distribute his weight. 'I think so. Shall I look?'

'But the house is built on solid rock,' said Theodore.

'Rock,' Isaac agreed. 'Not solid. I'll go down.' With
a last noble flap of the arm he slid into the hole.

'Be careful,' Theodore called, across the room, and
Isaac continued more rapidly, encouraged by the
thought that Theodore might be concerned for his safety.
His face reappeared dustily in the gap.

'Terrible. A great hole. Bring another light.'

'Where?' Theodore, who would not normally take
orders from Isaac, accepted the command without
offence.

Isaac contrived a gasp. 'One – in – the – kitchen. Behind the bread box.' Theodore returned with a second
lamp that Isaac had planted there before supper, with a
good strong cell in it. Isaac, his eyes at ground level, regarded Theodore's boots mincing gingerly across the

floor. He took the lamp and Theodore sprang back to the safety of the doorway. Isaac dived.

'Why didn't you tell me as soon as I came in?' Theodore was demanding, petulantly. 'The whole wall may collapse.'

Isaac squatted under the floor and threw a few loose rocks about to indicate furious activity.

'I didn't want to s-s-s-spoil your s-supper,' he stammered virtuously. 'An hour won't make any difference. It may be days before we can get a builder. Perhaps I can shore it up.' He waited a few moments for the idea to take and then looked out of the hole.

'Can you?' asked Theodore. 'Do you know how?'

'As well as anyone,' said Isaac, truthfully enough, since he had already done it. He began to climb out. 'There's plenty of stuff to use.' He dragged himself out of the recess and sprawled, twitching, on the floor. 'I know the house so well.'

'Of course,' said Theodore.

'I'll begin tonight.'

'Tomorrow will do if you think it's safe for now.'

'Oh, thank you,' said Isaac. 'We ought to shut the door now. The food should keep overnight. Cam – Master Cameron will let us store it in his cold room. I'll ask in the morning.'

Isaac dusted himself violently and they returned to the dining hall. Theodore insisted that Isaac drink more wine. While he sat snuffling into it Theodore produced from the file Isaac's contract of employment and signed it. There was no longer any suggestion that Isaac might walk out of the house tomorrow without a job. Isaac took up the stylus to put his name beside Theodore's at the foot of the sheet and wrote himself into the household as Theodore's steward and factotum.

Then he lighted Theodore to bed, took his dehydrated

dinner from the hot cupboard and retired to the curtained alcove where he slept, in the servants' hall, next to the kitchen. He was the only occupant and had been since the steward died. Isaac thought of the steward and of the pallid child who followed him about: a pallid, talkative child who had, for once, had the sense to keep his mouth shut and store his knowledge until it was needed, as he had later stored the explosive. He extinguished the light and curled up on the divan, but, unable to keep still even in sleep, he continued to rotate all night.

Outside, unseen, the moon came up and cast abrupt shadows in the streets where no one walked. Between its two hilltops the stony roads of Epsilon were empty, and the shadows were empty. There was no more life in Epsilon by night than in the desert below it or in the mountains that overlooked it.

No one walked by night in Epsilon. The flat houses, battened down against each other, stood apart, cold shoulders angled against the sky.

Envious Euterpe looked over the horizon, saw nothing to covet, and sank again.

2

An early morning dampness laid the dust. Isaac swept out the porch and, detecting warmth even in the long shadow of the house, decided to discard his winter cloak in favour of the loose, light coat that he wore in summer. Behind him, in the dining hall, Theodore nibbled at the socially acceptable parts of his breakfast and waited for his secretary to arrive with the mail on the morning carrier.

Isaac was going to the city to engage builders, empowered to bribe, coerce or threaten; armed with Theodore's warrant and a contract printed on the stationery of the Intergalactic Freight Company. Theodore might be a premier citizen in his own community, Epsilon, but in the city he was just another man who needed a builder in a hurry. Builders, like diggers, were never in danger of unemployment. If the name of Swenson proved to be powerless, Isaac could bring up the big guns of the Intergalactic.

He laid aside his broom, put on his coat and capered down the hill. Loukides, Sergeant of Colonial Police, stood at the door of the police station, watching his sousofficier rake the gravel frontage.

'Well, well; little Isaac,' said Loukides. 'A happy man, this morning.'

'Isaac-at-Swenson's: Theodore's steward,' said Isaac.

'That was some luck, wasn't it?' said Loukides, stressing slightly the word luck. He had fully expected to be obliged to send the Deportation Squad up the hill instead of seeing Isaac bound down it, buoyant with office.

The sous-officier, whose name was Casimir, propped his chin on the butt of the rake and stared at Isaac with a mixture of envy and disappointment. As an enthusiastic member of the Deportation Squad he had been primed by Loukides to make himself ready for a possible arrest in the next day or so, and the prospect had given him enormous satisfaction. During the three years of his employment he had grown to hate the frenetic scuffling that accompanied Isaac's progress up and down the hill. He watched him out of sight.

'How did he pull that?'

'That young fool up at the house,' said Loukides, referring to Theodore, 'must have missed the boat.'

'Where's he going, then?' said Casimir.

'He's not going anywhere. But there's a ship due in from Euterpe at the end of the month. If he wanted to replace Isaac he should have arranged for someone to be on it, two years ago. No foresight: he must have forgotten. Still, he could rent out a servant from Cameron, even now. That gardener's got nothing to do, for a start. Cameron wouldn't mind. He did it once before, when the steward was killed.'

'You told me,' said Casimir, gazing at Isaac's retreating dust storm. 'Why didn't he get another steward then?'

'He tried to,' said Loukides. 'He booked one onto the next ship out, but he went and died of some disease about three weeks before they reached Erato. I remember the row. The whole ship was put into-quarantine and they were stuck up there in orbit for a month before anyone could land. It must have been about then that Isaac started to take over.'

33

'And now he's finished taking over?'

Loukides nodded uneasily. Most miners employed two or three servants more than was necessary in case of having to deport one for some reason. Any of Theodore's friends would have been glad to loan him a servant. Was it possible that Isaac had suddenly become useful?

Loukides beckoned Casimir inside. 'Take over for a while,' he said. 'I'm going up to the house.'

The road forked at the police station. Isaac turned right and followed it as it climbed upwards again, past the church, a long low building with metal lettering over the door: First Church Secular of Epsilon. Isaac was incarcerated there once a week with the rest of the population, to hear the word of Pastor Aumer, the present incumbent, a bag-pudding in a soutane.

It was here that the miners had their houses, hewn from the hillside on rocky terraces, most of which were laid out with Intergalactic gravel in a variety of dun colours. Such households employed an outdoor handyman to look after the gravel and referred to him as the gardener. Master Cameron, as befitted the town magistrate, had many servants, one of them a real gardener, a glum and hairy young man called Moshe; and a real garden, the terraces banked with soil. As yet, Moshe had nothing to do but dig over the earth and wait for Theodore to import seeds, hence, perhaps, the glumness. Having no plants to grow in the garden he cultivated a beard instead. It was the only beard in Epsilon.

The Camerons' mansion was spread over the top of the hill, only slightly lower than Theodore's house on its own hilltop. From the upper terrace Isaac could look across the little valley to his front door. He just missed seeing Loukides turn in at the porch. Nearby, Madam Cameron was stalking up and down on her verandah to the rustle of her robes, studiedly ignoring Isaac. Isaac bowed at her back and scuttled round to the side of the house where Gregor, the Camerons' steward, was lounging in the shadows.

'You're staying on, then?' said Gregor, as Isaac stepped into his line of vision. It was beneath his dignity to turn his head at the sound of footsteps, unless they were made by miners' boots.

'Steward,' said Isaac. 'Like you. So pay me, pay me attention.'

Gregor permitted himself to sneer. Isaac was not like him. Yesterday Isaac had been a boy with no future. It would take longer than twenty hours to establish him as a man with a job. Isaac clung to Erato as it were with his toenails. Gregor was an immigrant, specially shipped out from Euterpe with work waiting. He had been with Cameron since his retirement from the mines, seventeen years ago, before the houses were built and Epsilon was a cluster of shacks littering the hillside.

'Steward?' he said. 'You didn't come here to tell me that.'

'We – I need to store meat in your cold room. I've had to, to s-s-s-switch ours off,' said Isaac.

'It'll cost you,' said Gregor. He didn't ask why Isaac's cold room was out of commission, since he didn't care.

'Cost me or cost Theodore?' asked Isaac.

'You've got a lot to learn,' said Gregor. 'How much will you be earning?'

'Three hundred and twenty dinars Ennead a year, from today.'

'Eight a week,' said Gregor. 'Slave wages. I'll make it a quarter dinar a day.' Up till now there had been no point in extorting money from Isaac. He had had no money to extort.

35

'I can't give it to you yet, till I get paid I don't – I don't get paid in advance,' said Isaac, panicking at his first commercial transaction.

'I can wait,' said Gregor. 'I'll make it a favour to a colleague and a half dinar interest on every week or part week. But if you don't pay on the nail I'll be round to collect. Meanwhile you'd better earn yourself some. Not everyone will give you credit. How about charging fares on that railway of yours?'

'I'll bring the meat up after noon,' said Isaac.

While they were talking the morning carrier had flown in from the city and waited at the airstrip on the other side of the hill. As Isaac left the Camerons' garden Theodore's secretary was breasting the hill, laden with attaché cases. They nodded anonymously at each other. The secretary never spoke to Isaac and Isaac did not know his name. He was always identified by pronouns. Isaac was not travelling by the Government-owned carrier. He had the railway.

To save walking back and round past the police station again he took to the hill path, a narrow gully that ran headlong down, sometimes emerging over a patch of waste land where survived the true natives of Erato, the rock vines that had blanketed the planet before the miners came: tiny rosettes of leaves above ground and fifteen-metre roots that wandered down among clefts in the stone to the water beneath. The path cut under the lower road in a culvert and came out in the valley at the railhead.

It was the old single-track freight line, operated by the Intergalactic Company in the days when it still had mining interests. Although the mine was derelict, nothing left but its name, the railway was still owned by Theodore.

The train consisted of three open trucks, one of which

was motorized, and since he had become strong enough to handle the brakes, Isaac had been riding to the city once a week to collect supplies. Being small, stateless and vulnerable to physical persuasion he had always been generous about giving free lifts to other servants. Now he was in a position to charge them for his services he had a backlog of old scores to settle.

For years he had dreaded the sight of lounging figures around the trucks. Once they would have been porters waiting for a job to turn up, but since unemployment had been abolished, and with it casual labour, their places had been taken by servants, waiting to impose themselves on Isaac. Today, armed with his new authority, he stepped briskly out of the gully almost disappointed to find that there was no one waiting.

He climbed into the leading truck and started the motor with the key that hung at his belt on its own string. He felt that the railway was properly his and kept the key apart; private. He had had the forethought to fill the fuel tank the day before, either for this very journey, or a last mad dash for freedom with the Deportation Squad at his heels.

The train moved out of the shadows of the hillside and into the morning sunlight. Isaac clambered up to his favourite driving position where he perched on the lip of the truck, clinging to the brake shaft. The train gathered speed, rolling towards the hills that lay between Epsilon and the city.

He would never have got as far as the railway, of course. The Squad would have seen to that. Isaac had never seen an arrest; no one ever saw an arrest, but he knew these things were done with discretion. He would never have got as far as the front door. He looked back over his shoulder without meaning to, and then the train was among the hills.

Isaac relaxed as the trucks clacked over the old dangerous rails, and dangled from the brake shaft, watching his shadow. He stuck out an arm, waved a leg, swung from side to side, so engrossed in the antics of his *doppelgänger* that he almost forgot to stop at Lambda Crag and had to slam down the brake in a hurry. The train had once possessed air brakes, but now it relied on a claw thrust down from above that ploughed' into the loose stones between the tracks at the risk of derailment. The train shuddered to a halt and Isaac, shaken from his seat, tottered above the line. The sound of the train would have alerted Mr Peasmarsh to his arrival. Isaac frequently had to hang about outside the house, coughing politely until he was noticed.

Old Mr Peasmarsh, the hermit of Lambda, lived in a cabin in a canyon, just out of sight of the railway. A disused branch line, running into the canyon, had once served the Lambda mine in the days before Mr Peasmarsh had bought it at a knockdown price because the ore was worked out. Unlike Mr Swenson, Mr Peasmarsh had no wish to share his retirement with his fellow miners and he lived on his land in decrepit seclusion, refusing any intercourse with Epsilon, although he had once worked there. Isaac had passed the canyon for months before he had discovered that anyone lived in it. One day old Mr Peasmarsh had risen from among the rocks by the track and flagged down the train, requesting that Isaac bring him back some salt from the city.

'You're the Swenson foundling, aren't you? Under age? Not allowed to pay you then, am I?'

'No, sir.'

'Bring it anyway,' said Mr Peasmarsh and Isaac, accustomed to obeying for the good of his health, had brought it. Mr Peasmarsh had been surprised when Isaac had handed him the correct number of dinars as change.

'An honest youth,' he had remarked, and since then he waylaid Isaac from time to time and gave him errands to do. Isaac had the odd impression that Mr Peasmarsh thought he was doing him a favour instead of the other way about. On his last trip the old man had said, 'Call in, next time you're passing. I'll have a job for you.' Isaac had agreed. It didn't occur to him to disagree, although it had crossed his mind that there might not be a next time.

He left the train and followed the branch line into the canyon. Saurian Mr Peasmarsh was sunning himself on a rock by his front door, and studying a wide sheet of paper draped across his knees. He heard Isaac skittering over the stones.

'How are you, this morning?'

'Fifteen,' said Isaac, pointedly. He looked over Mr Peasmarsh's shoulder and recognized the sheet of paper as the plan of a house.

'I shall have to start paying you, then,' said Mr Peasmarsh, taking the point. 'After giving you nothing but friendship all this time.'

Is that what it was? said Isaac to himself.

'Take a look at this,' said Mr Peasmarsh, holding out the plan for Isaac's inspection.

'You're not going to build a house, are you?' said Isaac. He couldn't imagine Mr Peasmarsh in a house, particularly a house as large as this one promised to be. The cabin fitted Mr Peasmarsh as closely as a shell. There was just room inside for a bent old man to turn round.

'Why do you want to build a house?' said Isaac.

'I don't,' said Mr Peasmarsh. 'But needs must where the devil drives, if you know what that means?' Isaac shook his head. Mr Peasmarsh had come from Euterpe, but before that, from Earth. He spoke a dying language, full of strange pictures. Isaac had devils to be sure, but they harassed him under their own names.

'I'll tell you what,' said Mr Peasmarsh. 'The Government's after my mine.'

'But there's nothing in it.'

'Ha. They tell me I'm sitting on some of the best building stone on the planet, not like that cheese you live in at Epsilon. Looks like cheese, cuts like cheese, crumbles like cheese. They want to start a quarry. Two of them came out here with a proposition. I ran 'em off, quick sharp.'

Isaac could understand that. The Government was the least loved aspect of life on Erato. 'Can they force you to sell?'

'So I'm told, as matters stand now. That is, I can't refuse to sell unless I've built on the land. No one, you see, could buy back Epsilon, but my cabin doesn't qualify as a house. Then I thought: if this is good building stone, let's build.'

Isaac could understand that, too. A house would be a millstone about the neck of Mr Peasmarsh, but it would also be a stone in the path of the Government. The people of Epsilon reasoned along similar lines and had denied themselves all main services in order to keep the Government at bay.

'I'm doing the job properly, mind you. I got an architect feller out here. You know, one of those lads who draws a picture of a house before it goes up. He did this for me. He was glad of the work, too. He'd just finished a job in the city and they were about to give him the bum's rush. It tided him over; he's got another job in Delta now. They're more easy-going out there. Trouble is, this is just a boot-box like all the others, like yours, for instance. I said to him, can't you do me domes and pinnacles, throw in a few statues if you like. Bring it alive.

It was no good; he couldn't. Only trained to do straight lines. He'd never even heard of a pinnacle. Get a sculptor, says he. Where from, says I. You can't dig them out of the ground with a pick. Euterpe, says he. There's hundreds there, screaming to get out, and no one wants them. He knew all about that. He'd had enough trouble getting out himself. Scared sick of going back, too.'

'Would a sculptor be an artist?' said Isaac.

'I should say so,' said Mr Peasmarsh. 'I bet you've never seen one, though. They're dying out, like writers, hey? Have you ever owned a book?'

'I know an artist,' said Isaac, thoughtfully.

'What does he art at?'

'Mosaic. Little bits of stone, all different colours. It had to be imported – it's very expensive. I s-s-saw the invoices.'

'Money I've got,' said Mr Peasmarsh. 'Bring him along. We'll have statues and mosaics.'

'I will,' said Isaac. The mosaic artist, Ansell, was making a mural for Master Evans who lived on the lower road, downhill from the police station. The work was nearly completed. Ansell would be glad of another job: glad enough to pay commission to whoever secured it for him.

'Meantime,' said Mr Peasmarsh, 'let's get us a sculptor. There's none about, you know. You'd think, with all this stone, there'd be plenty of jobs for a good sculptor, but there aren't.'

'Perhaps there aren't any good sculptors,' said Isaac. 'There's a thing in our church, carved. It's horrible.'

'Rubbish,' said Mr Peasmarsh. 'They sling 'em out, that's why. Artists work for themselves, don't they? They get unemployed, don't they? Can't have that, can we? Sling 'em out; deport them. No wonder you can't find one when you want one. No, we'll have to go back to the beginning and bring one out. So, you go to the Immigration Bureau and get me a list of applicants, the screaming hundreds. Here's my warrant.' He handed Isaac a card bearing his signature, without which no negotiations for immigration could begin.

'We'll do some poor devil a good turn,' he said. 'Bring me back a nice long list.'

Isaac began to leave.

'And some salt. Don't forget my salt.'

Isaac returned at mid-afternoon with the salt, a fat envelope and sticky fingers. Government adhesive was susceptible to Isaac's thumbnail. He had opened the envelope and read the list on the way back to the city but he had been unable to conjure any life out of the printed names.

'How much do I owe you?' asked Mr Peasmarsh.

'A demi-quarter dinar?' suggested the inexperienced Isaac.

'Don't sell yourself short, boy,' said Mr Peasmarsh, fondling the envelope. 'Never ask less than a quarter dinar for a job like this.' Isaac pocketed the first day's rental on the Camerons' cold room and departed, wondering how much he could squeeze out of Ansell in return for a job on the Peasmarsh house. Ansell's contract was due to expire within the month and Isaac knew he was desperate for work. If he didn't find any, Loukides would be telling Casimir to assemble the Deportation Squad and there would be no way out for Ansell.

The shadows were lengthening as he reached Epsilon. Usually when he returned home from the city he had to load the house trolley with provisions and lug it up the hill. Today he was empty handed, carrying only the builders' contract in the pouch at his belt. As he walked up the hill he looked out for Ansell although he knew that

Ansell, who had once worked feverishly until sunset, now made the work last as long as possible and spent much time poring over his diagrams, indoors.

He stopped beneath the long wall of the Evans' property and admired the mosaic that ran from one end to the other, with only a small unfinished patch in the middle.

That's odd. He hasn't touched it since yesterday, thought Isaac, looking at the space. He heard the wicket gate open and Barnet, the Evans' steward, looked out.

'Who's that?' demanded Barnet, half blind in the low light of Mnemosyne.

'Me, Isaac. Where's Ansell? I want to speak to him.'

'Ansell's finished.'

'No he-he-he hasn't.' Isaac skipped irritably. 'He's still got to, to do that bit in the middle.'

'Ansell's finished, I said,' Barnet repeated. 'He's gone, that's what.'

Isaac had come to know Ansell well in the last few weeks as the mural neared completion. Ansell, much in Barnet's company, appreciated Isaac's interest, and Isaac liked Ansell's appreciation.

'He'd never go, go, never go and leave it unf-f-f-finished.'

'He's gone, I tell you,' said Barnet. 'Went last night and owed me three dinars, the swindling skiver.'

He slammed the gate.

3

A week on Erato lasted ten days and Isaac had to trudge up the hill every day to fetch the meat for Theodore's meals. Gregor tried at first to charge him for the meat, but officialdom was hardening Isaac and it was only after bitter bargaining that they agreed on a season ticket at two dinars for the duration. One way and another, the by-products of Isaac's explosion were costing him dear. When Sachiko, the Evans' cook, came up to borrow offal he was driven to charge her a quarter dinar for the loan although the meat was at Cameron's and Gregor would undoubtedly charge her as much again for the effort involved in bringing it out of the cold room. Still, she could afford it. Barnet was known to pay her huge sums for unimaginable reasons. Isaac consoled himself with the thought that at least he had a job. Not everyone had a job.

'What happened to Ansell?' he inquired of Gregor, on the morning after his trip to the city. Ultimately all information filtered through to Gregor who made use of it as best he could.

Gregor held out his hand.

'Stick it on the bill,' said Isaac, resignedly. Gregor made a rapacious incision in his account book, a slate that hung by the back door.

'Deported,' he said.

'Deported?' said Isaac. 'Why deported? What had he done?'

44

'Outstayed his welcome,' said Gregor, grimly. 'Over-ran his contract. I heard it from Barnet.'

'He had nearly a m-m-m-month to go.'

'He must have been mistaken,' said Gregor. 'They came for him the night before last.'

'But he'd made a calendar of-of-out of his mosaics,' said Isaac. 'He showed me. It was all little blue stones, except for the last day. That was a red one.'

'He was wrong,' said Gregor. 'Now what do you want?'

'Mutton,' said Isaac.

'Well you can't have it,' said Gregor. 'I haven't got time to cut it.' Isaac had to content himself with frozen fish which he carried home by the tails in a rigid bouquet; thinking, as he went, that the Deportation Squad had not been entirely deprived of their prey on the night of his birthday.

At the end of the ten days the builders arrived: a merry rabble that came roaring in on the morning carrier with the secretary, who had to endure their company all the way from the airstrip to the house. Isaac had set aside an empty outbuilding for their use, but deriding his offer they set up a prefabricated hut in the middle of the lawn and proceeded to wear a deep path across the grass as they plodded back and forth. Nearby, they scraped out a fireplace and boiled black tea all day long. Theodore saw what was happening to his lawn and muttered. Isaac understood that it was his duty to reprimand them but he said nothing. No one dared cross a builder and Theodore knew this as well as he did. At the first sign of dis-pleasure they would merely fold up their hut and leave. Contracts were so much confetti to builders.

Inside the cold room they tore into the fabric with wanton glee, drilling, hammering, smashing; while the

45

dust rolled through the house in a gritty tempest. The apprentice builder, who could not yet be trusted to destroy anything, piled the rubble into carts, wheeled it through the kitchen and tipped it out all over the lawn. This went on for a further week and Isaac sensed their keen regret when it was time to halt the demolition and repair the damage.

The little grass that was left turned yellow and brought a threat of the heat to come. When he crossed the garden in the early morning Isaac felt fire strike up through the soles of his shoes. He prepared cold meat for Theodore's lunch, left it under a protective cover in the dining hall and set out on his weekly shopping trip.

He hastened past Ansell's mural, feeling unaccountably depressed when he saw it, and made his way to the train. A person was sitting in the front truck; it was Moshe, the Camerons' gardener. He was holding a two-dinar note in his hand, evidently informed by Gregor that this was expected in future.

'Where do you want to go?' asked Isaac, climbing in beside him.

'To the space terminal, to collect grass seed. How much?' said Moshe, addressing his beard. Isaac considered. Gregor was a bully and worked for a bully. Barnet was a twister and worked for a twister. Moshe was as communicative as a brick, but not surly.

'Are you bringing the seed back with you?'

'I hope so,' said Moshe.

'Half a dinar, then,' said Isaac. Judging by the state of Theodore's lawn, Moshe might prove useful in the near future. 'I didn't know we were shipping grass at the moment.'

'Nor did I,' said Moshe. 'There never seems to be any. I keep asking. Cameron sends me in about once a month.' Moshe suspended transmission and they made a speechless journey into the hills. The gardener had been on Erato for almost a year but Isaac, who saw him often, wouldn't have recognized him by his voice. His silence seemed to muffle the wheels.

'Diddlety-tum diddlety-tum diddlety-tum diddlety-tum,' Isaac droned, supplying his own accompaniment to the jolting of the trucks.

'Why do you do that?' asked Moshe at last, when he could bear it no longer.

'What?'

'Diddlety-tum.'

'Ah. For company,' said Isaac. 'It's worse than being alone, travelling with you.'

They were approaching Lambda Crag. Isaac applied the brake with a jolt that knocked Moshe from one end of the truck to the other.

'I have to s-s-s-see a person, here,' said Isaac, jumping down. Moshe nodded unquestioningly and watched him trot away between the broken rails of the old branch line.

Mr Peasmarsh was looking out of his window in readiness. He was holding the envelope which he passed to Isaac.

'Don't try to open it,' he said, amiably. 'It's got my seal on it.'

'Have you chosen?' asked Isaac, unabashed.

Mr Peasmarsh produced the list. 'This fellow,' he said, pointing to it, myopically.

' "Hsaio Pi-Teng, aged forty-three, calligraphy and ceramics",' Isaac read, doubtfully.

'No, no. You've got the wrong one.'

'You've got the wrong one,' said Isaac. 'Are your eyes failing?'

'Young man,' said Mr Peasmarsh. 'If you want to get on in life, modify your language. I won't be a prey to

47

oculists. Nine hundred dinars per lens! Trading in human misery.' He peered at the list. 'This is the one. "Elmer Ache, aged eighteen, clay modelling and plaster casting, stone carving." No choice really; all the others are old. Like me. I want young company, not someone who's going to drop dead at his work. I don't like the sound of him though, do you? Elmer Ache; what kind of a name is that? If I was young Elmer I'd change it. Where do you suppose he comes from?' It was bad form in the Ennead to recall one's national origins, but Mr Peasmarsh cared little for form. 'He might come from the Old Country. It'd be good to hear how it goes.'

Isaac didn't think it would do anyone any good to hear how any Old Country went. Such things were better forgotten.

'Perhaps he's from Earth, you never know,' said the old man.

'He's eighteen. He wouldn't be old enough,' said Isaac. He bent his head to the list. 'His name isn't Elmer, actually. It's Eleanor. Eleanor Ashe.'

'Is it?' Mr Peasmarsh, betrayed by his eyesight, sounded surprised. 'I could have sworn . . .'

'Eleanor is a woman's name, isn't it?'

'So what?'

'This may be a woman.'

Mr Peasmarsh appeared to revive. 'May it? Well, that'll be all right by me,' he said.

'No it won't. All alone here with you? It won't be – nice,' said Isaac, primly.

'On the contrary,' said naughty old Mr Peasmarsh, 'it will be very nice indeed. I didn't know that ladies cut stone.'

'She may not think it's nice,' Isaac pointed out.

'Why not? If she can carve she can do it here as well as anywhere else. In any case, she'll have nowhere else to go unless she fancies turning round and going straight home again. And if she does, I'll sue her for breach of contract, the trollop!' roared Mr Peasmarsh.

'She hasn't even left Euterpe yet,' said Isaac, soothingly, afraid that Mr Peasmarsh would work himself into a stroke and Isaac would make nothing on the deal. 'And she won't be here for another two years.' Mr Peasmarsh subsided, coughing.

'Nor she will. She'll be twenty by then. That's a good age, for a girl.'

'It's a good age for anyone,' said Isaac. He hoped he might see it. 'I ought to go now, I have a passenger.'

'Anyone interesting?'

'I don't know,' said Isaac. 'It's Moshe-at-Cameron's. I don't know what he's like. He won't talk and he's covered in hair.'

'All over?'

'No, only at the top. Now, what do you want me to do?'

'Take this to the Immigration Bureau at the terminal. Go straight to the top, it saves time. My instructions are in the envelope. They'll give you the transit papers and you bring 'em back to me. And fetch me five kilos of barley. I'm going to brew,' said Mr Peasmarsh.

When Isaac returned to the train Moshe had removed himself to the rear truck, out of the reach of diddlety-tum. They proceeded to the city. Isaac left the train at the junction, the knot of old railway lines where the mines had once unloaded their ore, and walked with Moshe into the pedestrian subway that led to the terminal. It was the oldest part of the whole complex and once a busy thoroughfare. Now Isaac was the only person to use it and it had been allowed to decay. Tiles had dropped from the curved roof and littered the floor, the ventilators were blocked and light fittings dangled blindly from dead wires. Isaac, even in the dark, knew every obstacle by heart and he hurried ahead, sure-footed, leaving Moshe to crash about behind him.

The subway joined one of the newer passages, brightly lit.

'Grain terminal's over there,' said Isaac, pointing down an adjacent corridor. 'I'm going up to Immigration. I'll meet you here later.'

Moshe shambled away, uneasy on the shiny floor after the dust and rock of Epsilon. Isaac made his way to the Immigration Bureau and traded Mr Peasmarsh's envelope for a Government folder containing the required papers. Then he went to search for Moshe. He found him in a loading bay, trying to avoid conversation with one Wensley, with whom Isaac was slightly acquainted.

In other circumstances, Wensley would have been a wharf rat, and the need for regular employment had not suppressed his instincts.

Wensley, in Isaac's opinion, was the biggest grafter on the whole planet, beside whom even Gregor looked like an unambitious amateur. Isaac quickened his steps, eager to see Wensley in action, although trying to get any reaction out of Moshe must be rather like wooing a pit-prop.

Moshe turned to him and, for once, spoke first.

'No grass seed,' he said, blankly. 'This is the fifth time. He said it would definitely be in this week.'

'You should have asked me,' said Isaac. 'I could have looked up the schedules for you.'

Wensley joined in, his eyes shifting round Moshe and over Isaac, from one to the other, and never resting until they were safely fixed on a point between them.

'It's an outbreak of Cereal Scab, on Clio,' he said. 'The Provincial Government's slapped an embargo on all grain trading.'

'Our Government, here?' said Isaac. 'Why should

they? It can't spread here, we don't grow anything –
except grass, of course.'

'The Government on Clio,' said Wensley. 'But what's
the odds? It's all the same bloody Government in the
end. They have standing orders from Euterpe about
Cereal Scab. They can still grow a bit there, and it'll lie
dormant for years.'

'Grass seed isn't grain,' said Isaac.

'All related species,' said Wensley, who knew just
enough words to confuse his victims. 'Rye, grass, barley,
wheat, oats, corn, rice even. Nothing goes in, nothing
comes out. Sorry, wack. Even if you was to pay me . . .'

'How else?'

'I couldn't swing it.'

'That doesn't sound like you,' said Isaac. 'I'd have
thought that, th-th-th-that by now you'd have had a line
going.'

'No profit in it,' said Wensley. 'A gramme here, a
gramme there.'

'When did the news come through?' said Isaac. This
was clearly something that Theodore knew nothing
about. Epsilon's rejection of all Government services
meant that news reached the town by word of mouth.
Isaac did not relish the thought of being the mouth on
this occasion. The Provincial Government might im-
pound contaminated freighters: Theodore's contaminated freighters.

'About an hour ago,' said Wensley. 'They've recalled
all grain transports to Clio and I hear tell they're deporting smugglers there as well.' He turned away.

'Can't he help us, then?' asked Moshe, who had
heard something of Wensley from the other servants.
Whatever one went to collect, Wensley also contrived to
be there, also collecting.

'Obviously not,' said Isaac. 'If anyone could it would

51

be Wensley, and if he could screw a demi-quarter dinar out of us he would, rot him. A s-s-s-smuggler could make himself very popular at a time like this.'

'Cameron won't be pleased.'

'Nor will Theodore,' said Isaac. 'And I'll have to tell him. That's the secretary's job, but he won't even know until he gets back here tonight. Look, there's going to be a shortage of everything, from now on, until that embargo's lifted. Get me a trolley, will you? I'm going to load up the train. You've got Cameron's warrant, haven't you, for the grass seed? I'd advise you to do the same. With luck he'll be a little less cross. Go home empty-handed and he'll be chewing the curtains.'

'But hoarding isn't allowed,' said Moshe.

'Is it not?' said Isaac. 'T-t-t-tell me another.'

When the train was loaded Isaac drove it a little way out of the city and then halted.

'Why are we stopping here?' Moshe called, hanging on for dear life to a pile of bulging sacks and fearing the worst. 'Do we have a breakdown?'

'I've got some reading to do,' said Isaac. He took the folder from the bottom of the truck, prised it open and sat back to examine the contents. His own arrival on Erato had been more or less accidental and this was his first sight of the customary proceedings. He read with deep interest while Moshe sat on the sacks, plaiting and unplaiting his beard.

The list from which Mr Peasmarsh had chosen the name of Eleanor Ashe was only one of many such catalogues of hopeful diggers, builders, craftsmen, servants and mail-order brides who wanted to start life again, or end it decently, on Clio or Erato. It was reckoned that the city Bureau held a hundred thousand such names at least. When a name had been selected the prospective employer, in this case Mr Peasmarsh, was sent an entry permit and a guarantee of work to endorse and return to the Bureau where it would await the arrival of the immigrant whose name it bore. As soon as this was done, permission to leave was transmitted to Euterpe, and as soon as a ship was ready to leave the said immigrant, one of a thousand, might begin his two-year trek.

Isaac resealed the folder, signalled to Moshe to hold tight, and started the motor again. He drove now with an increased sense of responsibility that was no less real for being unapparent. He felt that he carried a life in his hands.

When Isaac reached home he found the front door locked. He parked the loaded trolley by the porch and let himself in. The builders had departed in his absence, leaving trails of dust and rubble all over the floor, and Theodore's secretary had left a disagreeable note addressed to Isaac and tacked to the kitchen table. *Master Swenson is surprised that you were not here to supervise the departure of the builders and he would like to see the detritus removed by the time he returns.* It was signed with the cryptic initials F.B. which, Isaac maintained, stood for Fish Brain.

Isaac contemplated the detritus. There was no hope of sweeping it up; he fetched a shovel. While he was clearing the kitchen Theodore came home and stood watching him, dividing his displeasure between the abraded marble tiles in the hall and the ruined lawn where the remains of the builders' fire still smouldered.

'Look at that,' he said. 'This was the finest lawn in Epsilon before they came. It was the only lawn in Epsilon.'

'They've done a good job, though,' said Isaac. 'It had to be done.' He was only too aware that the Government had chosen an inauspicious time to ban grass seed.

'Do you know how to lay a lawn?' Theodore was asking.

'I saw it done before, when this one was planted,' said Isaac. 'I might be able to manage it, with Moshe to advise me.'

He had no idea how to lay a lawn, but the new indispensable Isaac was not able to admit this.

'But,' he said, 'I don't know when we can do it. You've heard about the Scab scare, of course,' he added, deferentially.

'What!' Theodore shied away as though the scabs were on Isaac.

'There's been an outbreak of Cereal Scab on C-c-c-clio. The Government there has stopped all trading in grain and seed,' said Isaac.

'The Government! Damn the Government! Half asleep for years and then waking up to interfere when it's not wanted.' Theodore found rage exhausting but he indulged occasionally. 'What do they know about it? What harm can it do, bringing seed out here, there's nothing to infect. What's this going to do to our trading figures? Make a note for the secretary to inquire about compensation. I would have thought,' he went on, evilly, 'that you could have found a way round this.'

'Round a Government embargo? They're turning back ships to Clio.'

'Just the grass seed. It's not asking much.'

Isaac was disconcerted by the personal tone that the conversation was taking.

'Master Cameron won't have-won't-won't have any either. Sh-sh-sh-shall I try to lay gravel until ... Gravel ... Until the sanctions are lifted?'

'Gravel! I'm so sick of stone.' Theodore began to yell. 'We live on it, we breathe it, we swallow it. I grew up in a garden. I want trees, grass, flowers. What have I got?

54

Grit, gravel, dust, rock and THAT!' He flung a shaking, dramatic finger in the direction of the Thalian core stone. 'Get rid of it. Blow it up.'

'What, here?' said Isaac. For a man who lived among miners, Theodore's knowledge of explosives was frighteningly slight. He had once found a detonator and reprimanded Isaac for leaving kitchen equipment about. 'We'll have the house down.'

'Good. I hate it. Bring it down, stone by stone. We might as well be living in a quarry anyway.' He flounced into the house to sleep off his tantrum. Isaac, left alone in the garden, wandered about, thinking furiously. The remains of the lawn sloped upwards, away from the house, to the edge of the terrace at the far end and the terrace was backed by the raw face of the hilltop. Isaac climbed up onto the terrace, then onto the wall, and then down again onto the block of core stone. It was his favourite resort on warm summer mornings when Theodore was out. By noon it became a hotplate, the air boiling above it.

He walked to the centre of the block and sat down, looking about him. Behind was the hilltop, ahead the township, rising and falling on the slope, a geometrician's playground of planes and solids, angles and apices. To his right the garden fell away downhill to the plain and the Omega mine. Isaac looked to the left, across the valley where his railway ran, an innocent thread winding into the hills of Lambda and Eta, Gamma and Theta, the old abandoned mines where no one ventured except the Government, looking for mineral pies to put its finger in, and old Mr Peasmarsh, decaying in his canyon.

Isaac's mind was much occupied with Mr Peasmarsh, or rather with Mr Peasmarsh's sculptor. He was due to collect the papers on his next trip to the city and return them to the Immigration Bureau. Within the day the message would be transmitted and the wheels of Eleanor Ashe's future would begin to turn. Mr Peasmarsh was in a hurry to set them turning because a ship was due to leave Euterpe in a week or two. He wanted to be sure that his sculptor was on it.

Isaac was not much given to star-gazing. Dark nights oppressed him, but he knew that tonight, when he saw Euterpe glowering above the horizon, he would feel a link that had not existed before.

He would never leave Erato now. How did it feel to swim out into the dark for the shores of a new world? How did one feel towards the people who made it possible?

Obviously, very grateful.

He stretched himself out with his hands clasped under his neck, but the bright glare of Mnemosyne drew red blinds across his eyes every time he blinked, so he turned over and lay with his cheek to the stone. It was very hot. Soon he would be unable to come up here after the eighth hour, but in the evenings he could sit in the shade of the block. He didn't want to see it blown up. It was, to him, as much a part of the house as the kitchen or the linen room and besides, it was a beautiful piece of stone.

Called red, it was only red in comparison with the white rock all round it. It was not even as red as his hair, but a kindly pink like the skin under fingernails: other people's fingernails. His own were white.

And it was soft: easily cut but not given to crumbling like the stones of Epsilon. A sculptor would love it as he did and make it live.

Isaac sat up again.

Why shouldn't a sculptor make it live? A sculptor, moreover, who would have Isaac to thank for his escape from Euterpe. True, he would have to talk Theodore into agreeing but if he could make Theodore happy, Theodore might agree to anything. The way to make Theodore happy was to get him some grass. This suddenly seemed a small problem and already, at the back of his imagination, a figment was starting to take shape, someone he had never seen before but who held out his hands in friendship and gratitude: someone who was beholden to Isaac. No one had ever been beholden to Isaac for anything, but an immigrant owed his very life to his employer and, more particularly, to the person who found him employment. He had failed with Ansell, he would not fail again.

'Listen,' said Isaac, serving Theodore with whisky after dinner. 'I've been thinking about that block.'

'Blow it up,' said Theodore. He was still hungover from his afternoon's outburst.

'Why not have it carved?'

'Carved? Who's going to carve it? You, I suppose, you useless freak. Loukides was right, I should have . . .' He stopped suddenly and plunged into his whisky.

Isaac heard alarm bells ringing.

'No one else would have one. We'd have the only sculpture in Epsilon, except for that mess in the church. Think of the size.'

'We had the only lawn, last week,' said Theodore. 'Where would we get a sculptor?'

'I know someone who's importing one from Euterpe,' said Isaac. 'Not someone in Epsilon,' he added, hurriedly.

'I don't know. More mess,' Theodore complained. 'You'd better get some gravel when you go to the city.'

'I've just been to the city.'

'Then go again. I don't know, gravel, grass, Goverment . . . gravelment . . . gass . . . govel . . . graver . . .'

The whisky was beginning to take effect.

57

4

Isaac, alone on the train, clutched the brake shaft and rocked from side to side, intoning his plainchant: diddlety-tum diddlety-tum diddlety-tum diddlety-tum. The line rolled ahead of him in a lazy curve. Beside the track sat a dark figure, propped against a boulder; it was Mr Peasmarsh, far from home. Isaac braked sharply and the resulting clangour roused the old man.

'You look like a monkey on a stick, up there,' he said, squinting at Isaac.

Isaac had never seen a monkey. He imagined it to be something like himself but hairier, with a tail. It was a fairly accurate guess.

'What – what are you doing out here?' he asked, dropping to the track beside Mr Peasmarsh.

'Taking a walk,' said Mr Peasmarsh. His face was bruised with fatigue and his rusty whiskers rose and fell breathlessly. 'I started out well enough. Couldn't get back. Crawled down here. Knew you'd be along sooner or later.'

'You've never done that before,' said Isaac. 'Never taken a walk before.'

'Have. Often. Just because I never told you … Keeping an eye out for Government trespassers.'

'You could kill yourself,' said Isaac. 'How will you get home?'

'It did occur to me,' said Mr Peasmarsh, 'that I might beg a lift in your infernal machine. If I make it worth your while,' he said, heavily.

'The train? Can you get into it?' said Isaac. 'You look as if you might die, doing that.'

'Not till I get back home,' said Mr Peasmarsh. 'Bend down by the track and I'll climb on your back – unless that will break you in half?'

'I only look weak,' said Isaac. He crouched beside the truck and Mr Peasmarsh hauled himself onto Isaac's shoulder and then into the truck.

'Astounding,' he said, between gasps, as Isaac clambered up after him. 'How do you do it – corsets? One touch of my boot, I thought, and he'll crumble to dust.'

'Is that why you stood on my neck?' asked Isaac, starting the engine again.

'Tell me,' said Mr Peasmarsh, from the bottom of the truck. What do you do all day now that you have a living to earn?'

'I cook, I clean. I tend the garden – what's left of it. I fetch, I carry, I do what I always did. Now I get paid for it.'

'That does surprise me,' said Mr Peasmarsh. 'Why didn't he get rid of you when he had the chance?'

'I don't know,' said Isaac. 'I thought he would. He kept me guessing right up to the very last minute.'

'Do you like him?'

'No.'

'Does he like you?'

'No. He needs me.'

'Tell that to the marines,' said Mr Peasmarsh. 'An old Earth saying. Blood is thicker than water – that's another; though it might not be in your case,' he said musingly, looking at the transparent face above him.

Isaac shrugged. Both sayings were meaningless to him. 'He needed me the night the wall collapsed. It was the night of my birthday, by coincidence,' he said, cautiously.

'Didn't the old man say anything?'

'Theodore's father? Not to me. And he didn't leave a will.'

'Of course he left a will. The only trouble is, Theodore doesn't know where he left it. While there's a chance it might turn up, he won't do anything about you.'

'Why should he? He's got a bargain. All that house and only me to look after it.'

'I knew old Swenson better than either of you two,' said Mr Peasmarsh. 'We started off in the Alpha mine together. Came over in the Mayflower, if you know what that means – no, of course you don't. He wouldn't have gone without leaving a will: he liked things tidy.'

'What else do you know?' asked Isaac, finally becoming aware that Mr Peasmarsh's slowly nurtured friendship might have hidden motives.

'Have you got a Bible at home?' said Mr Peasmarsh.

'What's that?'

'A book. Perhaps there's one in that church of yours?'

'Oh, that sort of book. It's not that sort of church.'

'So I've heard. What about your hairy passenger from last time. What did you call him? Moshe. He sounds as if he might.'

'I shouldn't think so,' said Isaac, who could hear nothing in Moshe's name to suggest that he might own a Bible. 'He doesn't know anything.'

'No more do you,' said Mr Peasmarsh. 'Try asking him what Cain said when the Boss asked him where Abel had gone. Then tell Theodore.'

'Cain? Abel?'

'Ask him,' said Mr Peasmarsh. 'Now you've got one more little job to do for me, haven't you?'

Isaac stopped the train and assisted Mr Peasmarsh

from the truck and into the canyon. The doors and windows of the cabin stood open and the sealed folder lay on a bench inside.

'You should take better care of that,' said Isaac, feeling a protective twinge on Eleanor's behalf. 'Anyone could have picked it up.'

'Not very likely,' said Mr Peasmarsh. 'The papers are no use without my warrant and I never leave that lying around. You'll need it again. Here you are.' Isaac put the warrant in his pouch. 'Now, you deliver those papers for me. I believe I owe you three dinars.'

'Four.'

'I'll give them to you when you get back.' He sat down on the bed and drew the plans of his house towards him. He handled the papers as though they were a great weight and a tax on his strength. 'I may have gone too far today,' he said.

Isaac stood by the door, in a hurry to be off. 'I'll be back soon,' he said.

'Too far,' said Mr Peasmarsh. 'Too far.'

Isaac hurried past the deserted grain terminal. The porters had moved elsewhere, so he was not too surprised to see Wensley the wharf rat superintending the arrival of a consignment of aggregates from an Intergalactic shuttle.

'No grass,' said Wensley, when he saw Isaac dodging lightly between the porters. 'No grass, no grain, only gravel and grit. Fifty dinars gets you a passage to Calliope if you want to go. Ever thought of stowing away?'

'What's the point?' said Isaac. 'No one cares if you try to get out, only if you try to get in. I want Grade A blue gravel, two tonnes, taken out to the junction. I've got a train there.'

'Hang about,' said Wensley. 'Does it have to be blue?

I've got a load of the stuff at the junction already, all bagged up and ready to go. Cancelled order. Have that, it's been there for months. I can't shift it.'

'Just as well,' said Isaac. 'Theodore knows how much gravel he's got, down to the last pebble. This'll be listed somewhere.'

'He may think so,' said Wensley. 'Shall we load it now?'

'No, give me twenty minutes,' said Isaac. 'I've got to go up to Immigration.'

'Taking on staff?' Wensley inquired. Isaac ignored him and ran up the ramp that led from the freight bays to the passenger terminal. By the number of spotty, grey-faced immigrants wandering about, he guessed that one of the Government ships from Euterpe was in orbit and a shuttle just unloaded. The heavy iron gates were locked across all entrances and exits. Isaac had no trouble getting in, but no one was allowed out unless he had un-impeachable proof of identity. He cut through a group of dazed diggers in the care of a mine warden and pushed his way into the Bureau. As usual, it was empty except for the clerk behind the grille. Isaac poked the folder through the slit at the bottom and addressed the clerk through the slit higher up, ostensibly at mouth level but above Isaac's hairline.

'Entry permit and guarantee for Ashe.'

'Identification?'

He posted Mr Peasmarsh's warrant through the slit. He had absentmindedly used it to gain admission to the terminal and no one had noticed, although it bore the particulars of one Virgil H. Peasmarsh, Miner (Retd.), aged sixty-three. It would not be wise to use it on the way out.

'You've made someone very happy today, Mr Peasmarsh. Sign please.'

62

'I'm acting for Peasmarsh,' said Isaac. The clerk looked through the grille and saw his red head bobbing about below.

'Sign on his behalf, then,' she said, less cordially.

Isaac fought his way out again, through the same group of diggers who were undergoing a rigorous *viva voce* before being discharged into the hospitable air of Erato. The mine warden profited from the delay by eating his lunch.

Isaac located Wensley, up to no good behind a fish truck, and they went out to the junction. Wensley knew his way about and shunted a heavy wagon onto the line alongside Isaac's train. He opened the door. The wagon was full.

'You're lucky this lot was due to go by Government carrier or it would all be loose,' said Wensley, bringing up a mobile crane that was mounted on the rails. While he was doing it Isaac looked in at the open door of the wagon. It seemed he was seeing Wensley's hidey-hole, his hedge against hard times. The interior was stacked with crates and barrels, sacks, carboys, all standing in a fertile litter of spilled pulses and grains. Isaac prodded a sack and felt beans inside.

'Get your mitts off,' said Wensley, climbing in. He began to manhandle the largest sacks towards the door. Isaac hooked them onto the crane and they swung them over and into the trucks. The last sack caught on a projecting bolt and tore. The contents began to trickle out.

'Oaf,' said Isaac to Wensley on the crane. Then he climbed down to examine the spillage. It was not gravel that lay between the sacks but long thin seeds.

'Wensley, you double-faced ratfink, this is grass.'

'Get away.' Wensley came to investigate and Isaac plugged the rent with his fist.

'How much more have you got?' he asked.

63

'I don't know. About eight hundred kilos, I should think, and don't ask me where it came from because I can't remember. It could have been here for years.' Wensley leaped into the wagon and rushed about, pummelling sacks. 'I'd forgotten I had this,' he said, whether honestly or not Isaac couldn't tell.

'Is that why you didn't tell Moshe?'

'Moshe? Your thick friend with the furry face? He didn't ask, did he?'

'Yes he did. I was with him.' Isaac didn't much care whether Moshe got his grass or not but he liked to know how things worked.

'He didn't ask properly,' said Wensley, rubbing fore-finger and thumb together with an unwinsome wink. 'He didn't say please. My memory has to be jogged, mate, jogged. Now I suppose you want it.'

'Not just yet,' said Isaac, thinking with unwonted energy. He closed his eyes and saw green: green lawns, green terraces, Epsilon green all over. Since the news of the embargo had officially reached the township, mining talk had been of nothing else. Now that nobody could have a lawn, everybody wanted one, even those who had been perfectly satisfied with gravel. He opened his eyes and saw Wensley watching him nervously.

'If I went home and told people that I'd found some grass seed they'd want to know where I'd found it, wouldn't they?' said Isaac. 'That wouldn't do you any good, would it?'

'Too right it wouldn't,' said Wensley.

'We'll have to think of something else, then, won't we? Let's up the price a little at the same time. People will pay anything for smuggled goods.'

'This ain't smuggled,' said Wensley. 'I told you, it's been here for years.'

'Who knows that? You and me. Open that last sack

of gravel.' Wensley whipped out a clasp knife and Isaac thought he was going to pay for his cleverness with a slit artery, but Wensley only took the top off the sack with a surgical swipe. Isaac gathered up two fistfuls of grass seed and spread them over the gravel, grinding them down.

'Adulterated aggregate,' said Isaac. 'No doubt an accident. Someone's been using old sacks. Easily done. Easily done again. Some of your mates on Clio could have been a little careless – right?'

'Gravel don't come from Clio.'

'No, but grass does. Gravel comes from Calliope and the ships call at Calliope after Clio.'

'I told you already, they're deporting smugglers.'

'This won't be smuggling. It will only appear to be smuggling, which is about to become the local pastime.'

Wensley's expression became one of grudging but intense admiration.

'A gramme here, a gramme there...'

'Multiply that b–b–b–by a thousand and we're in business. Like I said, people will pay a fortune for any-thing, so long as it's been smuggled, even if it's only bootlaces. But we can't do anything yet. First I'll have to report this – this – this adulteration to Theodore...'

'What?'

'Accidental shipment of infected seeds ...: plague spreading ... I've got to set this thing up.'

Wensley's hand shot out and took him by the throat.

'You half-witted little –'

'You half-witted great lout! He wants it smuggled in. This isn't going to be our little secret. Everyone will be in on it. The only thing they won't know about is this wagon. As far as they're concerned the grass is coming from Clio.'

'Miners? Conspiring to defraud the Government?'

'Every l-l-l-last one of them,' said Isaac, rubbing his neck. 'It's the only thing that makes life worth living. Don't imagine you're the only crook around. You just have the best opportunities. We'll be in good company.'

'And safe!'

'Exactly. They won't be able to say anything and we shan't have done anything anyway, so don't go throttling your business partners. Now, get out of my train. Keep quiet until I s-s-s-see you again. You know what to do.'

'Trust me,' said Wensley.

'You're joking,' said Isaac.

Rolling back to Lambda he began to tell himself tall stories. He could afford to; the situation was saved.

He wondered about the best way to invest his popularity. Theodore was going to be happy because people were going to pay inflated prices for the adulterated gravel, owing to the fearful risks that smugglers ran. He hoped that there would be enough grass to go round: Wensley might get over-enthusiastic and dump too much seed in the first consignments. It would look very odd if they suddenly ran out. He hastily invented a smuggler called Guiseppe Mecklenberg who could be caught red-handed and shot if necessary. Clio was a long way off.

Theodore would be in a good mood for a long time, long enough, with luck, for Isaac to talk him into having the block of Thalian core stone carved by a sculptor. He must borrow Mr Peasmarsh's list and choose a few. Mr Peasmarsh had said they were all old, but Mr Peasmarsh's eyesight had let him down once. Perhaps there was another girl on the list after all. She would be young, lovely; he immediately loaned her a succulent mile, borrowed from the clerk at the Immigration Bureau, although she had never turned the smile upon Isaac. A vague but shapely figure began to develop round the smile. Theodore would fall in love and marry her and she would owe it all to Isaac. She was going to be his hedge against hard times. He applied the brake and was down from the truck before the train stopped moving. He hurtled over the tracks and into the canyon.

'Mr Peasmarsh.

'Mr Peasmarsh!'

'Virgil H. Peasmarsh, miner, retired! OY!'

He sleeps sound, thought Isaac. He went over to the cabin and looked in at the window. Mr Peasmarsh was reclining on his bed with the plans for his new house spread over him like a stiff sheet.

Isaac leaned in across the sill.

'Mr Peasmarsh.'

He pushed open the door and went in.

'Mr Peasmarsh!'

The old man on the bed did not move. No breath disturbed the plans.

'Oh, Mr Peasmarsh,' said Isaac. 'You're dead.'

He leaned over the bed to touch the corpse on the shoulder and had a further shock as he realized that although the body was still there, Mr Peasmarsh had gone. That the thing on the bed was truly a thing and no more Mr Peasmarsh than the stones all round him.

He pushed himself away from the bed and went outside again. The walls of the canyon buckled and swooped towards him, and the sky turned black. He sat down by the door and ground his hands against his eyes.

After a while he took a more practical view of the situation. Mr Peasmarsh had often spoken sardonically of that Great Mine in the Sky and now he had gone to it, owing Isaac four dinars. He would never build his house. He would never employ his sculptor.

Isaac opened his eyes.

The sculptor was officially in transit. If no one prevented her she would be leaving Euterpe in the next few days to begin a journey that could end only in instant deportation. Unless she could find another employer.

Isaac looked at the angle of the shadows. Lambda Crag pointed a hooked finger into the doorway of the cabin. It was not long after noon. He had plenty of time to go back to the Immigration Bureau and stop the transmission. He knew how delighted they would be to rescind an entry permit.

The alternative was to do nothing, to do absolutely nothing, neither to stop the permit nor report the death until it was too late to prevent her from boarding the ship. A week; two? After that he would have two years in which to talk Theodore into employing her. Grateful Theodore; although Theodore's gratitude would be nothing compared with hers. She would owe him life, livelihood, just as his dream sculptor had done: what else was there? The thought of such an overwhelming obligation helped him to recover completely.

In the meantime, he would have to go on as usual, chugging up and down below the dreadful crag as if nothing had happened until it was safe, one day, to come home reeling with shock, to report the death to Loukides.

By the time he got to Epsilon and opened his doctored sack, the seeds had shaken so far down among the pebbles that it took him a long time to find any. When he had at last collected a handful in his shaking palm – why did it shake? – he slipped it into a sample bag with some gravel, scrambled them together and set off home, avertng his eyes from Ansell's mural as he passed the Evans property.

It could only serve to remind him that he had lost the nearest approximation to friends that he had ever had. Ansell had gone; Mr Peasmarsh had gone and there was no appeal against that deportation. If Moshe was a friend, as Wensley thought, he was keeping the fact to himself. No one owed Isaac anything. If he could wait out, survive, the next two years, accountable only to himself, the sculptor from Euterpe would owe him everything.

'Eleanor Ashe,' he murmured under his breath, as though it were already the name of a well-liked friend. She was going to owe him every breath she drew on Erato. While Theodore browbeat the secretary and Sachiko blackmailed Barnet and Gregor threatened Moshe, Isaac would turn confidently and say, 'Eleanor, do this thing for me', and she would do it; because she owed it to him.

And, of course, there was the grass. His sudden exuberance as he passed the police station was enough to make Casimir spit on the gravel. Loukides raised a solemn hand from the interior.

'That boy is euphoric,' he pronounced, when Isaac was out of sight. 'Take over for a while. I am going up to the house.'

Casimir leaned his rake against the wall and took Loukides' place behind the counter. He passed the time by fetching Isaac's dossier which had been meticulously kept since the day Theodore's father had returned to his cabin with the child Isaac: the cabin that had stood where the house stood now. There were speculations about Isaac's origins and notes on his development: aged six, unsuitable for civil education; aged twelve, unsuitable for military education; aged thirteen, unsuitable for

69

vocational training; aged fifteen, appointed as steward. This last entry, coming as it did as a coda to all the others, was surmounted by surprised red eyebrows and fenced with question marks.

Isaac swung down the steps into the hall and found that fortune was looking in his direction. Theodore was entertaining the magistrate, Cameron. Had Theodore been married already, his wife would have been entertaining Madam Cameron. We'll find you a wife, Theodore, thought Isaac.

Mnemosyne shone through the glass decanter where Theodore and Cameron sat at a table in the loggia drinking whisky and discussing grass. Isaac advanced with downcast eyes and an air of disaster about him but a spring in his step, nonetheless.

'What do you want?' said Theodore.

Isaac handed him the bag of samples.

'I got the gravel,' he said and bowed towards Cameron. 'I'm glad you're here, sir. There's something you should see.' Theodore opened the bag.

'Looks like gravel to me,' said Cameron.

'Tip it up, sir,' said Isaac. Cameron upended the bag on the table between them.

'That's seed.'

'Grass seed,' said Isaac.

The two men looked at each other.

'Have you reported this to Loukides?'

'N-n-n-no,' said Isaac, faltering convincingly, 'I thought you should – shought – ought to see it first. It came off an Intergalactic sh-sh-sh-ship.'

'Is there much of it?'

'Hardly any,' said Isaac. Seeing the drift of the questions he allowed a tinge of regret to invade his voice. 'I can't think how it got there. It must be old stock. I don't s-s-s-suppose it's infected.'

'No,' said Theodore. 'I don't suppose it is. Where do you think it came from?'

'Clio,' said Isaac. 'I expect the s-s-s-sacks came from Clio with the seed already in them, and the gravel got – got – got in on top. On Calliope. An accident.'

'You think that's how it happened?' said Cameron. Isaac squinnied sideways at his meaty scowl and nodded, unable to get out two words in the right order. Cameron often had that effect on him.

'Quite a lot could be shifted that way.'

Another nod.

'Using old sacks,' said Theodore, thoughtfully.

'Shall I report it to Loukides?'

'Not yet. Mustn't worry him. I'll tell him – don't say anything yet.'

'Why not?' said Isaac, seeing that it was safe to drop all pretence. 'He wants a lawn too.'

At that moment, chimes sounded at the front door. Isaac went out and found Loukides himself, mountain-ously filling the porch. He beckoned him inside.

'This is a terrible thing,' said Cameron, stirring the gravel with a stout thumb. 'Infected seed, perhaps. Should we inform the Government?'

Isaac left Theodore to explain the situation and made himself loudly busy in the kitchen. When he came back, the guardians of Epsilon's moral standards were smirking happily at each other. Loukides drank three glasses of whisky before returning to the police station. Casimir looked up expectantly and offered him the red stylus.

'Put it away,' said Loukides, leering. 'Nothing to report.'

'I won't ask you how it's to be done,' said Theodore, at breakfast. Summer was roaring all round and meals

71

were taken in the loggia. 'And I don't have to tell you to be discreet.'

'Of course not.'

'How and where the grass gets into the gravel is of no concern to me.'

Just as well, thought Isaac.

'You understand it's a matter of principle. A blow against dictatorship.'

'Of course,' said Isaac. He walked away from the table and found himself in the vicinity of the Thalian core stone.

'How it does block the light,' he said.

'I'm always telling you that,' said Theodore. 'Blow it up.'

'Imagine it cut down ... with holes in it ...' Isaac's only experience of sculpture was the ugly heap in the church, committed by a long-departed stonemason. Had he overrun his contract too? How feckless these artists were. His sculptor would take better care. 'Think how Mnemosyne would look, shining through it.'

'Well, maybe,' said Theodore. 'We've put up with it like that for five years. It might be improved. Who did you say was getting a sculptor?'

Isaac was too light-skinned to become any paler.

'Mr Peasmarsh.'

He remembered, too late, that he hadn't said.

'The hermit of Lambda? I didn't know you knew him.' Theodore looked decidedly put out and Isaac thought of the secret that had died with Mr Peasmarsh, the key to which might lie with Moshe. Isaac had been trying all day to remember the names, but they had been crowded out of his head by more pressing considerations. For a moment he wondered if he had been unwise in mentioning the old man at all, but he would be able to set Theodore's mind at rest in a week or two.

Just let her get on that ship, first.

'The railway passes Lambda,' he explained. 'I sometimes fetch things for him; salt and that. He has a porter
out from the city, once a month, but he forgets to order
some things.' He began to hope devoutly that the porter's
visit was not yet due.

'He ought to be dead by now,' said Theodore, fretfully.
'I mean, I thought he would have been dead by now.'

How right you are, thought Isaac, and put away the
little grief that haunted him now and then.

He didn't know what to do with it.

5,

'Moshe, how do you dig a lawn?'

'With a fork,' said Moshe, reluctant to give away trade secrets.

'Where can I get one?'

'Not in Epsilon,' said Moshe. 'Everyone's digging at the moment.' All over the hillside resentful servants were at work on the terraces and Moshe, as the single genuine gardener in Epsilon, was much sought-after, for advice.

Isaac had spent a busy week since Theodore had dispatched him to the city where he arranged for Intergalactic freighters to bring in soil by a circuitous route from the company yards, outside the city. The miners, overjoyed at this chance to flout the Government, planned enormous lawns. Every household possessed an illicit sieve, for in order to get the grass they had to order enormous quantities of gravel. Theodore's business was booming.

'Why all this gravel, suddenly?' asked a puzzled customs officer.

'Instead of lawns,' said Isaac. It was so reasonable, no one challenged it.

Only Moshe seemed to disapprove, vaguely, as if some forgotten aversion to impurities stirred in him. He looked sadly at Isaac, hopping about in the soil.

'Your earth's already prepared,' said Isaac.

'Not if you jump up and down in it.'

Isaac skipped onto the path.

'You don't need your fork,' he said. 'How much?'

'I don't want your money,' said Moshe. 'Take it.'

'Listen, Moshe,' said Isaac, startled. 'I think it's terrible too, but what can I do?'

'You didn't have to find that seed in the first place.'

'We aren't doing any harm,' said Isaac, who would have liked to confide to someone the true legality of the grass seed, but dare not.

'It's wrong. The Government weren't acting out of spite.'

'You'd b-b-b-better not let Cameron hear you say that.'

'He must know it himself,' said Moshe, who seemed more disgusted than upset. 'As well as you do. You're as bad as he is and now we're all breaking the law.'

'Loukides is the law and he's breaking it too.'

'You started all this.'

'I had to,' said Isaac. 'It was me that had to tell Theodore about that embargo. Now, the embargo was not m-m-m-my, wasn't my doing. But he was still angry with me. I couldn't leave it at that. I have to be useful every minute of the day. If you got deported they'd send you back to Euterpe –'

'God forbid.'

'Where would they send me?'

'Are you from Orpheus?' asked Moshe.

'Didn't you know?' Moshe's ability to keep himself in a state of perpetual ignorance had always amused Isaac, up till now.

'I didn't think anyone got out of that alive.'

'Oh, they did. I did. I was a child.'

'There weren't supposed to be any children.'

'Well, I can't go back,' said Isaac, abruptly. 'So stop preaching and let me borrow your fork. By the way, do you have a Bible?'

'Do I have a Bible?'

'A p-p-p-person I knew – know – thought you might have. There was a question I wanted to ask you, but I can't remember what it is. It doesn't matter.'

'I haven't got anything that you could read.'

'Never mind.' Isaac felt foolish. 'Just let me have the fork.'

'What is the hurry? Look, I'll tell you what I've told all the others, only they won't listen. This is the wrong time of year for planting grass. It won't grow. There's no rain for another eight months. I've been here a year. Once it's rained.'

'The seed won't be here for another three months at least.'

'If it's planted in the autumn the wind will blow it all away. And when the rain does come it is like a flood: everything swept downhill.'

'Moshe. That grass will grow even if you have to hold it down with your bare hands and water it with your own spit. Everyone's grass will grow, otherwise the next ship that goes back to Euterpe will go back full. But there are no ships to Orpheus. Do you understand me yet? Right? Now, lend me your f-f-f-fork. I'll take it for a week and give you a quarter dinar. You must need it, living in the same house with Gregor.'

'How very true,' said Gregor, oozing out of a shadow. 'You were never a child, Isaac, not even on Orpheus. Don't you believe him, Mo. He was hatched out of an egg in the hot sand. Never knew his mother. Never knew his father. Doesn't matter though, does it? He's the end of the line. There won't be any little Isaacs, will there?'

Moshe seemed about to hold out his hand in a spasm of sympathy, but Isaac turned quickly and ran away; across the terraces and down the hillside.

'When does the ship from Euterpe leave?' he asked

the clerk in the Immigration Bureau. She consulted a list.

'It's been in orbit for fifteen days. The last shuttle goes the day after tomorrow.'

'No, not that one,' said Isaac. 'I mean the one that's leaving Euterpe; leaving now.'

'Well then, it's leaving now.'

'When?'

'Three days ago,' said the clerk, who had become familiar with Isaac and didn't like him any the better for it.

'Do you have a passenger list?'

'It won't have been transmitted, yet.' She began to look busily in other directions.

'I'm inquiring for Peasmarsh.' He still had the warrant and slid it under the grille. The clerk sighed loudly and took it.

'What name is Peasmarsh inquiring about?'

'Ashe.' Surely she knew that by now. It was not an unusual inquiry, after all. Many immigrants did not live long enough to get on board. She went into the inner office and called to him from the door.

'Ashe is on board.'

Isaac took the warrant and walked away. There was no longer any need to close his eyes and hold his breath as the train passed under Lambda Crag. He must go and discover the body.

He went into the passenger terminal on his way to collect a consignment of dried beans. An altercation in one corner arrested his attention.

He went over to investigate and found a sale in progress. A digger, travelling in steerage on the ship from Euterpe, had lost his footing and beat out his brains on a bulkhead. He had been buried in space: had he died of any communicable disease his few belongings would

77

have been buried with him. As it was, they had passed into the possession of the steerage steward who supplemented his income by selling them off.

They were laid out on a makeshift table: a holdall, two changes of clothing, a hairbrush, a bag of washing materials, a book, a razor and a coat. Isaac's fingers went to work.

'Are you going to bid?' asked the steward who stood close by.

'Very probably,' lied Isaac. He liked the look of the razor, but had no need of it. The book? It was written in a language that he did not know. He owned a hairbrush and the clothes were too large; antiquated, foreign. He was about to leave when his fingers touched something sewn into the hem of the coat. He had no idea what it might be and ran his thumb round the seam as if testing the fabric. There were about two dozen of them, like teeth. He held up the jacket against himself. It was an old-fashioned workman's coat, with buttons and revers, originally brought from Earth, perhaps, and cherished ever since. It reached his knees.

'Two dinars,' he offered.

'Stick it,' said the steerage steward. 'The cloth's worth that alone. What do you want with it, anyway?'

'Two and a half?'

'Four.'

'Three.'

'Three and three quarters.'

'Three and one quarter?' He had to know what was in the lining. He felt an affinity with contraband at the moment.

'Three and a half,' said the steward, fairly sure that he would never unload it onto anyone else. Isaac paid up and took the coat away.

On the way home he stopped the train at the Lambda

branch line. It was necessary to visit the cabin one last time to leave the warrant, and to make sure that no one else had been there in his absence. He could hardly risk reporting the death only to have Loukides roll out to Lambda and discover that the body had gone.

Unable to face the prospect immediately, he took the jacket from where it lay across the sack of beans, and ran his thumbnail under the stitches. The thread was good but old. Isaac's talon, honed on Government gum, slit it in a moment. The contraband was embedded in fluff. He raked it out onto his palm.

More seeds.

He was about to fling them away, then thought again. They were not grass seeds. Moshe would know what to do with them, but why should he give them to Moshe? He ought to get something out of this malarky besides public approval. Public approval could have withered away by this time next year but the seeds might blossom. Eleanor was *en route*, but it was still by no means certain that Theodore would agree to employ her. He needed some reminder of the palmy days. He put the seeds into his pouch and climbed slowly out of the truck.

As he walked along the rails, into the canyon, he rehearsed his story.

I run into the police station greatly distressed.

Would anyone believe that he could be distressed?

Excited.

I run into the police station, greatly excited, clutch the counter and croak, 'Mr Peasmarsh is dead.'

Let's hope Loukides is on duty. It's harder to lie to Casimir.

Loukides says, 'How do you know?'

I say, 'I went up to the house to see him and he lay there. Dead.'

Loukides says, 'When was this?'

79

I say, 'Just now, on the way back from the city.'

Loukides says, 'Was he alive when you went to the city?'

I say, 'Yes.' No, I can't say that. He's been dead for fifteen days. He'll look as if he's been dead for fifteen days. I'll say I don't know.

Loukides says, 'Don't you normally call on your way to the city?'

He wouldn't know that.

He might. Theodore may have told him.

Why should he?

Theodore didn't like it when I said I knew Mr Peasmarsh. I don't know what he tells Loukides. Oh god.

Loukides says, 'Don't you normally call on your way to the city?'

I say, 'Yes, but today I was late.' No, I say, 'I went to the city every day last week. I saw him then.' No, he was dead last week. 'I went to return his warrant.' I'm not supposed to have his warrant. No one knows I've got it.

The girl in the Immigration Bureau does.

Surely they wouldn't check on that?

They might.

Oh god.

Perhaps they won't be able to tell how long he's been dead. Why am I doing this? Eleanor Ashe, you'd better be worth it.

He was standing by the cabin. He looked in at the window, not looking, and dropped the warrant under the table. Then he did look.

Mr Peasmarsh was still there, obviously dead for fifteen days.

Isaac clapped his hands over his face and ran back to the train, his rigmarole forgotten.

When he finally reached the police station it required

no art at all to stagger in, fall against the counter and wail, 'Mr Peasmarsh is dead!'

Casimir was sent off to examine the body. Isaac gave him the key of the train and hoped he would crash it.

All over the hillside men were digging. Loukides and Theodore were standing on Cameron's lower terrace, discussing lawns. No one gave a damn about Mr Peasmarsh, except, possibly, Theodore, and Isaac was not too far gone to notice that when he heard the news his look had been one of pure relief.

No one had wanted to know of Isaac's part in the death of Mr Peasmarsh.

No one cared.

He sat in the police station, with his forehead resting on the counter, awaiting Casimir's return in the evening light. Nearby, someone was clearing a terrace of gravel. He heard the astringent rattle of stones and wondered where they would put it, and the many tonnes to come.

After a while he got down from his stool and went outside. Here too a section of the gravel frontage had been cleared and soil laid down ready for the grass seed, when it should arrive. Isaac took his seeds out of the pouch and scattered them over the earth.

'Grow,' he said. 'I can't do anything for you.'

He went home.

PART TWO

ISAAC,
ELEANOR

6

The seeds had flowered twice. Not knowing their real name, Isaac called them sun flowers because they were round and as yellow as Mnemosyne. They blossomed in a row at the foot of the police station wall, golden stars in a white sky.

The hillside was not quite so white now. It was patched here and there by slips and slashes of green; Isaac's illegal lawns. Colour had come to Epsilon.

Isaac liked the sun flowers because they were obliged to him. He had received divers favours from the miners in the last two years, especially this spring when the lawns were well established, but already it seemed that people were beginning to forget how they came to be there.

'We make the desert bloom,' said Cameron to a visitor, with no reference to Isaac. The sun flowers, however, went on shining, and he particularly enjoyed seeing Casimir having to water them.

Madam Cameron had presented him with sixteen metres of lightweight brown cloth, via Gregor, so that it was down to twelve when it reached Isaac. He cobbled himself a suit from it and sold the rest to Sachiko. With the proceeds, added to his wages and savings, he bought a pair of boots, at last being robust enough to walk in them without keeling over.

From time to time he measured himself against the kitchen wall, scraping a knife blade into the stone, but he didn't need to consult the rising scale of marks to know that he was up to Theodore's ear and able to look

Moshe in the eyebrow. Moshe was not very tall himself, but being powerfully thickset he looked large, and Isaac felt large beside him. He put on his new suit, and his boots, and prepared to meet his sculptor.

'More money?' said Theodore, when he went to request his fare.

'For the carrier.'

'What's wrong with the train?'

Isaac didn't want to travel by train in his new suit. Also it seemed improper to bring home a young lady in a freight truck. Insofar as anyone could look her best after two years in steerage, he wanted her to look her best when she met Theodore.

'I'm paying for myself,' he said. 'I need the sculptor's fare.'

Theodore nodded and took a roll of dinars out of the drawer. Isaac had sprayed the hall with water and the curtains were drawn back so that the summer sun, shining through the loggia, threw moist reflections into the study.

'Six dinars?' said Isaac. 'For me too?'

'Why not,' said Theodore. 'Come to think of it, I don't suppose she'll feel like a ride in your train. I know I wouldn't.'

You've never been on my train to find out, thought Isaac. When Theodore required transport he got his secretary to order up one of the Intergalactic freighters to meet him at the airstrip. Isaac assumed that he was making a joke. He sometimes did, these days. He had been noticeably more light-hearted since the death of Mr Peasmarsh and Isaac often thought of Mr Peasmarsh's secret, but the clues, the names, had escaped irrevocably from his memory and as such thoughts were no aid to the pursuit of happiness he put them aside.

Instead, he lay in wait for the jokes, received them

with rapture and used each one as a cue for a talk about sculpture, so that Theodore was gradually coming to think of sculpture as something enjoyable, associated with the making of jokes.

'I may not be here when you get back,' said Theodore. 'If I'm not, make her welcome.'

'Of course.' Isaac performed a skimpy bow and left.

In the porch he paused, getting the feel of his new boots, and then set off downhill towards the green and gold of the police station. Perhaps it was the reflected light from the sun flowers that made Casimir look more jaundiced than ever. Two years had not increased his affection for Isaac. He was still Loukides' sous-officier and likely to remain so until Loukides turned up his toes of all-over fatty degeneration.

Isaac turned right, uphill again, past the church on his left, the Osingas' house on his right, the steep track that led to the da Vincis, the lower terraces of the Cameron estate where Moshe also had coaxed flowers into bloom. Moshe's flowers were close to the ground, like Moshe, and lacked the debonair gloss of Isaac's little suns.

He reached the top of the hill and went down once more towards the airstrip. In the distance an Intergalactic ship was loading ore from the Omega mine, and nearby stood the carrier. Deaf to all but the sound of his new boots, Isaac was not aware that he was being followed until he reached the booking hall, when a heavy hand fell on his shoulder. Gregor.

'Now why is he all dressed up?' said Gregor, loudly enough for the counter clerk to hear. 'Is he emigrating? N-o-o-o, couldn't afford it. Absconding? No, hasn't the guts. Is he going to meet a lady, perhaps?'

'A return,' said Isaac to the counter clerk. 'And a single.'

'Who's the single for?' asked the clerk. 'Him?' He pointed at Gregor.

'I was right,' said Gregor. 'He's bringing someone back with him. A lady. A mail-order bride for Master Swenson? For you? Oh my.'

'Our sculptor,' said Isaac. 'The ship from Euterpe went into orbit yesterday and the first shuttle docks this morning.'

'How do you know she'll be on it?' asked Gregor.

'Theodore can arrange these things,' said Isaac, knowing that Cameron couldn't. 'How do you know it's a she?'

'Oh, we've all heard about your sculptor, Isaac,' said Gregor as they crossed the airstrip to board the carrier.

'Are you coming too?' asked Isaac.

'On a similar errand,' said Gregor. 'A dressmaker for Madam and a gardener for Master Evans.'

'Shouldn't Barnet be meeting him?' Just as well he wasn't. Barnet *and* Gregor. Dear god.

'He was, but then his Old Man heard that I was coming and you know how he loves to save a couple of dinars. I'll meet your sculptor too, if you like.'

'No, thank you,' said Isaac.

'Want to keep her all to yourself, do you?'

'It's my job to meet her.'

'You're devoted to your work, aren't you?'

'I don't do more than I need to.'

'Ah, but you need to do so much. What's she like?'

'The sculptor? I don't know. I haven't seen her, have I?'

'How old?'

'Twenty.'

'That's young. I thought they took years to train. That ham-fist who worked in the church was older than Cameron. Still, nice for Theodore.'

88

'That's what I'm hoping,' said Isaac, rashly. Gregor pounced.

'Hoping to take Theodore's mind off his troubles? By which I mean your tiny self. What happens if she doesn't like him?'

'She won't have anywhere else to go unless she fancies turning round and going straight home again,' Isaac quoted, dismayed at seeing his careful plot stripped bare in seconds by Gregor using nothing but his nasty mind.

'You'd better take care of her,' said Gregor. 'Artists don't last long round here. Do you remember Ansell?'

'Always.'

The doors closed: the carrier began to whine and shudder dismally. Very few people took the morning flight out of Epsilon but there were enough passengers to keep Gregor entertained. One after the other eyes, ears, noses, hair, carbuncles, warts and moles were presented to Isaac for ridicule. People who had looked quite normal five minutes before assumed grisly deformities. Isaac was still slight enough to sink down in his seat so as to disassociate himself from Gregor, thanking chance that he was the audience and not one of the victims, forced to hear a broadcast recital on the lowness of his forehead, the set of his ears, his funny eyes and funnier teeth.

He wished he had the nerve to draw attention to Gregor's moustache. Gregor had tried to grow a beard, prompted, Isaac thought, by envy of Moshe's dense foliage, but his chin wouldn't take it and he was left with a bristly outcrop of whiskers over his lip.

All one saw of Moshe nowadays was the end of his prominent nose. The rest was hidden under his hair that grew ever longer and wilder, erupting from his head in all directions. Gregor had an unendearing habit of grabbing a handful when he wanted Moshe's attention.

89

The journey that took two hours in the train lasted less than a quarter of that time in the carrier. They disembarked at the inland airstrip and walked through one of the new, well-maintained subways to the passenger terminal. A bored customs official was watching the bay where the shuttle would dock, in case some manic immigrant tried to get out in advance. Isaac went into the Immigration Bureau, closely followed by Gregor. They joined the queue of employers' employees, mine wardens mainly, Government clerks and stewards like themselves, who had been detailed to meet the new arrivals. Gregor waited until Isaac reached the grille and then took his place.

'Permit and papers for Müller and Hamble.'

He handed over the warrants of Evans and Cameron. They were returned at once with the papers for the new servants. Gregor leaned on the counter and watched Isaac.

'Permit and papers for Ashe.' The clerk looked at Theodore's warrant.

'But this permit is made out to Peasmarsh,' she said. 'Is this an illegal entry?'

'Peasmarsh died,' said Isaac. 'Swenson took over the contract. It was all arranged months ago.'

'I don't know. You'll have to wait,' said the clerk, and took the papers away. The queue behind began to shuffle and mutter, dividing its wrath equally between Isaac and the Government.

'This could only happen to you,' said Gregor.

'I bet it happens all the time,' said Isaac. 'Bloody Government!' he said, eager to efface himself by adding to the barrage of insults.

Eventually the clerk came back.

'All in order,' she said, passing the documents.

'I told you so,' said Isaac, snatching them.

90

'We can't be too careful,' said the clerk.

'Bloody Government,' cried the queue, in chorus.

During the delay the shuttle had docked. Isaac and Gregor, coming out of the Bureau, found themselves in a maelstrom: mine wardens looking for diggers, clerks looking for clerks, stewards looking for servants. The newly-hatched immigrants stood in speechless huddles, some gazing with confidence at this brave new world, others with terror, wishing perhaps that they had never left the old one.

This terminal was the real melting pot, a stew of men and women of all kinds and colours whom deprivation had turned a uniform shade of grey; all stooped, all shuffling, except for the very tall who loped about uncertainly as if expecting their knee joints to turn disloyally and bend the other way.

Red-eyed, pallid, stippled with spots, they stared perplexed at the uniformed men massed against them, at the great gates locked against them.

The confusion began to resolve itself. The warden from the Omikron mine found the Omikron diggers, the Tau warden found the Tau diggers: one by one the immigrants identified themselves and were herded away.

Gregor became impatient.

'Sheep!'

'When did you last see a sheep?'

'Where's that gardener? How am I supposed to find him in this mob?'

'Look for someone with earth on his boots,' said Isaac, who had decided that the easiest way to identify his sculptor was to wait until there was only one person left. He withdrew against the wall.

'Pssssst!'

Wensley the wharf rat was addressing him from behind the gate that led to the freight bays.

'What do you want?' said Isaac, faintly surprised, as he always was, to find that Wensley was still at large.

'Long time, no see.'

Isaac had thought it prudent to stay away from Wensley after the grass-running episode and they seldom met. Wensley was the link in the chain that Epsilon knew nothing about; front man for the ephemeral Giuseppe Mecklenberg. They had done extremely well out of it, dividing Giuseppe's earnings between them, and it would not do to let anyone find out exactly what had happened, or rather, hadn't happened.

'Hiring and firing?'

'Hiring,' said Isaac. 'A sculptor.'

'That won't last long,' said Wensley. 'One deported last week – caught hiding out in the city after his contract expired. When they got him in here he broke away from the Squad and got down among the loading bays. Fell under a truck – or chucked himself.'

'Killed?'

'What do you think? You've seen those trucks. Still, I suppose anything's better than going back to Euterpe.'

'Where were they taking him? There was no ship in, last week.'

'There's always ships, matey. You should know.'

'Intergalactic?' Of course he had known, or had he? Theodore doing his duty to the community by allowing deportees to be transported on his ships. This was a cargo that never appeared on the invoices.

'You'd best make sure your sculptor knows what they think of artists round here.'

'Mine won't be deported,' said Isaac.

'Take good care of him, then.'

'It's a her.'

'Really? Hot stuff, my son,' said Wensley. 'How did you swing that?'

'Low cunning,' said Isaac, honestly.

'Have fun,' said Wensley and sidled guiltily away as he always did, even when there was no need.

Gregor came up towing his two charges; a tall man and a short woman.

'Heinrich Müller, Margaret Hamble – Isaac-at-Swenson's. We're going on the town,' said Gregor. 'There's two hours before the carrier leaves.'

'It'll take you two hours to get them through the gate,' said Isaac.

'Not me,' said Gregor, flourishing a fan of notes. 'See you later.' They walked off, the gardener beaming at the thought of what a good bloke this Gregor had turned out to be, the dressmaker looking altogether more shrewd.

The crowd had left the body of the terminal and become five separate crowds at the exit gates. Isaac watched Gregor bribe his way to the head of the queue and then turned his attention to the immigrants who remained. There were very few of them left and most of them had gathered in the middle of the hall, clutching the holdalls that were the only luggage they were allowed. Isaac ran his eye over them.

Three women, two young, one middle-aged, were pressed together in the centre of a bench. Beyond them five squat, short-legged men, obviously diggers, stood defiant. None of them spoke but they were all asking themselves the same question. What happens if nobody claims us? On the next bench a youth with dirty hair and enviable leather boots had carried nonchalance to the uttermost by falling asleep, his legs stretched across the gangway, and his feet propped on a square leather bag.

Isaac stepped over the boots and was about to approach the women when an uproar broke out at one

of the gates. Among the jostling bodies Isaac saw the
black uniforms of a Deportation Squad and the sight
made him draw back, in common with everyone else;
even the immigrants who didn't understand the significance of what they saw. He tripped over the boots whose
owner woke up swearing and removed himself and his
baggage to a safer place. His hands were filthy, too,
although the boots were polished like marble.

The Deportation Squad broke out of the crowd and
advanced towards the gate where the shuttle stood
waiting. There were six of them and in the centre walked
another man, dazed and handcuffed, with a bruised jaw.
Isaac made sure that it was no one he knew and turned
his head aside, unwilling to see the gates clash shut
behind the Squad as they boarded the shuttle.

One of the diggers accosted Isaac.

'What's he done, then?'

'How should I know?' said Isaac. 'He's probably
lost his job,' he said, without thinking of the effect this
information might have. 'Or overrun his contract.'
Ansell had overrun his contract. Was this how Ansell
had left Erato?

He went up to the three women who were gazing
in terror at the gates of the shuttle.

'What did he do?' asked the older one.

'A common criminal, ma'am,' said Isaac, bowing.
You won't be ma'am much longer, he added, to himself.
You're a cook if ever I saw one. He smiled at the girls.
'Is either of you Eleanor Ashe?' Unfortunately, for they
were both pretty under the spots, they shook their heads.

'Eleanor Ashe?' he asked again, in case fear had made
them half-witted. 'Is one of you a sculptor?' The very
idea made them giggle.

Half-witted in any case.

Isaac left them wittering and tried the guard at the

shuttle. He was standing under a poster put up to welcome, or warn.

ONE MAN, ONE JOB
NO UNEMPLOYMENT

'Has Eleanor Ashe landed?' He was becoming nervous. Perhaps she hadn't boarded the shuttle in spite of his arrangements. Perhaps she had died in space like the steward who never arrived. The guard looked at his list.

'Well,' he said. 'She got on and she's not likely to have got off half-way. Maybe she's got in with the wrong lot. Check at the exit gates. You've got her permit and she won't get out without it.'

'Did you notice what she was like?'

'Have a heart,' said the guard. 'There were nigh on a thousand people in that steerage and a hundred came down on the shuttle. Would you remember one above the others?'

'She's a sculptor.'

'In that case,' said the guard, 'I wouldn't have gone near her. They've got the kiss of death on them, those types. People stay away from them – in case it's catching, if you see what I mean. I don't know what it is about artists. For every one we bring out here we seem to take two back. I don't know why your people hire them.'

'We aren't savages,' said Isaac. 'We like art.'

'You don't like it enough, it seems to me. Why bring the poor devils out here if you don't want them to stay? Diggers don't get sent back. Or doctors. Funny that, isn't it?'

'Diggers and doctors don't run out of work. Anyone without work gets sent back, it isn't just artists.'

'No unemployment,' said the guard, slapping the poster. 'That sounds nice, doesn't it? Especially if you've

95

never been able to get a job in your life. Come to Erato where work is waiting, it says. Erato welcomes workers. One man, one job. It strikes me that you and I interpret that differently. Unemployment is illegal on Erato – they don't explain how it's done.'

'Don't blame me,' said Isaac. 'I only work here. I'd better go round again, she must be somewhere.'

He went across to the exit gates. Two were completely cleared and the others were almost empty. There were only a few women left, already ill at ease in their foreign clothes, the short dresses and coats that looked mean beside the long sun-resisting robes of Erato. Isaac hurried from one woman to the next, brandishing the permit.

'Eleanor Ashe? Excuse me, Eleanor Ashe?' He was beginning to think that it was a rotten name anyway.

'Go outside, you're not supposed to do that in here,' said a mine warden who thought he was recruiting for immoral purposes.

A laugh broke out among the immigrants; a ragged, half-tearful laugh, but they were glad to let it go; the first laugh on Erato.

Isaac, startled, backed off. People were less inclined to laugh at him these days and to find himself once more a butt came as a shock. He went angrily to the benches in the centre of the hall, colliding again with the dingy young man.

'Why don't you put your feet elsewhere?' he asked, thinking revengefully that anyone with legs that long was going to regret a career in the mines.

The young man planted his boots on the floor and stood up, grabbing for the handle of his leather bag and lifting it as he rose. Isaac thought he was going to brain him with it and side-stepped.

'You wouldn't be looking for me, would you?' said the young man. From small, hostile eyes he stared down at Isaac over the scarp of a high-bridged nose. Isaac looked at the archipelago of spots across his jaw and reflected that no one in that condition could do much damage.

'No, I wouldn't,' he said, disagreeably, returning the stare with a scowl that deepened as he realized that it wasn't a young man; not a man at all.

'Oh god,' said Isaac, and sat down heavily on the bench.

'Are you looking for me?'

'I hope not,' he said, without hope. He looked round, but the other benches were empty. There was no longer anyone left to choose from. He thought he had made a reasonable mistake. She was wearing a heavy workman's shirt, belted over trousers which were tucked into the tops of the boots that Isaac had so admired. They seemed less admirable on a woman. Ladies on Erato wore neither boots nor trousers. Legs were out of fashion although Isaac had known city girls show their knees when they ran.

'Are you a sculptor?'

'Yes.'

'You've come to work for Virgil Peasmarsh?'

'Yes.'

'You are Eleanor Ashe?' The very last of the magic in the name trickled away.

'Yes I am.' Now he had heard the worst Isaac had time to be angry.

'I've been running round this place for the last half hour looking for you. Didn't you hear me?'

'Are you Peasmarsh?'

'No,' said Isaac. 'Peasmarsh is dead.'

This was the bad news, preserved to wait on his perfect timing and he had let it go too soon. He had meant to pay it out gently, with tender sympathy for her plight,

97

watch her break and then mend her with tenderer assur-
ances that he had taken her future in hand. Instead she
stood before him, feet apart like a pair of calipers, and
said, 'Do you mean I have to go back?'

Now was the moment when the investment should
have begun to pay interest, but it was in the wrong
currency. In a voice that held nothing but threats she
said again, 'Have you come here to tell me that I have
to go back?'

At the back of his imagination a figment began to
dwindle away; a tremulous, tearful little figment with
upraised, pleading hands. Eleanor's hands were like
mechanical grabs. Her sleeves were pushed back, reveal-
ing a granite ridge of muscle along each forearm, that
ended in a fan vault of tendons between wrist and
knuckle. A stone carver's hands.

'You haven't to go back,' he said. He stood up. She
was much bigger than he was.

'What have I to do then?' she said, cutting in on
him before he was fairly in his stride. 'Stay here and
carve up the floor?'

The protective arm which he had held in readiness
was tensing into a weapon of destruction. More than
anything he wanted to punch her in the teeth. 'Listen,'
he said. 'Listen, I've got you another job. You won't
have to go back. I persuaded my employer to take over
your contract.'

Now fall on your knees in gratitude and thank me
with tears in your eyes.

'Peasmarsh is dead?'

'It doesn't matter,' said Isaac. 'I've got work for you.
You won't be sent back.' He realized at last that
he had indeed shocked her horribly and that she
had failed him only in being unable to show it, but

his plans had gone too far awry to be put back together.

'Sit down,' he said. He took her by the arm and pushed her towards the bench. The bag slipped from her hands and hit the ground between them. 'What have you got in there?' It sounded like spanners and certainly weighed more than the regulation ten kilos per passenger that was all the ships permitted. He bent to pick it up but the hands were there first.

'Get off it.' She knocked his own hand away and he felt a kind of unhealthy strength in the blow.

'You don't have to stay,' said Isaac, savagely. 'If you don't like it here you can turn round and go straight back again. No one says you must stay.'

It would be very easy at this moment to leave her sitting there and walk over to the guard at the gate. There's been a mistake. This young woman has no work after all. Then he could go away quickly before they called the Deportation Squad, and return home to report to Theodore that the sculptor had unfortunately died in transit. No one would mind particularly, and given a day or so it might be true. Immigrants came out of steerage in a weakened condition, and going back again might finish her off. But Isaac had lied about death before and no good had come of it. That was why he was here.

He had a sudden vision of the boots standing forlornly on a makeshift table in the corner of the terminal, while a steerage steward stood nearby, selling off the contents of the black leather bag.

'We'd better be going,' he said. 'Have you got your landing card?' She drew it out of a pocket and gave it to him and stood up again, still clinging to the bag. Although thin she was very wide across the shoulders. The thought of Theodore making advances to this monolith caused him an angry snigger.

99

'Are you laughing at me?'

'Oh god, no,' said Isaac. He nudged her towards the gate.

He was passed through without any trouble. Eleanor was detained on the other side and systematically relieved of any small dignity she might have tried to smuggle in, by two guards who evidently shared Gregor's sense of fun. Isaac hoped they might demand to see inside the leather bag but they were more concerned with her appearance which, he thought, hardly needed advertising. At last the gate opened and she was allowed out.

'You got off lightly,' he said, thinking of the bag..

'What's the heavy mob like, then?' said Eleanor, almost concussed with fury. 'What was that for? Why do they do it?'

'What, make a fool of you? They'd do it to everyone if they had the time. We were the last. It's your own fault, you should have spoken up when I called you. Anyway, they were right,' he went on, brutally. 'If you go about looking like that you must expect to be noticed.'

'But,' said Eleanor. 'Two years in steerage. Everybody looks like this.'

'They don't,' said Isaac. He wondered when she had last looked in a mirror. She had certainly cut her hair without the aid of one. It was gnawed off short and hung in ragged fronds, possibly brown, possibly not. 'Come on, we'll be late for the carrier.'

'Where are we going?'

'I told you, to the carrier. We aren't going to walk home. Now, wait here,' he said, steering her against a pillar. 'I'm just going to find a friend of mine.' He meant Gregor. The exact nature of the friendship was too complicated to explain.

' "Erato welcomes workers",' said Eleanor, reading

100

aloud from a nearby poster. 'I suppose they put that there to remind people who haven't noticed.'

Isaac left her and ran up the steps to the front entrance. In the old days, when miners were miners, there had been some attempt made to improve the frontage with lawns and bushes and decorative stone work, courtesy of the Intergalactic Freight Company which had needed the publicity in those pioneering times. Now that miners were diggers the lawns were bald, the stone eroded, the bushes expiring in unpainted tubs. Isaac looked up and down the road for Gregor and his company but his view was blocked by a traffic jam of trucks and pedestrians. The only people he recognized were the members of the Deportation Squad, dusting their hands and promising each other a drink; men with a job well done. He hurried inside again.

'Now where?' said Eleanor, kicking herself away from the pillar as he came down the steps. 'Leave that bag alone.'

'Along here. All right, carry the thing yourself.' The corridor to the inland airstrip sloped downwards for a way, under a low ceiling. The footsteps behind him grew slower and slower, then stopped. Isaac turned. Eleanor was standing in the middle of the subway, looking giddy.

She said, 'Why is it all underground?'

'All what?'

'Everything. The shuttle went underground when it docked. The hall was underground. This passage slopes down. Where are we going?'

'To the carrier.'

'Is that underground?'

'Yes.'

'It all is. You live underground, don't you? You've got no atmosphere.'

'Don't be so stupid!' Isaac bellowed. 'Of course we

101

don't live underground. When we get on the carrier it goes up to the surface. It has to. It's a helicopter. Have you ever seen anything fly underground? It's only to save space for the freighters. When I went up those steps I was above ground. I could have shown you.'

'You didn't. What are those pipes for?'

'Pipes?' He followed her feverish gaze. Along the middle of the ceiling ran a fat master pipe, low slung and suspended from brackets; on either side a lean attendant pipe, clinging coyly. Nearby, a tributary passage joined the corridor and from it issued several little tributary pipes. Turning smartly to the right they ran alongside the serpent in the centre.

'They're only the mains.'

'Mains what?'

'I don't know.' He had never thought about it. They were just pipes, but they gave the declining subway a heady perspective. Eleanor was staring sickly at them with her hand pressed over her mouth. Isaac felt his own stomach turn in sympathy; he could see only too clearly what was about to happen. He went back and seized her by the belt.

'Not here,' he said firmly, and walked backwards, drawing her after him. 'You're not used to solid ground, that's all. Everyone feels strange at first. We're nearly there. Come on.' He was afraid that someone would come round the corner and witness their idiotic progress.

I hope Theodore's out when we get back.

The ride home on the carrier was all that he had anticipated. The entrance was in the rear and they boarded unobserved, taking seats at the back. Eleanor lifted the leather bag onto her lap and clung to it.

'I'm not going to run off with it,' said Isaac. Her grip did not relax at all but she leaned back against the

102

bulkhead, eyelids dropping shut. A few minutes later, just before take-off, Gregor's party came on board and sat in front of them. Gregor twisted round and looked over the back of his seat.

'If it isn't our Isaac. You should have come with us. There was a fight at the eating house, between Tau diggers and Sigma diggers. Blood flowing.' He looked at Eleanor. 'Is that it?'

'Yes,' said Isaac, with foreboding. 'This is Eleanor.'

'It's a man,' said Gregor, flatly. Having made the same error himself, Isaac was not inclined to blame him, only he knew that Gregor was not speaking in error.

'She's not well,' he said.

'I shouldn't think she was ever well,' said Gregor. 'Is this what you got all dressed up for? Oh, Isaac, you do have some luck.'

Isaac nudged Eleanor. 'He'll go on all the way like this. Don't take any notice.' There was no reaction.

'Gone to sleep, or died,' said Gregor. 'They used to fumigate. Why ever did they stop?'

Eleanor looked up with a start.

'Are we flying?'

'Just taking off,' said Isaac. 'Go back to sleep,' he urged her, looking at Gregor.

'I wasn't asleep. We're still underground, aren't we?' said Eleanor. The carrier, built on the cheap by the Government, had no windows in the second-class section.

'That's right, we always fly underground,' said Gregor, knowing nothing of the scene in the subway. 'We swim in solid rock. We breathe water and drown in fresh air. Ugh. Ugly and stupid,' he said, turning to Müller the gardener.

Eleanor waited until he looked her way again and then reached out, planted the heel of her hand squarely in his face and shoved. Gregor's head disappeared.

'You fool!' Isaac hissed. 'We'll pay for that. I'll pay – and you'll pay me.'

Eleanor rested her face against the bag in her lap and ignored him. He waited for reprisals from the front seat, but none came. For the rest of the journey there was an evil silence in the second-class compartment.

7

When the carrier touched down at the airstrip Gregor's party left, without another glance at the back seat. This unnerved Isaac more than a frontal assault would have done. Gregor was giving himself time to think. He pinned Eleanor into her place with his elbow until the compartment was empty and then snarled, 'We're home now. This is Epsilon – and everyone here knows me. Pretty soon they'll know you. Behave yourself. Just remember, if it weren't for me you wouldn't be here.'

'You told me that.'

'I'm telling you again. I didn't bring you here to make trouble. Keep your fists to yourself. I can get you deported like that.' He snapped his fingers. 'Now, look out of the door. See, daylight.'

'Leave the bag alone.'

'Suit yourself. You see, we don't live underground.'

'It's two years since I saw daylight,' said Eleanor. 'Were you ever two years in the dark?'

'Don't they give you lights in steerage?'

'Lights, yes. Not light.' The noon sun rang on the hills and terraces of Epsilon, splintered in the dust and lay in a million fragments round them.

'It gives you a headache the first time, so I'm told,' said Isaac. 'Don't look too long.'

'I have a headache already,' said Eleanor. Isaac stumped down the steps, leaving her to follow.

'Where are we going?'

'To our house. It's at the other end of the town.'

'This is a town? It's all rock.'

'You should like that. You're a sculptor, aren't you? Look again.'

She looked again and saw the houses.

'You can't see ours from here. Wait till we get to the top of the hill and I'll show you.'

'The hill? Have we got to climb it?'

'Yes. And when we get to the top we go down again and when we've gone down there's another hill and we have to climb that,' said Isaac, relentlessly. 'So the sooner we start, the better.' He moved off across the airstrip. Eleanor hooked her fingers through the handle of the bag so that it rested over her shoulder, and came after him. Ahead of them, Gregor mounted the hill with Müller on one side and Hamble on the other.

. 'You stay out of Gregor's way,' said Isaac, as they toiled upwards. 'You never hit him again. You never ever hit him again.'

Eleanor looked down at him out of the tail of her eye. 'Why not?'

'I don't know what you're used to on Euterpe, but you don't hit anyone here and especially you don't hit Gregor. He's Cameron's steward, for one thing.'

'Cameron?'

'Our magistrate. He's a big man in Epsilon. He's got ten servants; eleven now. He doesn't need them, but he's got them.'

'Does whatshisname, your employer, have as many?'

'Theodore Swenson. You call him Master Swenson. He's not a miner but you call him Master Swenson. No, he only has me. There's a secretary too, but he doesn't live with us.'

'Is Theo – is Master Swenson poor, then?'

Isaac laughed. 'Poor? He's richer than Cameron. You've heard of the Intergalactic Freight Company? He owns it. He owns Epsilon – and he owns you.'

'No he doesn't. I came here to work for him, for some-one. He doesn't own me.'

She stopped walking and stood in the dust, out-facing him. Isaac took one look at the sullen thrusting underlip and lost his temper.

'Do you think so?' He gave her an ill-natured jab in the ribs with two fingers, forgetting the weight of the bag. She overbalanced and sat down on a boulder.

'Nobody owns me.'

Isaac came in close. 'Listen. You're nothing now. Nobody owns you? Nobody wants you. Nobody cares what happens to you. Nobody needs a sculptor. You're a luxury like – like grass.'

'Grass?'

'You wouldn't understand. Theodore only took over that contract because he wants something no one else has got. He wants a sculptor, yes, but he doesn't want you. There's plenty more where you came from and any one of them could do your job. I don't know what he'll do when he sees you – you – you wreck, you r-r-r-ruin. S-s-s-send you back, I should think.'

Isaac's conquered enemy, the stammer, sniped at him.

'He can't do that – the contract . . .'

'The contract's not signed yet. Until it is you've got no rights, nothing. If I left you here it would be quite legal. Now get up, you can't stay here.'

'You just said I could.'

'I said I could leave you here. That's not the same thing at all.'

Isaac stalked ahead and she limped after him, stumbling. Mistaking her bewilderment for obstinacy, he let her stumble. As they approached the police station, Casimir glared out at them with yellow loathing.

'Open a new file,' said Loukides. 'That must be the sculptor.'

'Nothing's been signed yet,' said Casimir.

'Open it anyway. I believe it may fill up very quickly. Eleanor Ashe.'

'A woman?' said Casimir, looking at Eleanor's flat-sided figure. 'In trousers?' He sucked his teeth.

'Here we are,' said Isaac, halting in the shadow of the porch. 'This is our house.'

Eleanor looked up at the door and the barred windows. 'It's a fortress.'

'No, just a house.' The door was shut. Theodore's out at any rate, thought Isaac, reaching for his key with some relief. He unlocked the door and pushed her in, dropping the curtain behind him. Eleanor looked across the hall to the loggia and the garden.

'It's all open. Why have that great door? Why lock it? Anyone could get in.'

'No one would. We only shut it to show we're out, and at night. Now don't stand there putting down roots. Come through to the back.'

'But if people know you're out, mightn't they break in?'

'You're not on Euterpe now. There's no one here to break in.'

'No thieves?'

'Who'd give a thief an entry permit? This is my kitchen.'

'Is this where you live?'

'This is where I work. I sleep next door in the back hall. So will you.'

'In the same room?'

'It's not a room, it's a hall. After two years in steerage I wouldn't have thought you'd care.'

'I don't care, but it's such a big house.'

'It's a big hall and there's no one in it but me. Come on.' He led the way into the servants' hall, drawing back

108

the curtains of an unoccupied alcove at the opposite end from his own. 'This will be yours. See, it's a room on its own, really.'

Eleanor looked in. The alcove was half filled by a semi-circular divan.

'It's very small,' she said, doubtfully.

'It's big enough for most people,' said Isaac. 'I didn't know you'd turn out to be this length.'

'I shall have to curl up.'

'Well, curl up, then. Stand on your head, hang from the ceiling. You can sleep on the floor if you like. I don't care,' said Isaac. 'Sleep in the garden, out on the road ... What are you doing?'

Eleanor sat down on the divan and made ready to lie down.

'I'm doing like you said. Going to sleep.'

'Get off that quilt.'

'What's wrong with the quilt?'

'There's nothing wrong with the quilt,' said Isaac, clenching his teeth. 'That bedlinen is fresh. I put it on this morning. Go and wash. Go and wash your hair. You don't go to bed until Theodore's seen you and he doesn't see you until you are clean.'

'You talk as if I'm filthy,' said Eleanor, looking down at her immaculate boots.

'You are filthy,' said Isaac. 'I never saw anyone so filthy, not even in the mines.' He retreated a few steps as she started to get up, but all she said was, 'So where can I wash?'

'Well, I wash in the kitchen,' said Isaac. 'But I don't know that you should.'

'Can't I have a bath?'

He was taken aback.

'Theodore baths.'

'Don't you? Can't I?'

He towed her into the marble magnificence o
Theodore's bathroom. She stood in it, a blot on th
brightness, and asked ashamedly, 'Can I borrow
comb?'

'Haven't you got one? You can borrow my hairbrus
if you wash your hair first.'

'Of course I'll wash my hair first.'

'As far as I can see there's no of course about it.' H
fetched the brush from the drawer under his divan. Whe
he returned, Eleanor was foraging in the leather bag
Seeing him, she slammed it shut.

'What have you got in there?'

'Is there any soap?'

'We don't have soap. You'll find a tin of crystals i
the cupboard. That's as good if you don't use to
much.'

'What does it do?'

He thought of Madam Cameron whose face wa
apparently veneered in sandstone. 'It doesn't do you an
good.' He started to leave and then stopped in the doo
way. 'But use as much as you can,' he added. 'Ca
borundum might help.'

'Tell me something,' said Eleanor, digging her blac
fingernails into her palms. 'How have you lived s
long?'

Balked of his position as patron and saviour, Isaa
assumed the executioner's mask. He strode back into th
bathroom and spun her round until she was facing th
mirror that hung beside the doorway.

'There. Look at that. That's you,' he said, hatefully
'Isn't it pretty? Isn't it nice?'

'I left a note for you on my desk,' said Theodore
coming home not long before sunset. 'You were suppose
to meet me.'

110

'I'm sorry,' said Isaac. 'I haven't been into the study. Have you had a pleasant evening? What can I get f-f-f-for your supper?'

Theodore noted the catch in his voice and looked at him suspiciously. 'Anything you like. I'm not hungry.'

'May I have your coat? Would you like a drink? It's a very warm evening.'

'Naturally. It always is at this time of year,' said Theodore. Then, 'Well, where is she?'

'Who?'

'The sculptor. She did arrive, didn't she?'

'Oh yes. Yes, she arrived.'

'Where is she then?'

'Ah.' Isaac examined a stain on the wall, some way beyond Theodore's left shoulder. 'She's in bed. She's very thin – I mean very tired – after the journey, you know. And not at all well. Ill. I made her go to bed.'

'Ill? What's wrong with her?' Theodore began to back away. 'Something infectious?'

'Oh no. Only steerage fever. It's coming out of steerage that does it. All immigrants have it. It isn't s-s-s-serious.'

'It's very unhealthy on those ships,' said Theodore. 'Someone should do something. I'll see her tomorrow then, if you're sure it's not catching.'

'Oh no. Not catching.'

'I'll see her tomorrow, then. I'll just have a snack now, and go to bed myself.'

Isaac served the food, saw Theodore put away for the night, and went out into the garden. The moon had not yet risen but the sky was lit by the dusty afterglow that hung above the distant city. He climbed onto the block of Thalian core stone that lay so massively, awaiting Eleanor's attentions, and sat down. He had almost forgotten, in the day's mishaps, why she had come. It

111

seemed impossible that he had told lies and taken risks in order to bring her there. He had actually compromised himself in order to get her a job. Looking back, it seemed equally impossible that he had once mined the cold room wall to secure himself a job, but then he had been dealing with known factors; himself and Theodore. Eleanor had been an unknown factor since the day he had first seen her name on Mr Peasmarsh's list, Elmer Ache, and what he hadn't known he had invented, with frightening inaccuracy.

He felt sadder than he had done since the day, which he couldn't remember, when Theodore's father had found him wandering in the ruins of his home on the blasted moon, Orpheus. Now he sat in the ruins of two years' planning. He looked for the foundations of his dream and found only rubble. He looked for the flaw in the structure that had brought the whole thing crashing down and saw that from the beginning it had been jerry-built, jury-rigged, haphazardly knocked together and ready to collapse from the moment it was begun. She was not what he had intended. Now she was paying for his errors.

He slid down from the block and went into the back hall to look at his protégée. Pulling the curtains of the alcove aside he saw that she was lying as she had foreseen, curled up; her arms were still locked round the leather bag and her spine pressed against the straining cloth of her shirt like knuckles in a glove. Asleep she looked less of a bargain than ever, an exhausted, emaciated young woman, but violent. It was the violence that he feared most, the absence of brakes. She was like his train; restrained only by the most primitive methods. He had been right to show her the mirror, although the thought of his cruelty almost troubled him when he recalled the stricken face that had stared into, and out of, the glass.

Raising his hand lamp he leaned over and saw what she had seen; the sunken eyes, the spots, the ill-treated hair.

You'll have to grow that, he thought. No lady wore her hair shorter than waist length, pinned up in complex whorls and curls. It'll keep the sun off your neck.

'Are you all right?' he asked, and she answered without waking, 'Go for his throat. That way makes no sound. We'll follow you.'

Life on Euterpe, thought Isaac. Not only had she been out of polite society for a long time, quite possibly she had never been in it.

Maybe we should make allowances.

She had brought Euterpe with her, the nightmare they all tried to leave behind.

'What do you want?' said Isaac, when he opened the front door next morning and found Gregor propping up the porch. Gregor thrust a steel finger into his chest.

'I think you should grovel a little,' he said. 'No one hits me in the face.'

'Eleanor did,' said Isaac, wishing he could derive more pleasure from the recollection. 'But I didn't,' he went on. 'So don't take it out on me. She's Theodore's responsibility, not mine.'

'You're the steward,' said Gregor. 'Perhaps you understand my position now. The buck stops at you. You have to take the rough with the smooth, and she's certainly rough.'

'That's what Euterpe does to you.'

'Don't give me that. We all came from Euterpe once. Think of a better excuse.'

'Maybe it's worse now.'

'Worse than what? You were never there,' said Gregor. 'The orphan from Orpheus.'

'She didn't realize what she was doing.'

113

'If she weren't so big you could knock her about a bit,' said Gregor. 'I've come to get oil. Get, not borrow, and don't try to charge me.' He walked into the kitchen, uninvited. 'Where is she, then?'

'In there,' said Isaac, jerking his thumb towards the back hall.

'At this hour? Shall I go and knock her about a bit for you?' Gregor suggested.

'No thank you.' Isaac was not anxious for them to meet again so soon. 'She's got steerage fever – she's sleeping it off.'

'Is that what you told Theodore?'

'I had to tell him something.'

'And what does he think?'

'He hasn't met her yet.'

'If I were you,' said Gregor, 'I wouldn't let him wait too long. He might build up false hopes.'

'I can handle Theodore,' said Isaac, who had been thinking precisely the same thing.

'This is wildly unsatisfactory,' said Theodore, at tea-time. 'She's been here a whole day and I haven't seen her yet.'

'You could always go and look,' said Isaac. 'She's still here.'

'Don't be saucy.' Theodore finished his tea in offended silence and retired to his study. Isaac cleared the plates and put them in the sink. He usually washed them at once; instead he went into the back hall, treading warily. Eleanor was awake, sitting on the edge of the divan.

'Are you better?' he asked, with a convulsive attempt at a look of kindly concern.

'I haven't been ill. Who are you?'

'You can't have forgotten.' Forgotten me? The mirror?

'No. Theodore, isn't it?'

'Isaac. You'd better come into the kitchen and have something to eat,' he said. 'Then you can meet Theodore.'

'Who's Theodore?'

'The kitchen's this way. Theodore is your employer.'

She looked puzzled. 'I thought my employer's name was Peasmarsh.'

Isaac turned. 'You really have forgotten everything, haven't you? I suppose you don't remember smacking Gregor in the eye.'

'That slob on the carrier? No, I haven't forgotten him.'

'He hasn't forgotten you.' He flapped his fingers in front of her eyes. 'Look, you'd better wake up properly. Things happened yesterday that shouldn't have done. For a start you went to bed without meeting Theodore. That was stupid.'

She walked behind him, overhanging. 'May I sit down?'

'Of course – no, not on that.'

'There's nowhere else.'

'It's my chopping block. Will you get off?'

'Well, you'll have to go and chop somewhere else, won't you?'

'That block,' said Isaac, 'is worth more than the rest of the kitchen put together.'

'It's only wood.'

'We have no wood on Erato, this was brought from Euterpe. It's half a tree trunk. Cameron's got the other half. Here you are, eat this. Well go on, eat it.'

Eleanor examined the plate that he handed to her.

115

'What is it?'

'Bread. I made it this morning. What do you want to drink, tea, whisky, fruit juice, wine?'

'You have all that?' said Eleanor. 'Where does it come from?'

'We import it. Everything we eat is imported, nothing grows here. We get a better choice than most because Theodore owns the ships. Now, what do you want?'

'Water,' said Eleanor, with a certain amount of malice. 'Don't tell me you import that.'

'We have our own well and cistern at the back,' said Isaac. 'Everyone does in Epsilon, but we have to be careful with the supply. In the city it's rationed.'

'Does that mean I can't have any?'

'No, no.' Isaac drew a cupful from the sterilizer. 'Why aren't you eating your bread?'

'I'll have it in a moment.'

Isaac watched her drink. 'I thought you would be starving.'

'I never said so.' He could see every bone in her face.

'We're always told that food runs short during the last months of the voyage.'

'For some of us it was short all the way. Are you sure this is bread?'

'What's wrong with it?' Even Cameron praised his bread.

'Nothing. I just don't want it. Haven't you got something softer?'

'Why?'

'My teeth ache.'

'Yesterday your head ached.'

'What did you expect? Steerage is steerage, we weren't travelling for our health.'

'Didn't you get fruit on the ship?'

'It was there. I didn't get any.'

'We have it dried. And we get the juice canned or frozen. We have to have it. You get a disease otherwise; I can't remember what it's called but your teeth fall out,' said Isaac. 'Are yours falling out? Have some fruit juice.'

'No.' She dipped a piece of bread in the water and sucked it. Isaac looked away.

'If you tidy yourself up we'll go and see Theodore. He's waiting. I can let you have some flour if you like.'

'Whatever for? Not to eat.'

'To cover your spots,' said Isaac. He saw she was about to protest and stopped her. 'Look at them,' he said. 'Here, use this spoon. It's polished.'

Eleanor examined the rash, spot by spot, in the back of the spoon.

'Everyone on the ship had spots, even the crew. They aren't so bad as they were.'

'They look very nasty and they won't go away for at least a week. Have the flour.'

'Look here,' said Eleanor. 'Will your Theodore throw me out because my face is spotty?'

'I want to explain something to you,' said Isaac. 'Try and understand. Mr Peasmarsh was a friend of mine. He was going to build a house and he wanted to decorate it, to have carvings and statues round it. It was a nice house – it would have been; I saw pictures of it, only he died before it was ever begun. He chose your name from a list because he couldn't find a sculptor here. I don't know why, but artists don't seem to keep their jobs; remember that. Other people don't get deported like artists do. Anyway, he died, soon after you must have left Euterpe. I didn't think anything of it at first,' he said, editing the story as he went along. 'Then I remembered you, that you were coming, and that there would be no work for you. You know what would have happened?'

117

'Yes. They make sure of that on the ship. Everyone knows what will happen.'

'I suggested to Theodore that he took over your contract. He didn't want to at first but then I did him a favour and he agreed. I made him realize,' said Isaac, 'that no one else in the town had a sculpture. We'd be the first. He liked that. After a bit he began to think it was his idea in the first place. There are a lot of things in this house that no one else has got. But he hasn't got the sculpture yet – he's only got you. He doesn't need you. Nobody actually needs a sculptor. It would be a different matter if you were nice-looking; he might not care if you couldn't carve at all.'

'But I can. I'm good. Since I was a child –'

'That's not the point. Everyone is rich here. They have servants, pottery, glass, grass –'

'What's this with the grass?'

'They have what they like. They don't have what they don't like. You've been here only one day and already you've made enemies. For all I know, Theodore's one of them.'

'And you're another?'

'Whatever they told you on the ship, it didn't sink in. Did you come from Euterpe on a one-way ticket?'

'No, they make you buy a return so you can be sent back if you don't suit.'

'Who says you'll suit? You could go back today, how would you like that? On the same ship. How would you like that? Steerage, more spots, more fever, more dirt, starving again. How would you like that?'

'Isaaaac!' Theodore's voice fluted through from the study.

'He's calling me. Get off there, brush your hair and come in when I tell you.' He left her with the hair-brush and ran to answer the summons.

'Who are you shouting at, Isaac?' asked Theodore.

'Was I, was I shouting? I didn't mean to,' said Isaac. 'Eleanor has got up. Would you like to see her? D-d-d-do you wa-want, shall I get you a drink?'

'I suppose I should see her,' said Theodore peevishly. 'Fetch some wine up. If she's been so ill she won't want whisky. Bring it into the dining hall and we'll see to the contract too.'

Eleanor was walking tentatively up and down the kitchen.

'Are you feeling ill again?'

'Lightheaded, that's all. You were the one who said I was ill, I didn't.'

'You said you didn't feel well.'

'That's not the same as being ill. No one feels well in steerage, you don't expect to. It's all part of the great adventure, like drinking recycled water.'

'Theodore thinks you've been ill. Let him go on thinking it. And come away from that crockery, it cost a fortune. Can't you walk straight?'

'I'm not ill!'

'We're going to have some wine. That will make you feel better.' He opened the trapdoor in the kitchen floor and reached in. The wine was stored in racks, row upon row, but he kept a few bottles near the entrance to save time.

'Is that imported too?'

'From Clio. I told you, nothing grows here. You can't make wine out of rock. The really old stuff came from Euterpe. I bet there's no wine there now. Don't drink too much. You've got a contract to sign in a minute, that is, I hope you have.'

'Do you really?'

'What?'

'Do you really hope he'll sign me on?'

119

'I went to a lot of trouble to get you here. That doesn't seen to have sunk in either.' He put the bottle on a tray, with cups, and minced into the dining hall.

'This is Eleanor,' he said, watching Theodore. Theodore was watching the doorway. Eleanor drifted in.

'I hear you've been ill,' said Theodore, craning his neck to take her all in. Eleanor stooped over the table accommodatingly. 'Sit down. Do sit down.' Isaac booted a stool towards her and she folded up on it.

'Get your elbows off the table,' hissed Isaac, serving wine with one hand and prodding her with the other.

'Fetch a cup for yourself, Isaac – oh, you have,' said Theodore. He raised his goblet. 'I hope you have a successful term of employment with us.'

'So do I,' said Eleanor. She waited a moment and then said, 'Is that all?'

'What more do you want?'

'Shut up,' whispered Isaac.

'Don't you want to know anything more about me?'

'What is there to know?'

'Shut up.'

'About my work . . .'

'So long as you can do what you say you can do I shall be satisfied,' said Theodore, bemused. 'I don't need to know anything else. Isaac said you could carve stone. Can't you?'

'Yes, but . . .'

'Shut up!'

'I don't want to know anything else.'

Eleanor began to get the measure of his indifference. 'What am I meant to be carving?'

'Hasn't Isaac shown you?'

'I would have done but you went to sleep,' said Isaac.

'My late father,' said Theodore, interrupting him, 'imported a block of Thalian core stone.'

'It's that big pink thing in the garden,' said Isaac.

'It was to have marked a new stage in the development of the Intergalactic Freight Company – you've heard of Intergalactic? Father called it megahaulage. He'd produced a new kind of hoist and he decided to try it out by bringing the stone here. He was going to have it standing on end at the top of the hill, as a kind of landmark. Unfortunately,' said Theodore, 'the hoist failed and the stone fell. He fell with it.'

'Was the stone damaged?' asked Eleanor.

'My father,' said Theodore, 'was killed.'

'Oh. But was the stone damaged?'

'Not much. At first I wanted it destroyed. I couldn't bear to look at it. Then I decided to have it made into a memorial to him. It can't be lifted, but if you can make a tasteful, dignified work of art, I shall be well satisfied.'

'How big is it?'

'How big is it, Isaac?'

'Twelve metres long, f-f-f-four metres high and five acrosh,' said Isaac. 'Itsh enormoush, en-n-n-normoussss.'

'That's enough wine, Isaac,' said Theodore.

Eleanor said, 'How long have I got?'

'As long as you need,' said Theodore. 'Which brings us to the contract. Isaac, you can leave us now.'

Isaac withdrew to the hall, hovering near the doorway, but the voices never rose high enough for him to overhear. He was particularly interested in the signing of contracts. His own had been simple enough: he was guaranteed employment for five years and neither side could terminate unless a criminal offence could be proved against one or the other, and this clause was, in his case, more of a guarantee than the contract itself. Since the grass-running, it was in no one's interest to put him in a position where he might be tempted to talk. But Ansell had gone very suddenly. It seemed to Isaac

that all artists went very suddenly. What was it abou
their contracts that made them expire unexpectedly
Would Eleanor's?

He pottered about, doing unnecessary jobs, and afte
a while the curtains flew apart and Eleanor spun ou
He caught her as she hurtled towards him and pushe
her into the kitchen.

'You're drunk.'

She hung round his neck. 'I can't be. I only had on
cup.'

'On an empty stomach. They're big cups. Sit dow
and I'll get you something to eat.'

'Not your bread.'

'How long did you get?'

'The contract? It's for a year, but he said it can b
extended if needs be.'

'Don't you believe it,' said Isaac. 'It's more likely t
be cut short. Are you sure it said a year?'

'Ten months, it said.'

'Is that how many months you have on Euterpe?'

'No, we have twelve, like Earth. But you have ter
I know that much. What's this?'

'Soup. We have forty months a year, here. Surely yo
know the times are different?' He suddenly saw how
was done.

Poor Ansell, and others like him, straight off the shij
ill, confused, required to sign documents committin
them to times that didn't exist.

'Our moon goes round once every ten days, so that
the real month except you can't call ten days a mont
so we call it a week, and four weeks we call a month
Your contract doesn't mean anything after a hundre
days.'

'Don't you have a contract?' said Eleanor.

'Mine really does say years,' said Isaac. 'Yours is wha

122

you might call a special artist's contract and it's not the only one. Once those hundred days are up they can get rid of you when they like. Eleanor, I beg you, behave. Be good. Don't argue, don't fight. Just go out there and carve your stone and be nice to Theodore and nice to Gregor and pay up when you're asked to pay – how much is he paying you? Eleanor?'

He caught the soup bowl as it slid towards the floor. She had fallen asleep again, even while he warned her, and he wondered then if anyone else would have warned her.

If anyone else had ever been warned.

8

'You told me a block,' said Eleanor. 'This is a mountain.'

'You have a whole year,' said Theodore.

'Ten months?'

'Certainly.'

'Or a hundred days?'

'That's just a loophole,' said Theodore, with a nasty look at Isaac. 'The very nature of your calling makes you unpredictable, you must see that. It's just a loophole, rarely used. You have a year, or more if you need it.'

'I should think I would need it.'

'Grovel,' muttered Isaac. 'Grovel.'

'What do you want me to do with it?'

'Well ... carve it,' said Theodore, whose knowledge of statuary was only marginally greater than Isaac's.

'Yes, but what do you want me to carve? I'm not short of ideas; I've done nothing but think for the last two years. I could do anything with this, but it would be a pity if I spent a year carving and you didn't like it.'

You may think you're being funny but he doesn't.

'I imagined you would understand my requirements. Something dignified, tasteful. It is to be a monument to a great man.' He walked away, displeased. Isaac waited until he was out of earshot.

'Be nice to him. Make him think he likes you.'

'I didn't come here to be liked. I came here to work.'

'You will not see the truth, will you?' said Isaac. 'If you aren't liked you won't work. That's the truth.'

124

'The contract's signed now.'

'If you ask me, that loophole as he calls it is always used, sooner or later. If not the first hundred days then the second or the third. They get you somehow.'

'You're the youngest old woman I ever met,' said Eleanor calmly, looking down at him. She was walking up and down along the top of the block, seemingly getting accustomed to it. 'What did he say this was called?'

'Red core stone.'

'From Thalia? There's no air on Thalia.'

'I know. Three men were killed getting it.'

'But what's it for? Why did Theodore's old man need it so badly?'

'He didn't,' said Isaac. 'It was an experiment. He wanted to see if he could get it and he did. Those were great days. Great ships. We've nothing like it now.'

'And men were killed?'

'So was he.'

'There's some justice on Erato, then.' Her head appeared darkly over the edge of the block like a bad sun setting.

'Who says there isn't?' He had some reservations himself on the subject, but he was affronted by her criticism. How could Euterpe criticize Erato?

'There's no justice on Euterpe, come to that,' said Eleanor. 'Only lynching.'

'Is that what happens to people who get sent back?'

'I don't know.'

'Did you ever hear of people who came back? If you'd been sent back, what would have happened to you?'

'I don't know.'

He inferred that either she did not know or refused to tell him. He had been looking forward to hearing about the horrors of life on Euterpe, the better to point

125

out the service he had done in getting her away. Now it seemed that she scarcely regarded it as a service at all.

'You saw that man in the terminal, in handcuffs?' She nodded. 'You saw the men with him?'

'Yes.'

'That was a Deportation Squad. If it hadn't been for me they would have got you too. You would have been sitting there waiting and they would have got you. There's a Squad in every town and that includes Epsilon. There's still time.'

'I've heard that line before. Now, where can I get clay?'

'Clay?'

Eleanor kneaded her hands together. 'It's a kind of plastic earth.'

'Plastic earth?'

'Not that kind of plastic. You can mould it, model with it. I shall have to make maquettes.' Isaac recalled Mr Peasmarsh showing him her name on the list. Eleanor Ashe, aged eighteen, clay modelling, plaster casting...

'We haven't got any.'

'Then where can I get it? No, don't tell me. You import it along with your food and your drink and your pots and your pans and your blood and your sweat —'

'I don't import anything,' said Isaac, wearily. 'I take what I can get and so will you. But Theodore will order clay if you need it for your work. I believe it comes from Clio. It will take at least three months to get here.'

'What am I supposed to use in the meantime, your horrible bread? Have you got any paper?'

'Why do you want paper? It's terribly expensive — far more than clay. I might be able to find some bit in Theodore's study.'

'What use is bits? I wants sheets of it.'

'You can't have sheets. How was I to know you'd want clay and paper? We ordered tools.'

Eleanor laughed abruptly.

'I don't need tools.'

'They're power tools. They'd run off the generator.'

'Still more I don't need power tools.'

'What are you going to carve with, your teeth? Maybe you look at stone and it cracks,' said Isaac, spitefully.

Eleanor jumped down beside him. 'Let me show you something.' Isaac saw that the power tools were being rejected.

'We offer you stone and you want clay. We get you equipment and you refuse it,' he growled, following her into the house.

Eleanor beckoned him into the back hall and opened the drawer under her divan. Isaac kept clothes in his. Eleanor's contained only the leather bag.

'Are we going to see inside?'

She hooked a finger inside her collar and brought out a key, hung round her neck on a twist of string.

'I needn't keep it there any more, need I?'

'I won't steal it.'

She broke the string and opened the lock on the bag. Isaac peered in. The bag was full of short metal rods, few of them much longer than his hand, with blunt ends. At the other end of each was a cutting edge of some kind. 'This is what I use. These are my tools.'

Isaac looked at them. 'But how do they work?'

'You hit them,' said Eleanor. 'With a hammer. You hold the chisel in one hand, like this . . . and the hammer, here it is, it's called a lump hammer, you hold that in the other hand . . . and you hit it.' Isaac observed a row of mauve scars down her left thumb. 'Sometimes you miss.'

127

'You'll never carve that block in a year, by hand,' said Isaac.

'Want to bet? He said I could have longer if I needed it.'

'In that case you'd better make sure he likes what you're doing.' Isaac looked further into the bag. Under the tools lay other equipment; more hammers, oil stones, files, a hand drill, even a can of oil. He thought of the bag's immense weight. 'How did you get this lot onto the ship? Immigrants aren't allowed more than ten kilos in luggage. Most people bring clothes.'

'I brought clothes.'

'Just about.' Isaac lifted the bag experimentally. 'There's twice ten kilos here.'

'Yes, well, when I first boarded the ship I was wearing most of it.'

'Most of the clothes?'

'No, most of the tools. In my boots, in my sleeves, under my belt.' Eleanor smiled faintly. 'I could hardly move; I felt like stone myself; carved. But it worked. The bag weighed ten kilos and I weighed seventy-five. No one queried that. I wasn't so thin then.'

'I said you'd got off lightly,' said Isaac, but she didn't see the joke.

'What do you mean, lightly? I hadn't been so clever as I thought. All I had besides the tools was soap and a comb; and a few clothes. And I had no one to tell me that you needed things to barter.'

'Even on the ships?' Isaac had imagined that it was a local problem.

'Especially on the ships. When you get onto a ship you get into a gang – any gang that will have you, only I didn't know that. I had to make my own way. The first night I traded my dinner for somewhere to sleep, and the next night, and the next. I went on like that for a week but one night I was hungrier than I was tired so I sat up all night. Every time I fell asleep someone punched me awake, so I gave him my soap to leave me in peace. Then I had to give up the comb. It was a steel comb. I couldn't really do without it because my hair was so long then, but I borrowed a knife and cut it. There were other rackets. You could buy your way into the washroom for the cost of a meal, or you could pay a man not to slash your luggage open or you could pay a man not to beat you up too often. I was paying to keep my tools. I never let that bag out of my sight, out of my hand. In the end I hardly dared sleep at all for fear I should wake up and find it gone. I'd almost stopped eating altogether.'

Isaac listened to her furious monotone in astonishment. 'But all those tools,' he said. 'Surely you could have spared a few.'

'I never opened the bag. No one knew what was in it. If anyone had found out, I shouldn't have been sparing a few. The whole lot would have gone. They're sharp,' she said.

'But I thought there were stewards to stop that kind of thing.'

'You misunderstand,' said Eleanor. 'It's the stewards who start it.'

'But ten hundred of you . . . ?'

'Was it only ten hundred? It felt like ten thousand, but then, there wasn't much room. But at least you knew it couldn't last forever. And it didn't last forever. One day I stepped out of that stinking shuttle and that was when I realized what had happened to me. You showed me.'

'I did?'

'You showed me a mirror.' She began to replace the tools in the bag, wrapping them in oily rags with trembling hands.

'Was it worse than Euterpe?'

'Like I said, on the ship we at least knew it would end, even the very day it would end. It never ends on Euterpe till you die.'

'Would you have died?'

'Most people do, eventually,' said Eleanor, pushing the drawer shut on the leather bag. 'But I didn't. I'm here. Let me get on with my work and stop telling me how lucky I am. I know how lucky I am.'

Casimir loitered negligently by the front door.

'Loukides says to remind you that she hasn't signed on yet.'

'We haven't forgotten,' said Isaac.

'Then why hasn't it been done?' said Casimir, filtering away through the shadows. Isaac made sure he had properly gone before going back into the house to find Eleanor. She was standing on the block, kicking away loose fragments with the heel of her boot.

'Come down off that,' said Isaac. 'There's something you have to do.'

Eleanor, he noticed, was incapable of obeying without stalling first. She temporized by sitting on the edge of the block, feet dangling.

'What do I have to do?'

'You have to go down to the police station to sign on. It's for the records.'

'What records?'

'The town records. To prove that you're here and not somewhere else, so come on down and don't argue.' She came down, very slowly. 'It's not something you can choose to do, it's the law.'

130

'Oh, the law.' Eleanor followed him through the house and out onto the road. 'I'm not used to law.'

'You'd better get used to it,' said Isaac. 'There's a lot of it about. And every time you break it they make a note in your file.'

'It's not against the law to make loopholes?'

'Not if the people who make the loopholes make the law.'

Loukides and Casimir were drinking whisky at the counter as they went in.

'This is Loukides, Sergeant of Colonial Police,' said Isaac. 'And this is Casimir, his sous-officier. Loukides, this is Eleanor Ashe, our new sculptor.'

'Good morning,' said Loukides. 'What a good morning. The file, Casimir.'

Casimir had seen them coming and the file lay ready on the counter.

'We've already had a complaint about you,' said Loukides. 'Gregor-at-Cameron's says you hit him in the face on the carrier.'

Eleanor opened her mouth and Isaac cut in hurriedly.

'She was ill . . . dreadfully ill . . . c-c-c-can't remember a thing.'

'She wasn't too ill to hit him.'

'He asked for it. I was there. It was gross provocation; we ought to lay a-a-a charge against Gregor.'

'Gross provocation does not constitute an offence,' said Loukides. 'There is no provision in the statute book for gross provocation, undesirable though it may be. Physical violence is no answer to gross provocation, otherwise we'd all be at it,' he added, cryptically. 'The fine is two dinars.'

'But I haven't got any money,' said Eleanor. Isaac was pleased to see some signs of apprehension in her tiny eyes.

That'll learn you. Aloud he said, 'Can't you let her off, this time? She's only just arrived – doesn't know our ways.'

'We can't have leniency,' said Loukides, pursing his lips as though speaking of a filthy habit. 'If we show leniency towards a first offence, the second offence may be that much greater. Two dinars.'

'Master Swenson won't like this,' said Casimir, happily.

'Penniless –'

'Two dinars,' said Loukides.

'Not the best way to start one's term of employment.'

'– overlook it?'

Eleanor stood among them in a state of miserable confusion, looking at Casimir who sat grasping the red stylus like an assassin with a reeking knife.

'What happens if she can't pay?' said Isaac, who knew very well what would happen and wanted to be sure that Eleanor knew too.

'We shall have to arrest you for non-payment,' said Loukides to Eleanor. 'And hold you in custody.'

'How long for?'

'Ah. Until you pay.'

'You can't pay if you aren't earning, and you can't earn if you're in gaol. Master Swenson won't like this,' chanted Casimir.

'How can I pay?' said Eleanor. 'I haven't earned anything yet.'

'Well then,' said Loukides. 'You should have earned something before you assaulted Gregor.'

'If you're in gaol you can't work. If you don't work you're in breach of contract, in which case,' Casimir sang, 'you'll be deported.'

Seeing that Casimir was beginning to enjoy himself, Isaac decided that the episode had gone far enough.

'I'll pay it,' he said, handing the notes to Loukides. Casimir appeared disappointed. Loukides simpered.

'What it is to have friends.' He put the notes in a drawer. 'You'd be well advised to make some more, instead of enemies. Now, sign the file, please.'

Casimir was recording the transaction. When he had finished he pushed the file and the stylus across the counter. Eleanor wrote Eleanor Ashe in the space provided. Loukides took the stylus and put a line through 'Ashe', cutting it out.

'Among us,' said Loukides, 'you are just Eleanor. Eleanor-at-Swenson's. Isn't that comradely? Good morning.'

'Out,' said Isaac, pushing. They stood in the sunshine, among the sun flowers.

'Would they? Could they? Why didn't you warn me?'

'Would and could and what was the point of warning you?' said Isaac. 'You wouldn't have taken any notice. As it happens, I've never heard of anyone being imprisoned for debt. We always bail each other out.' He didn't explain that this was a source of income from earned interest. 'It didn't do you any harm to learn the hard way.'

'Can we go home now?'

'If you want. Or would you like to see the town?'

'I'm seeing it, aren't I?' said Eleanor, looking all round with deep dislike.

'All right; we'll go home. Well come on, then,' he said. She had turned and was looking in the opposite direction, towards Cameron's terraces. 'What are you staring at?'

'That,' said Eleanor, pointing upwards, to the top terrace. 'Who is it?'

'That's Cameron's gardener,' said Isaac. 'Moshe.'

'What's he doing?'

'Planting something, I expect.'

'He looks as if he's trying to plant himself,' said Eleanor. From their angle Moshe, who was kneeling down, resembled a tangled crop of vegetable growth in the middle of the flower bed.

'He's got a good hedge on his shoulders,' said Isaac, and in the pleasure of a shared joke they so far forgot themselves as to smile briefly at each other.

Isaac had lost his sun lounge. After the breakfast was cleared away and Theodore safe in the study he went out to the block and climbed on top. There he found the open tool bag, scattered chisels and the few scraps of paper that he had managed to salvage from Theodore's study; old letters, unscrewed and laboriously ironed flat on the hot pipe above the stove. They had been drawn on, screwed up again, and abandoned.

'Eleanor?'

'Down here.'

He looked over the edge of the block and saw her below him in the wedge-shaped hollow between the stone and the wall. The gap had silted up over the years and in the dust Eleanor, knee-deep, burrowed at the base of the block.

'What are you doing?'

She looked up, whey-faced in the smiling sunshine. The spots on her jaw glowed unkindly.

'I'm looking for flaws. I can't believe it wasn't damaged when it fell.'

'I don't remember,' said Isaac. It had been months before any of them had felt able to look at it. 'Theodore says it's all right.'

'Would he know?' Eleanor snorted slightly and a little cloud of dust blew up and powdered her hair.

'You ought to buy a hairbrush,' said Isaac.

134

'I haven't got any money, you should know.'

'You haven't been using mine, have you?' Isaac resolved to lock it away.

'No. I use my fingers, like I did on the ship.'

'You ought to get some decent clothes, too. What you did on the ship won't do here. When will you get paid?'

'After four weeks, he said. Or is that four months? I don't know.'

'Weeks,' said Isaac. 'You'll just have to manage with what you've got until then. Perhaps you could wash them more often. There's nothing of mine will fit you.'

'Can't you lend me any more money?' Eleanor was coming up, one foot braced against the wall, one against the block.

'I haven't got any more. I used nearly all I had to buy these boots. Mind you,' he went on, complacently, as she climbed up beside him, 'if I want any more I can squeeze it out of the others.'

'How squeeze it? Could I?'

'We charge each other for services rendered, favours, information, little things like that. We have to. Miners live on money, we live on our wits. We all do it, although Gregor does it best. You can't do it at all.'

'Why not?' Even when they were both sitting she could still look down on him.

'Why should anyone give you money?' he asked, resentfully. 'As far as I can see you've got nothing that anyone would want.' He surveyed her up and down. 'Nothing.'

'Live on your wits?' said Eleanor. 'It seems to me you live on each other. Parasites.'

'Don't throw that word about,' said Isaac. 'It doesn't mean what you think it does. Which reminds me, when you do get paid you'll need to buy a dress, for church.'

'I don't go to church.'

'Yes you do. Everyone goes to church, once a week on the tenth day.'

'If you think I'm going to spend my hard-earned cash on something to wear once a week you can think again. What do you worship, money?'

'We don't worship,' said Isaac. 'We just go to church.'

'I don't.'

'Yes you do.'

9

Isaac put on fresh clothes for church and polished his boots. He intended to hint that Eleanor might do the same, but she was nowhere to be found and he wondered if she was hiding from him.

He searched the house with mounting exasperation that anyone should go to such lengths to avoid attending church. She had claimed that she was too busy to take a day off, but when he looked in the garden there was no sign that she was working. Then a sound close by drew him round behind the block of stone and there he found her, drawing on the wall.

'You can't do that. Stop it,' he shouted, running forward. Eleanor was working with a stump of something that left gritty black streaks on the white stone. 'You can't draw on the wall.'

'Those little bits of paper are all used up. What else can I draw on?'

'Not the wall. What are you drawing with, anyway?'

'Charcoal. It's burnt wood.' She saw his expression. 'No, I didn't make it, I brought it with me. I haven't been stealing bits of your precious tree trunk.'

'But the mess ...'

'No one will see it round here,' said Eleanor. 'When I've finished I can clean it off – no, you can clean it off. It's your job, isn't it?'

'Draw on the stone.'

'Not until I'm sure of what I'm doing. I'll work at this, first.'

'You shouldn't be working at all today. It's the tenth day. We're going to church.'

'I told you, I'm not going to church. I'm going to work. Surely Theodore won't mind so long as he gets his money's worth?'

'People will notice and he'll mind that. They'll say he can't control his servants.'

'He hasn't had much practice, has he, with only you to control. You'd go down on all fours if he told you. Anyway, I'm not one of his servants.'

'Please come,' said Isaac. 'At any rate, stop working.' Eleanor laid down another line, thicker and blacker.

'You'll regret this,' said Isaac, turning back to the house, but later, as he followed Theodore downhill, he knew that he was the one who would regret it. It was his job to make sure that she went to church: he mentally listed the excuses that he could make for Eleanor's absence and waited for Theodore to notice it. She's too tired. Ill? Ill again. Nothing to wear; that's true, at least. She sleeps in that shirt. The one reason he could not give was the real one. She's working. No one but servants worked on the tenth day, and then only as much as was needed to keep their households running. Eleanor, as she was fond of reminding him, was not a servant.

They were passing the police station before Theodore turned round, discovered that there was only one person behind him and remembered that there should have been two.

'Where's the sculptor?'

'She's not coming,' Isaac mumbled, trying to give the impression that the words were, in fact, being spoken by someone else.

'Not coming?' said Theodore, with icy indignation. 'Everyone comes to church. I suppose you told her it was statutory?'

'I don't think she understood.'

'Then go back and fetch her.'

Isaac went right off the rails.

'She c-c-c-can't come ... in no fit state ... she's – she's – she's –' he could hardly say it. 'She's working.'

Loukides was leaving the police station, Casimir three paces behind.

'Make a note of that,' said Loukides, and Casimir went inside again.

The Reverend Aumer, shepherd of his flock or more precisely, whipper-in, stood in the church porch. As Isaac entered behind Theodore, he was mopping and mowing in front of the Camerons. His hands fanned the air like fish fins, but when he saw the Swenson household approach the fins became fists, and bowing to the Camerons, he barred the way, very politely.

'A happy and reposeful tenth day to you, Master Swenson. I understood you had another, er, person in your house this week.'

Whenever Isaac saw Aumer he seemed to see also crawling things without legs, that moved round the hem of his robe. He could not name them, but supposed them to be an unlovely though apposite memory from an earlier time. Aumer's pronouncements crawled out in a similar manner.

'Is she not to be among us on this blessed day of rest?' Aumer made the mistake of swaying sideways and Theodore contrived to get past him with an embarrassed smirk before Aumer's bulk rolled back again, trapping Isaac who was left to do the explaining.

'She's been ill,' he began. He kept a close eye on Aumer, wondering if he was going to get away with it. 'She might be taken ill again ... in the heat of the day ...'

'Sickness? Suffering?' said Aumer, hopefully. The

jelly of his eye seemed to radiate with an inner light. 'She needs consolation?'

Isaac wouldn't have wished Aumer's consolation onto anyone. 'Sleep,' he said firmly. 'She needs sleep.'

At that moment the bright white morning rang with a distant but distinct note. The chime of a hammer striking a chisel striking stone.

'I had an idea while you were out,' said Eleanor. 'For the design.' She had clouted a lump of stone from the corner of the block, about the size of a head, and making a vice of her knees, was clipping at it experimentally with a small chisel.

'Damn your ideas,' Isaac shouted. 'You missed the sermon.'

'Good.'

'We shall have Aumer up here before long and you'll get a sermon all to yourself. Then see what sort of ideas you have.' There came a crash, inside the house. 'That's Theodore, throwing things. Oh, you're for it, all right. You're for it.'

He went indoors to pick up the remains of whatever Theodore had broken and there was Pastor Aumer, standing at the front door with his hand on the bell.

'Child,' said Aumer, addressing Isaac; his voice booming across the tactless insistence of the chisel. 'Where is she?'

'In the garden,' said Isaac, caught unprepared, without a lie.

'Take me there,' said Aumer. 'Take me to her.' He raised his hand in a kind of flaccid benediction and Isaac saw a note under his thumb on which he thought he recognized Casimir's scurvy handwriting.

'Come this way,' he said, and led Aumer into the garden. Eleanor had prudently stopped carving but the

140

stone head was rocking slightly, while a rising cloud of dust told Isaac where she had gone to earth. He directed Aumer to the cool chasm between the stone and the wall, made a great noise going away and then climbed quietly onto the block where he lay, full-length, his hand muffling his bunch of keys, and looked down at the fore-shortened figures below him.

Aumer drew breath.

'Child,' he said, on tiptoe to lay a fat hand on Eleanor's shoulder. 'As I looked at my little flock this morning, I saw an absent face.'

'Oh yes?' Backed into the extreme end of the wedge, Eleanor was trapped. Isaac wondered if she would try to climb over the wall to get away.

'Child,' said Aumer. 'The church is the heart of our life, here in Epsilon; the soul of our society. The well-spring of the joy that takes us from one week's end to the next. Can you, my child, go ten days without a drink? Here on Erato, water is our jewel beyond price. Can any man say "I can live without water"? Can any man say "I have no need of refreshment"? All men come to church to drink at that well, each tenth day.'

Eleanor, looking for a way out, misheard him.

'Isaac said that every house had its own cistern.'

'Child,' cried Aumer, fingers entwined. 'You cannot mock in the face of spiritual thirst. Of course, if you don't wish to attend it will cost you two dinars a week, payable to me.'

'I haven't any money,' said Eleanor, alerted by the familiar sound of two dinars.

'Then come to church and labour not upon the tenth day. It was given to us by the Government for rest and contemplation. When do you get paid?'

'At the end of the month.'

'And there are yet three more tenth days between now

141

and then. I shall see you among the brethren a week hence,' said Pastor Aumer. 'Another sinner saved from perdition by penury. Blessed are the poor. Amen, amen.' He strode away.

Eleanor yelled after him. 'Do I get reduced rates if I never come at all, you God-bothering drone?'

'Amen, amen,' very softly, echoing among the pillars of the loggia.

'You can come down now,' said Eleanor. Isaac sat up.

'You'll have to go next week, it's the law. Aumer doesn't care whether you go or not, and as for God-bothering, God's got nothing to do with it. Aumer's an official, that's all, like Loukides.'

'He's like Loukides, all right.' Eleanor was absent-mindedly scrubbing at the moist patch on her shirt where Aumer's hand had rested. 'But what's he for?'

'We used to have a real chaplain years ago,' said Isaac. 'All the towns did; left over from the mines. But he wasn't much good to anyone. He used to pray and a lot of people didn't like that, so Theodore and Cameron sent off to Euterpe for someone who wasn't religious at all and we got Aumer.'

'Yes, but what's he for?' Eleanor persisted. 'There's no law on Euterpe about going to church at the weekend. Not that it would make any difference if there were, but there isn't. Why should the Government care what happens to my spiritual welfare if I work ten days a week?'

'It's not a Government law,' said Isaac. 'It's our law.'

'And Aumer's your collective conscience?'

'He reminds us of how things should be.'

'He reminds you of how things are, not how they should be,' said Eleanor. 'I don't need reminding. I won't go.'

'I don't think you can afford not to,' said Isaac. 'Eight

dinars a month. You know what happens if you don't pay a fine.'

'It's a fetter, your church, a fetter. Can't you see that?'

'No I can't,' said Isaac. 'I'll tell you what I can see. Aumer's annoyed, Theodore's angry, Cameron's laughing and Casimir's making notes. What Aumer said to you just now was just a bit of what he said to us all this morning. But we all knew he was really saying it to Theodore. He was saying "It's your sculptor who's breaking the law. Keep her in order or you'll be sorry."'

'How will he be sorry?'

'He won't but you will be. Let's go for a little walk; I want to show you something.'

Eleanor began to climb back onto the block. He caught her arm. 'Did I ever tell you about Ansell?'

'No.'

'Ansell was an artist too. He made murals in mosaic. Let me show you his mural, you ought to see it.'

'I want to get on with my own work. I'll see his another time.'

'You should see it now. Ansell was a very hard worker; he used to work ten days a week if there was something he wanted to finish. But he never did finish. Come on. I mean it.' He tugged at the resisting arm. 'Come on.'

They stood before the mural that stretched the length of Evans' wall.

'What happened to the middle?' said Eleanor, pointing to the empty patch which someone had filled by plastering it with brown pigment.

'I told you, he never finished it. And I'll tell you why he never finished it – he was deported. I used to wonder why. Now I'm beginning to guess.'

'He was good. It's good work.'

'Come to church and I'll show you some bad work.'

Eleanor walked up and down below the mural, critical, appreciative; the first person to see it, perhaps, who understood it.

'He knew what he was doing.'

'That didn't save him. One day he was here – the next he was gone. It could happen to you.'

'Didn't he have a contract?'

'Yes he did, and it hadn't expired. At least, he thought it hadn't expired. He was looking for another job when he went. It must have been one of those funny little contracts like yours.'

The door in the wall burst open and Barnet burst out.

'Who's this?'

'Our sculptor, Eleanor,' said Isaac. 'Eleanor, this is Master Evans' steward, Barnet.'

'What are you doing, looking at our wall?' Barnet demanded.

'Isn't it meant to be looked at?'

'It's only out here because Evans didn't rightly know what a mural was,' said Barnet. 'He said if he liked it he'd have another done on the inside where he could see it. Seems he didn't like it.'

'Do you know what happened to this Ansell?' said Eleanor. Barnet slammed the door shut.

'He doesn't know how to say good-bye,' said Isaac. 'We can go home now. I just wanted you to see; it doesn't matter how good you are, how hard you work, if you don't suit, out you go.'

After tapping and scraping at the little lump of stone for a few days, Eleanor went back to drawing on the wall. Theodore sulked, Casimir hovered, Isaac watched them all, dreading the end of the week when they must go to church again. His dread was not diminished by a visit from Moshe.

Isaac knew Moshe a little better after two years; enough to get two consecutive sentences out of him on occasion. He appeared in the kitchen one morning about the middle of the week with the request that Isaac should bring him some seeds when he went to the city.

'How many? What kind? Write it down,' said Isaac at the table, up to his wrists in dough.

Moshe picked up the memo pad, fiddled with it and put it down again. 'Just cabbage,' he said. 'They've been ordered. They only need collecting.' He turned to go.

'How are you?' said Isaac, awkwardly, as he reached the door.

Moshe seemed to have no answer to that but he stopped and came back into the kitchen. They stood one each side of the table, looking at the dough.

'Nice bread,' said Moshe.

'Eleanor doesn't think so,' said Isaac. The key had turned in the lock. They both looked up.

'Where is she?' said Moshe, lowering his voice. Isaac waved his hand towards the garden and a piece of dough detached itself from his finger, flew across the room and stuck to the wall.

'She's in trouble already,' Moshe went on, quietly. 'Does she know?'

'She knows. She doesn't care. Trouble for her is trouble for Theodore. Trouble for Theodore is trouble for me. She doesn't care about that either,' said Isaac, trouncing the dough as though he had Eleanor's neck under his knuckles. 'Who's complaining? Aumer?'

'He'll make an official complaint if she isn't in church this week. Sean told me.' Sean was Aumer's cross-eyed steward who made a comfortable living out of

145

fleecing Aumer. 'Gregor will like that,' said Moshe.

'Now tell me something I don't know,' said Isaac.

'Why won't she go? Is it on religious grounds?'

'You can't refuse to go to church on religious grounds,' said Isaac, manhandling the dough into a wooden bowl.

'I don't know. Aumer's an affront to anyone's religion,' said Moshe, surprisingly. He had no more religion than anyone else, so far as Isaac knew. 'Does she worship something odd?'

'You could say that,' said Isaac, thinking of Eleanor's impregnable self-regard. He went to the cupboard and took out a cloth which he wrapped tenderly round the bowl, more to protect the wood than the dough. Then he set it on the window sill, still warm, although Mnemosyne had swung high above the house, long before.

'Make her go,' said Moshe. Isaac leaned on the window sill and sighed.

'Make her? Have you seen her?'

'The other day, when she went to sign on. But in the distance only.'

'Then you'd better come out and meet her,' said Isaac. 'See if you can get anything into her thick head. By the way,' he said, as they crossed the hall, 'do you know of anyone who wants to sell a dress?'

Eleanor was kneeling on the block with her back to them, grinding chisels on an oil stone. Isaac and Moshe climbed the steps to the terrace and came up under her nose.

'Ah, the hedge,' said Eleanor.

Moshe, innocently unaware of her meaning, thatched his eyes with his fingers and looked up into the full light of the sun. An unprecedented giggle came out of his beard.

'You've got a halo,' he said.

146

Isaac looked at him in disgust. Eleanor leaned down and extended her hand.

'His name's Moshe,' said Isaac.

'Hello, Moshe.' Moshe took the hand and shook it, formally. They smiled shyly at each other along the length of their two arms.

'He's going to get you a dress –'

'I never said that,' Moshe protested.

'– so you can go to church. Shut up, Mo. You must know someone.'

'I don't know anyone.'

Isaac reflected that this was nearer the truth than Moshe supposed. Certainly no one knew him. Then he noticed that they were still hanging on to each other.

'Well, you won't know anyone big enough, that's for sure,' he said, loudly. 'Still, anything will do so long as it's a dress. Obviously it won't fit, what would? It doesn't matter, she won't notice. I could run her up a little something out of dish rags and she wouldn't notice.' It was the nearest he could get to knocking their hands apart.

'And she wouldn't wear it,' said Eleanor, letting her fingers fall open.

'Oh no, it must fit,' said Moshe. He stepped back and his moustache came down over his smile and brushed it away. 'But I really don't know anybody who wants to sell one. They're so hard to get and fabric is so expensive.'

'It would cost a year's wages to cover that lot, anyway,' said Isaac, and was gratified to see Eleanor contract and stoop. 'It's no good trying to make yourself look smaller,' he bawled. 'Especially with the light behind you, halo or no halo.'

What little he could see of Moshe's sallow face turned red with embarrassment and he began to go.

'Count yourself lucky,' said Isaac to Eleanor, 'that he didn't meet you last week, before the spots faded.' He left her kneeling there, wretchedly fingering the scars, and went after Moshe to escort him to the door.

'Isn't she an eyeful?' he said, meaningly. 'Seriously, though, we've got to get her to church.'

'I don't think you will ever get her to do anything,' said Moshe, peering hesitantly at Isaac from under his hair. He had very dark eyes and rather thick eyelids. Isaac had never stood so close to him before. 'Why don't you be . . . kind?' he said.

'Why should I be kind?' demanded Isaac, and stood in astonishment by the porch, watching Moshe, who knew he was being watched, stump down the hill, his feet becoming more unwieldy with every step.

Outside the police station, fly-eyed Casimir was watering the sun flowers.

The next morning Eleanor began to carve. Isaac had imagined carving to be a similar matter to the careful whittling of the stone head, which had finally been split and thrown away; and wondered more and more if even ten years would be long enough for his block to become a sculpture. He was soon undeceived.

Theodore was sitting at his ease in the loggia, over the remains of his breakfast, while Isaac washed curtains in the kitchen and Eleanor crawled about on the block, clinging to the edge with prehensile toes. She wore her boots only when the stone became too hot to stand on. The charcoal had reappeared and the surface of the block was scored with black marks.

Isaac watched them peacefully ignoring each other and turned his attention to the day's work. On the window sill he arranged a row of small bowls: beans soaking in oil and wine, strips of frozen beef thawing back to meat, dried fruit fattening in syrup. In the distance Omega shuddered behind its veil of dust as the first of the day's blasting rocked it underground. Isaac felt the reverberations through the floor and thought, as he rarely did nowadays, of his own explosion in the cold room. How long ago, how lucky. I should always have such luck, said Isaac to himself. Theodore rang his little bell that stood on the table at mealtimes and Isaac went out to clear away the plates. The secretary had arrived and sat portentously beside Theodore with a dispatch case poised on his knee. He and Isaac stared past each other to opposite ends of the hall.

'It's a pleasant morning,' said Theodore. 'We'll work out here for a while. Bring out the document case, will you. It's on my desk.'

The first hammer blow fell before he could finish speaking, to be followed by a fusillade of such sustained violence that the three of them could only stand there, hands over ears. There was a final, deliberate slam, and a slab of stone, as big as a man's torso, detached itself from the side of the block and slid to the ground. Then the dust reached them. Theodore and the secretary fled to the study and Isaac ran the other way, into the garden.

'What are you doing?' he shouted. 'What are you doing?'

'I'm carving,' said Eleanor. 'What did you think I was doing, cutting my toenails?'

'Very funny,' said Isaac, running to the terrace and climbing up to stand beside her on the block. 'You have such a perfect sense of timing. Why begin while Theodore was having his breakfast?'

'He'd finished eating. I made sure of that,' said Eleanor, who was plotting further incisions with the stump of charcoal.

149

'He was sitting three metres from you. Don't do it again.' He looked at the raw scar where the stone had fallen away. 'How did you manage to shift so much at once?'

'It was flawed. I cut in along the flaw. I'm going to do it again in a minute, just where you're standing.'

Isaac looked down. 'You can't cut along here, you'll ruin the lawn. All the bits will fall on it.'

'Yes, well, they won't float,' said Eleanor. 'What did you think would happen?'

He hadn't thought. He suddenly saw the block diminishing while a pile of rubble grew up round it, obliterating the lawn.

'You don't know what I went through to get this lawn.'

'No, but you know what I went through to get here. What can I do about it? Watch this come down.'

The hammer struck again and again, round Isaac's feet. He blinked and bounded backwards as a second boulder fell to the ground and embedded itself in the grass. Isaac jumped down after it and tried to drag it free.

'You must stop. Will they all be this big?'

'To begin with. I have to take away what I don't need.'

'Theodore –'

'Theodore must have known what would happen. If he didn't, you'd better take him on one side and explain gently that stone, being subject to gravity, falls. Unlike dust, which goes up.'

'Dust falls too, in the end. Don't I know it.'

'When will it rain?'

'Not till spring.'

'It would lay the dust.'

'I can't make it rain.'

The heat made Isaac crotchety, like the rest of the

inhabitants. Eleanor rolled up her trousers to the knee and pushed back her sleeves but he, in his position as steward with the honour of the household to maintain, was obliged to remain fully clothed. When he set out for the city he was tempted to forget propriety and leave off the long coat that presentable persons wore in the street. Only manual workers like Moshe went out in their shirt sleeves; or oafish outlanders, like Eleanor. Seeing her wander about half dressed, as it seemed to him, his own clothes felt more oppressive than ever.

At the bottom of the hill he fell in with Moshe. Even without a coat Moshe seemed to be steaming inside his heavy working clothes. He was too dark skinned to become sun-tanned but under the thick coils of hair his face shone with sweat.

'Why don't you shave off your beard?' said Isaac. Moshe looked at him uncertainly for a while before deciding to answer.

'I'd be cold in winter.'

'Well, do like Eleanor does,' said Isaac, watching him closely. 'She stays cool enough.'

'What does Eleanor do?' asked Moshe, almost as if he would prefer not to know.

'She doesn't wear a coat,' said Isaac. 'Or boots, or a robe, and the sun doesn't strike her down dead like they told us it would. Let's all do it.' He laughed, and made as if to take off his coat. Moshe did not laugh. He swung himself in front of Isaac and grabbed his arm.

'Why doesn't she wear those things?'

'Well, she hasn't got them to wear,' Isaac admitted. 'Except the boots, and she doesn't bother much with them, either.'

'But we've got them, and like it or not, we'll wear them,' said Moshe. 'Listen, Isaac. She may be a nuisance, but don't let her be an influence. Don't let

151

anyone point at you and say, "He does that because Eleanor does it." An influence is not a good thing to be, here. Isaac, please.'

'I don't know what you mean,' Isaac stammered, drawing away. 'You talk too much. Yaah, I couldn't have s-s-s-said that once, could I? What's the matter with you? Who's being influenced?'

He left Moshe standing in the road, still grasping at an arm that was no longer there.

Sean, one blue eye, one green, each looking in a different direction, stood behind a pillar in the loggia, fanning himself limply and watching Eleanor attack the stone. Isaac came up behind him.

'What do you want?'

As Aumer's steward Sean availed himself of Aumer's right to enter a house uninvited in the service of the church. He turned one insolent eye on Isaac and continued to watch Eleanor with the other.

'I am delivering a message from my master to yours. I took it to him personally.'

Theodore called from the study, 'Is that you, Isaac?' Isaac went in and found Theodore at his desk, hands clenched on the marble top.

'Aumer's just sent me a letter. Do you know what's in it?'

Isaac looked at the hands and at Theodore's jaw, as tightly clenched.

'No,' he said.

'Aumer was supposed to be visiting us tonight to play cards. So were the Camerons. We arranged it weeks ago. Now he tells me this.' He read from the sheet of paper before him. ' "Although it grieves me to fail in friendship towards a valued and respected member of the community I cannot, as spiritual leader of that community, be seen to confer approbation, by entering it, upon a household where the tenth day is set at nought." Do you know what he means?'

'It means he's not coming.'

'I know that, but where does it leave us?'

'One short this evening. Do you want me to play?'

'Isaac!'

He realized, with a start, that he was not responding in the prescribed manner. If Theodore was angry and worried so should Isaac be angry and worried, and Isaac was being undeniably light-minded, flippant even. The memory of Moshe's urgent voice stung him. *Don't let her be an influence.*

'She's got to go to church,' said Isaac, quickly.

'This week,' said Theodore. 'What kind of a fool do you think I'm going to look in front of Cameron? He's got eleven servants and never a moment's trouble. I've got two and nothing but trouble.'

'Couldn't you order her to go?' Isaac suggested.

Theodore leaned so far forward that Isaac thought his feet must have left the ground on the other side of the desk.

'Tell me,' said Theodore. 'Do you find the work here too difficult? Would you be happier with fewer responsibilities?'

'No,' said Isaac, quietly. 'Not at all.'

'Then tell her yourself and see that she does as you say. If Gregor can handle ten, you should be able to manage with one.'

Gregor.

Isaac left Theodore composing a suitable reply and went to find Sean.

'What, precisely, made Aumer feel that he shouldn't enter a house where the tenth day is set at nought?'

'I did,' said Sean, modestly. 'I didn't feel it was

153

commensurate with the office of steward to the pastor of the First Church Secular of Epsilon, to allow the silly old fool to be seen coming here.'

'Ah. And who suggested that it wasn't commensurate with your office and how much did he pay you?'

'How much will you pay me to tell you?'

'Nothing. It was Gregor, wasn't it? Did Cameron put him up to it or was this a bit of private enterprise?'

'Is that a question? One quarter dinar; thank you. Gregor thought of it by himself, though I daresay he took his cue from Cameron. Cameron's been saying some funny things about this household in the last few days. You can't expect Gregor to let a funny thing slip through his fingers.'

Isaac left him lounging against a pillar and went out to the garden. The square edge of the block had become a rough shoulder and a row of rocks lay beside it on the grass. He put a hand on one and found it too hot to touch. Eleanor, evidently of the same opinion, was sitting in the shade, putting on her boots. Isaac planted himself in front of her.

'You're coming to church tomorrow.'

'I'm not,' said Eleanor, without looking up.

'You are, or to put it another way, if you don't you'll be in gaol by tomorrow night.'

'I shall work tomorrow,' said Eleanor. 'I can't stop now.'

'Listen.' Isaac sat down beside her. 'If you work tomorrow I don't believe you'll ever work again. You'll owe Aumer four dinars and you won't be able to pay him. I can't bail you out and no one else will.' He thought of Moshe. 'No one else will. Loukides may – what have you done to your shirt?'

'It split.'

154

'You can't go out like that.'

'I'm not going out.' She collected the hammer and chisels that lay beside her and climbed back onto the block. 'You can pray for me tomorrow, if you like.'

'I wish I could break your neck.'

He returned to the house. By the voices from the study he guessed that Theodore was talking to Sean, so he tiptoed past and went to the linen room by the servants' hall. After the kitchen, Isaac liked it best of all the rooms in the house. It was a big windowless cupboard with racks on three sides to hold the clothes and bedding that were currently in use. He got the most peaceful pleasure from standing among the dim shelves, smelling clean cloth and admiring the neat folds, stacked to the ceiling. Its only drawback was that it had no handle on the inside of the door, so he could never entirely seclude himself there. He had to prop the door open since the day the wind had swung it shut and locked him in for an hour before Theodore heard him calling. He had liked it less that day.

One side of it was occupied by the curtains that had to be changed so frequently during the summer months. Underneath them, in a cupboard, he kept the thick winter drapes, one of which he knew was beginning to fray along the folds. He pulled it out from among the others and spread it on the floor in the back hall, watching the heavy fabric billow and settle. Then he fetched his shears from the kitchen and began to crawl round the edge of the cloth, hacking at it and muttering as he went, 'The Camerons have a dressmaker; the da Vincis have a dressmaker; so do we. So do we!'

'Don't you want to know what I'm making?' he asked Eleanor later, as they rested in the kitchen. He had

155

learned to prevent her from sitting on the chopping block by sitting on it himself and he perched there crosslegged, stitching busily. Eleanor sat on the floor.

'No. Why, is it a shroud?'

'A dress,' said Isaac, marvelling at her lack of curiosity. Most people in their position coveted cloth and eagerly encouraged their employers to put on weight, in order to inherit outgrown garments. Isaac was still using up clothes that Theodore had been wearing at the time of his father's death, and before.

'You might lend me your needle,' said Eleanor. 'I could mend my shirt.'

'I'll do it for you, if you like,' said Isaac, who had assumed from Eleanor's appearance that she didn't know how to sew.

'Just give me the needle.'

'You can't reach round to the back,' he argued, but she could, and he watched in dismay as she basted the rent with five stitches and bit off the thread, leaving a long end dangling.

'I could have done a better job with a blunt bradawl and string,' he said, re-threading the needle. 'Why didn't you let me do it?'

'Stop nagging and get on with your dress,' said Eleanor. 'I suppose it is for you?' Isaac ignored her. 'For Theodore?'

Theodore had gone to the city after lunch and Isaac awaited his return with one ear cocked towards the front door. When he heard footsteps crossing the hall he got up quickly, and thrust the curtain behind him. Gregor stood in the doorway. Eleanor saw him over her shoulder and was on her feet before he was fairly in the room.

She's learned something, at any rate, thought Isaac. Gregor took no notice of him but stood looking at Eleanor, rocking back and forth on his toes.

'A word to the wise,' said Gregor. 'In the form of a short question. What will annoy Theodore more: losing his sculptor or losing face?'

'No question,' said Isaac. 'No question of either.'

'All right, no questions. Just a plain fact.' Gregor moved forward until he stood nose to chin with Eleanor. She had been sitting down the last time they met. 'The ship to Euterpe, yes, that's right, the one you came on, should have left orbit yesterday. I hear, however, that it's been delayed and won't be going until tomorrow night. That leaves plenty of time for a really bloody-minded stone carver to be on it, and as Isaac says, no questions asked.'

Eleanor stepped back and Gregor advanced again. 'Wouldn't you say that two weeks is rather a short stay after two years' travelling to get here? And two years back; assuming you want to go back, of course.'

'Why should I go back?' said Eleanor, looking considerably less sure of herself than she had done for some days. 'I have a contract.'

'You have a piece of paper,' said Gregor, 'which can be shown to any Government official who wants to know why you are here. Conversely, you have a file at the police station which can be shown to any Government official who wants to know why you are not here. When the annual census is taken you will have to be accounted for whether you are in Epsilon or half-way back to Euterpe. That's all. I thought you'd like to know.'

'What's going on?' said Isaac. He clutched at the curtain material and ran the needle into his hand.

'Nothing's going on,' said Gregor, mistaking the reason for his gasp. 'But your friend here is treading on thin ice, sailing close to the wind, leaping before she looks. Old Earth sayings,' he explained, strolling out of the room. Isaac pursued him into the hall.

'Was that a warning?'

'In a way. How much do you think it's worth to her, to have been warned what will happen? Two dinars?'

'I've warned her. She hasn't got two dinars and she's already in debt to Aumer. Why did you set him up? To annoy Theodore?'

'Just tightening a screw here and a screw there,' said Gregor. 'As to your friend – she is your friend, isn't she? I don't care if she goes or stays, but if she stays I'd like her to know who allows it.'

'You don't allow it.'

Gregor shook his head. 'I'm afraid I do. Tell her, will you, two dinars on pay day.'

10

After a brief, powdery sunset Mnemosyne dropped below Lambda Crag so suddenly that one expected a dull thud to come booming up from the valley. Isaac switched on the lights and finished his sewing in the kitchen. Eleanor had long ago retired to her alcove where she slept restlessly, choking, calling out, sometimes letting go a short, hoarse scream. Isaac could hear her voice from where he sat and he wished, even in the depths of his dislike, that she could sleep more easily.

For a while his wish was granted and he sewed in silence. Then the voice rose again; not nightmares this time but fragments of a querulous conversation. Typical, thought Isaac. She even argues in her sleep. He bitterly pitied her dream opponent who was clearly getting the worst of it.

He shook out the folds of fabric and held up the curtain that had become a dress. It was a simple garment, stitched up straight at the sides with two holes for the arms and one for the head, and although entirely grace-less, had the undeniable virtue of concealing everything from the neck down. He hoped that on Eleanor it would fall in stately lines, stopping just clear of the ground.

He locked the front door, switched off the lights and went to bed, sucking his perforated fingers. He lay in the dark and made his plans for the morning. At the other end of the hall the unhappy voice insisted, 'It won't do any good.' And, 'It hurts. It hurts!'

*

As Mnemosyne rose again beyond Omega, Isaac left his bed and made strenuous preparations for his day of rest. Then he took a saucepan, ran into the back hall and began beating the wall beside Eleanor's alcove. It was unthinkable that he should draw the curtains and look in; the alcoves were the last, if not the only, refuge of privacy, never to be violated. He waited for Eleanor to burst through the curtains in a rage but his tone-deaf carillon had no effect.

Now where's she gone? Surely she's not going to spend the day in hiding? He became aware of voices from the garden. Hurrying outside he found Eleanor sitting on the wall and talking to someone below her in the road. She must have crept out, if it were possible for her to creep, while he was busy in the kitchen. He went to the front door, opened it quietly and looked out, round the corner of the porch. Eleanor was talking to Moshe. He stood at the foot of the wall, groomed for churchgoing in a clean shirt and a coat, his hair slightly combed.

'Shabbat ought to be every seventh day,' he was saying, seriously. 'It used to be every seventh day that no one worked. I would prefer that, myself.'

'Who wouldn't?' said Eleanor.

'You wouldn't,' he said.

'I stop when I feel like it,' said Eleanor. 'Today I don't feel like it.'

'But you will rest?' He spread his arms, hopefully. Eleanor stood up, dangerously balanced on the narrow causeway of the wall.

'How's my halo this morning?'

'Come down,' said Moshe. 'Come down before you fall.'

Eleanor said, 'Why don't you come up?'

Isaac hopped out of the porch and poked Moshe in the small of the back. 'What are you after?' he demanded, with black suspicion. Eleanor, surprised by Isaac's sudden eruption from the porch, lost her balance and fell off the wall. Moshe was confused and concerned. He stooped to help her up.

'Are you hurt? Your elbow . . . ?'

'Leave her alone,' Isaac growled, pushing between them. 'If you start counting bruises you'll be here all day; she's always knocking holes in herself. What are you doing here, anyway?'

'Just passing,' said Moshe.

'Oh yes? Going somewhere interesting, were you?' Once past the house the road petered out in an aimless track that lost itself among the stones of the hillside. If it had ever intended to go anywhere it had given up the idea, long since.

Moshe gnawed his thumb. Eleanor scowled.

'I'd better go back,' said Moshe. He turned to Eleanor. 'I'll see you in church.'

Eleanor nodded and muttered something inaudible to him as he set off down the road.

'How did you know he'd be out here?' said Isaac. 'Did you arrange to meet him?'

'No, I was out here anyway, and he came up the hill.'

'Did I hear him say he'd see you in church?'

'Yes.'

'Does that mean you're going?'

'Yes.'

'I thought Gregor would make you see reason.'

'Gregor be damned. It wasn't Gregor.'

'Wasn't it?' Isaac felt ill at ease. Blackmail he could understand; he was on familiar ground. Persuasion was another matter. He recalled Moshe's suggestion, *Why don't you be kind?* Where would kindness take them? 'Well, whoever it was, don't forget that Gregor wants two dinars off you at the end of the month. Now, come inside. I want to show you something.'

'Moshe didn't charge me anything,' said Eleanor, but she followed him indoors meekly enough.

'What's this?' she said, when Isaac held up the dress. 'Oh, it's your shroud, isn't it?' Then she understood him. 'It's not for me?'

'Try it on.'

'I can't wear that.'

'Why not? You don't seem to mind what you wear. There's a mirror in the dining hall, there's a mirror in our hall, there's a mirror in the bathroom. For pity's sake, Eleanor, when did you last look at yourself?'

'The day I came,' said Eleanor, and Isaac knew that she hadn't dared to look since.

'It's just for church, just for wearing in public. You can put your rags on again afterwards. No, take them off first,' he wailed, as she plunged head first into the dress. 'Oh, you are disgusting.'

'I could carve in this,' said Eleanor, lost inside. 'Perhaps if I cut the bottom off ...' To his surprise, her head emerged through the right hole and the skirts settled round her feet. Hanging straight from the shoulder it still looked exactly like a curtain.

'Could you make it shorter?'

'I could, but I won't' said Isaac. 'That's just the right length. Now you look like everyone else – well, nearer like. Don't wear it for work; keep it nice for going out in.'

'I shall trip over. Can I belt it?'

'No, it's meant to be worn loose.'

'I shall belt it. Have you got any string?'

'Leave it alone!' said Isaac sharply. 'Go and practise walking in it, and have a look in the mirror.'

'I shall belt it.' She went out treading awkwardly, as if on water.

162

'Don't say thank you,' muttered Isaac.

The church was as hot as a bakehouse. As soon as his congregation was seated, Aumer closed the doors at the back and processed up the aisle. Mounting the pulpit he spread his arms and rose on his toes as though he were about to blast off and soar through the roof, leaving a small cloud of oxygen vapour.

He filled his bellows with hot air and began to speak.

'Friends, in these prosperous times, let us not forget our harsh beginnings, the frugal nativity of our planet. Let us not forget the giants that were, in those days, men of true steel who gave their lives that our land might live.'

'Theodore's old man?' said Eleanor, behind her sleeve, while wiping the sweat out of her eyes. In the unaccustomed folds of the curtain she must be suffering more than Isaac had allowed for. He drove his elbow into her side to silence her.

'In these days, as another generation comes to maturity, let us ensure that the labours of our comrades were not in vain, that the land they wrought for us shall be passed on to our children as they would wish to see it; a land fit for free men to stand tall in.'

'Where are these children?' said Eleanor. 'I never see any.'

'Sssh. On Clio.'

'Oh, you import them. I might have guessed. There doesn't seem to be any other way of getting them.'

'Shut up.'

'Friends, we are all from the same cradle. In our time we have seen three homelands destroyed, laid waste, despoiled, violated. Shall we see it happen a fourth time, here on Erato?

'No, my friends. I say to you, no, no, no! It is our sacred trust, laid on us by our comrades, to preserve our

163

planet, to save it from defilement. We are alone in this; we must stand shoulder to shoulder and fight for it.'

'What's that rubbish at the front, by the pulpit?' Eleanor whispered.

'Sssh. That's a sculpture.'

'Who did it?'

'I can't remember his name. He disappeared.'

'He deserved to.'

'Don't say that. Don't ever say that.'

'Friends, our master, the Government, sits in Euterpe among the ruins of a once-great civilization.' He lowered his voice. 'Let us not be unduly harsh on them, when we think of their dilemma. Was it not that same Government that sent us out here thirty years ago to plumb the depths of Erato, and later gave us its blessing when we declined to go back as others had done, but swore instead to stay and bring life to this barren land?'

'I thought you said he wasn't here then.'

'So I did. Will you shut up.'

'But we and they see different aspects of the same dilemma. On Euterpe, beset by riot and violence, they care only to help people escape. But friends, how will that help us? In the old days they said to us, Go forth and be fruitful and multiply.'

'No one ever said that to me,' Eleanor murmured.

'I'm not surprised,' said Isaac.

'When we came here they said, Go where work awaits you, and what has happened? Whether there is work or not, they still send us their poor, their defeated, the lees with the vintage, the dregs with the cream. Beset, I say, by ruin, they seek to inflict that ruin upon us. *Friends! There shall be no ruin here!*'

The simmering congregation stirred violently as if coming to the boil, although moved by the sound rather than the fury. Aumer leaned over the edge of the pulpit like a man so exalted that he could skim the length of the church without touching the floor.

'To those of you who serve I say, beware the sin of dependence.

'To those of us who are set in authority I say, beware of the parasite.

'Let no man look to another for his comfort. Let depart from among us the parasite who lives off the charity of others. Let us stand by and support our brother Loukides who watches over us, who sees the infirm foot, the faltering purpose, who plucks from among us the parasite who seeks sustenance when his labours fail him. There are many such who would sap the life-blood of our community.

'Friends,' said Aumer. 'These people are not happy. They are sent as a snare and a delusion to trap the senses.'

'We're coming to your bit,' whispered Isaac. 'We haven't had it since Ansell went.'

'Will a man prosper who turns his back on the community and serves only himself? Consider a miner, a good and honest man, who has laboured long and hard in the service of the Government, who has laboured long and hard to cleave for himself a place in the community.

'That man may say, "I have laboured long and hard and my working days are done. I wish to cushion my declining years with sensual pleasures, with artifice. I am discontented with the abundance of nature, poured out before me."' He waved a hand towards the windows which looked out on the yellow lawns and withering flowers of Cameron's terraces. 'I say unto you, that man's foot is set upon the downward slope, for he brings among us the man who labours for himself. Now the man who labours for himself is a man and who shall gainsay him? And when that man's work is finished, should he not return whence he came, rejoicing that his travail is done? Verily he should do this thing, but no! He remains here, if he can, and tries to entrap others in his toils; a sore, an open wound upon the healthy flesh of the community, dependent upon those he once served as a free man, enslaved by his wilful passion for self-determination.

'Friends, the answer is so plain: if nobody wants him, why should he stay?

'I say to you, cut out this infection.

'Bid him go, and if he will not, repatriate him.'

'Oh god, when will he stop?' Eleanor moaned, clutching her head.

'I wish you'd pay attention,' said Isaac. 'Casimir's watching.'

'I would say also to those who have newly come among us, take the work that is offered and labour in the time appointed. When that time is over, accept that it is over, and do not seek a foothold on a sheer slope where there is none. That we may say at the end of the day, Let thy servant depart in peace.'

Eleanor started to get up, but Isaac jerked her down again.

'Not yet. Aumer goes first, then the miners, then us.'

'Does it constitute an offence, going out first?' said Eleanor, pulling away. Moshe leaned over from the seat behind and touched her on the shoulder.

'Wait.'

'You get your beard out of this,' said Isaac, turning round. The three of them cracked heads, and in the midst of the subsequent recriminations, Gregor's head was suddenly there as well.

'Two dinars, Eleanor. On pay day.'

'You can whistle for it,' said Eleanor. She was out of her seat and halfway down the aisle while Isaac was still

166

studying Gregor's reaction. He bounded after her and caught her up at the door.

'Do as I tell you, for god's sake,' he said, in the porch. 'You'll pay him all right. Didn't you listen to a word of that sermon? Didn't you understand?'

'I understood it very well,' said Eleanor. 'It's not dependence they're afraid of, it's independence. People like me setting up on their own. Look here, if Theodore foxed that contract, why shouldn't I find other work?'

'How? Where would you live if you couldn't? What would you live on? I knew you weren't listening. Do you remember that poster? One man, one job? Well this is the other side of it. No job, no man.'

Eleanor reckoned up her debts in charcoal on a slab of stone.

'Well then, how much do you owe?' said Isaac, observing that her mathematics were of the same standard as her sewing.

'Six dinars, I think, so far.'

'So far's right. Gregor will charge interest. And how much will that leave you when you do get paid?'

'Forty-four. That's not too bad.'

'It's not good. If you go on at this rate you'll owe it all. It's an expensive pastime, upsetting Gregor.'

'He's an unforgiving so-and-so, isn't he,' said Eleanor.

'No. He's just realized that it's more fun keeping you here than getting you kicked out. And he's only a steward. Don't try hitting a miner.'

'What would happen?'

'What do you think would happen?' said Isaac. 'It wouldn't be a fine.'

'Aha; the ultimate deterrent,' said Eleanor. 'Marching orders.'

'It's still better than lynching.'

'Has anyone ever done it?'

'Not in my time,' said Isaac. 'You may laugh, but that deterrent's a real deterrent.'

'No, but suppose that one of your miners was a bad employer, a real bastard –'

'Keep your voice down.' They were on top of the block and he looked nervously over the wall.

'– and somebody did him in, wouldn't the others close ranks? Wouldn't they all side with one of themselves, rather than see him taken?'

'And run the risk of being deported too?' said Isaac. 'No they wouldn't.'

'And you?'

'Nor would I.'

'And the Government? Doesn't the Government care about all these deportations?'

'I dare say, but the Government's on Euterpe. What we call the Government here are our people, immigrants. They don't care about Euterpe any more. No one likes them, of course, but they don't really do much harm. Except the Customs and Excise,' he added thoughtfully.

He climbed down from the block and went indoors, leaving Eleanor to her arithmetic, and as amazed as ever by her refusal to accept a situation that suited everyone else. He was not familiar with the term 'to do in', but he could guess what she meant. Did she perhaps think that he ought to do Theodore in?

He entered the kitchen and opened the trapdoor to the wine cellar. It held more than wine now. Theodore had come by some sacks of rich and gravid mould with instructions to keep it in damp darkness and see what happened. Isaac had spread it in trays on the cellar floor and found one morning that little pearly globes had appeared on the top. For a few days they had led a pointless existence, growing up and dying as he watched, marvelling at the microcosm, until he showed one to Eleanor who had seen such things before and told him that they were mushrooms; food.

It was the first fresh food that he had ever eaten. He gathered a bowlful of them and took them upstairs to be prepared for lunch. The secretary was eating with them today and although Isaac grudged him even one of his little foundlings, there might be unpleasantness if he didn't get any.

He placed the mushrooms on the chopping block, first brushing away the ring of stone granules that appeared like spores wherever Eleanor sat, and sliced them skin-thin with a razor.

'Five for Theodore, three for me, two for her and one for you, Mr Secretary Fish Brain.'

Fish Brain didn't speak to Eleanor either, which was some comfort.

While he was making a dressing to serve with the mushrooms he heard voices outside, and then the wholly unexpected sound of a woman laughing. He went out to investigate and saw a stranger sitting at his ease in the gap between the block of stone and the wall: a dark-faced young man with dark hair that curled over his neck and forehead, and with a smile so entrancing that Isaac's heart struck him once, hard, in the chest.

However, he was not smiling at Isaac; he hadn't seen him. His eye was fixed on someone else, out of sight behind the block, and entrancing or not there should be no strangers in Theodore's garden. Isaac wondered how to get rid of someone so obviously at home. The woman laughed again so he went forward with a fine air of determination and confronted them.

The laughter was Eleanor.

The stranger with the beautiful dark face was Moshe.

'Ssssss,' said Isaac. 'I see you've been pruning your hedge.'

'You suggested it,' said Moshe. He put his hand in front of his mouth but his eyes went on grinning.

'I didn't think you'd do it,' said Isaac, almost unable to believe what he had seen. He had always imagined that Moshe suffered from some disfigurement and wore the beard to conceal it. 'What are you doing here, anyway? You're supposed to ring the bell and wait for me.'

'The door was open.'

'It's always open. Don't do it again.'

'You've got the rats in you,' said Eleanor. She had stopped laughing when Isaac looked round the end of the block, and the customary scowl was fissuring her face. 'Look what he's brought you.'

'I've grown a lettuce,' said Moshe.

'Rats?'

'Dozens of them.'

'Dozens of rats?'

'Lettuces,' said Moshe. 'Under that glass you got for us. But this is the first.'

'Shouldn't Cameron have that?' Moshe looked as naively pleased with himself as a clever child. Isaac knew he was twenty-five and was surprised that cutting the hair should so weaken a man. He took the lettuce. It was a flabby green thing, with leaves. 'How do I cook it?'

'Put it in cold water,' said Moshe. 'It will improve.' He came out from behind his hand to look at Eleanor, tentatively, as if uncertain of the reception he would get.

'It won't cook in cold water.'

'You don't cook it, you eat it raw. I had one once. It was nice.'

'Well, thank you,' said Isaac. 'If you come back tomorrow I'll give you some mushrooms.' He regretted saying it immediately. He didn't want Moshe back tomorrow, or any other day.

'I will,' said Moshe, too eagerly. He began to stand up.

'What else can you grow?' said Eleanor, as if to detain him.

'Hair,' said Isaac. 'It'll all be back by the morning. Wait and see.'

'Only small things,' said Moshe. 'The soil is so shallow – water is so scarce. At Delta they have a reservoir, they grow trees. I wish I could grow a tree.'

'What would you do with a tree?'

'I'd sit under it,' said Moshe.

'Better than sitting here,' said Isaac. Moshe took the hint and went, after one last smile that made Isaac wish, for a second, that he could have his tree and sit under it all day long, if only they could watch him do it.

'Did you really tell him to shave?' said Eleanor.

'No. I only made a joke about it,' said Isaac, hearing the footsteps die away on the road. 'He knew it was a joke. He just used it as an excuse.'

'Why an excuse?'

'I think he wanted to be seen,' said Isaac, looking sideways at her.

'If I looked like that,' said Eleanor, sadly, 'I'd want to be seen, too.'

Nights and shadows grew shorter. One day the secretary succumbed to the climate and hard labour and had to be sent home prostrated in the carrier. Isaac found

171

himself with a portfolio of clerical work in addition to his own duties, since he understood the workings of Intergalactic at least as well as Theodore did.

Theodore rested on a couch in the study that evening, the hottest evening of the summer so far, and still many weeks in which worse might come. Isaac sat in the kitchen, the furthest he could get from Mnemosyne's fierce pyre. On the table before him a pile of invoices grew soft and damp under his hand.

Eleanor had given up trying to carve about tea-time and had gone to her alcove where she lay with the curtains drawn. Had Isaac liked her better he could have suggested a dozen ways of making the hot season more tolerable: the curtained alcoves were the most stifling places in the house, but she was less trouble asleep than waking so he left her there. Now she wandered into the kitchen to join him, blundering against the corner of the table as she passed.

'There's nothing so big but you don't walk into it,' said Isaac, soothing his disturbed papers. 'Can't you see what you're doing? You can hardly pick up a spoon without cutting your hand open.'

Eleanor leaned on the window sill, looking out at the hot sky, the hotter hillside.

'Do you have any friends, Isaac?'

He thought she was being personal. 'Of course I have friends.'

'Where are they, then? Where do you meet them? When do you meet them?'

'Everywhere. Any time.' Isaac couldn't see where the questions were leading and was puzzled. 'In Epsilon; in their houses, in the streets.'

'But never here. Do they never come here?'

'No,' said Isaac. 'Only Theodore's friends come here.'

172

'I see. So there's nowhere you could meet? Where you could all meet?'

Isaac watched a globe of sweat gather on the bridge of his nose, roll down to the tip and drop onto the paper in front of him. What she was suggesting was not illegal, merely unheard of. Any like gathering would certainly be attended by Casimir, notebook and stylus poised to catch conspiracy.

'No, there isn't.'

'Why are you all so afraid of each other?' Eleanor turned her back on the sky and sat on the window sill, watching him.

'Stop kicking, you'll mark the whitewash. Who says we're afraid of each other?'

'Well, I'll assume that not everyone is like Gregor, but why does no one here do anything on anyone else's behalf? Moshe said there was a reservoir at Delta. Why isn't there a reservoir here?'

'We've all got our own wells and cisterns, I told you.'

'That's what I mean. There's a generator too, isn't there?'

'At the back. We all have one.'

'But there's a power station in the city, Moshe said. Why not have electricity from that?'

'You spend too much time talking to Moshe. Gregor won't like it. While we all have our own supplies, we don't have to rely on anyone else. If we all shared everything, we'd all run out together.'

'If they can grow trees at Delta, why not here? Think what this place could be like if you all pooled your water. What happens to sewage?'

'Shafts, boreholes,' said Isaac briefly. 'The old workings.'

173

'And what happens when the boreholes are full? Does your past come surging up to confront you?'

'Don't be more repellent than you can help,' said Isaac. 'Delta isn't Paradise, whatever Moshe may think. They depend on the Government for everything, and they pay for it. They've got telephones and sewage works and water mains and electricity, and they've got the Government. Delta's not much bigger than Epsilon and it's got a population of fifteen thousand. There's three hundred of us. We make our own laws, they don't.'

'We? You and who else?'

'Anyone can go to Delta and anyone does.'

'I think I will,' said Eleanor.

'That would be very silly,' said Isaac. 'I didn't say anyone from Epsilon could go. Anyway, things will have to change there soon. Better to be here where there's nothing to change.'

'What about your friend Ansell? If he'd been in Delta he might not have disappeared so suddenly.'

'Eleanor, you cannot go to Delta.' He finally got the drift of the conversation. 'Don't even think of it. You are here, and here you stay. Unfortunately.'

'And when I've finished here?'

'I shouldn't let anyone hear you talk about finishing. You've hardly started.'

Left alone again, Isaac finished his papers and returned them to the darkling study. Theodore was asleep on the couch, his slumber punctuated by a high-pitched whistle between his front teeth and by the murmurous whirr of the fan above his head. There was no reason why Isaac should not have had a fan in the kitchen, except that Theodore had never considered it necessary to install one. Isaac put the portfolio on the desk and slipped out again. In the hall he ran against Eleanor, heading for the front door.

'Where are you going?' he said. She glanced down at him without replying and went on.

'You're not going out?' She mounted the steps, lifted the curtain and disappeared, in a hurry. Isaac ran after her. When he reached the road she was already halfway down the hill, a dark streak in the white night.

Anyone might see her. He raced to catch her up.

'Eleanor, where do you think you're going?'

'I'm going to see Moshe.'

'What? You can't do that.'

'Why can't I visit a friend?'

'How can he be a friend? You hardly know him.'

'Perhaps when I know him better I'll like him less.'

'You can't go there.' He overtook her again.

'Is that the law? Is it in the statute book? Who's to prevent me?'

'I'm the steward. I prevent you. Anyway, Gregor won't let you in.'

'Sod Gregor. Moshe's out on the terrace, I've been watching him.'

'Eleanor!' She swept on; he could barely keep up. 'People don't walk alone at night. It isn't allowed, and I can't come with you. Theodore thinks I'm at home, th-th-th-thinks you're at home.'

'Go home then. I don't want you to come with me.'

'Be quiet.' Isaac looked towards the police station. The windows were shuttered and the building silent. Only the dying sun flowers hung their heads in the moon's light, but who knew where Casimir lurked after dark?

'I must go back. Eleanor, come back with me.' He stood still in the roadway, but Eleanor walked on and did not look round.

Isaac went home and hovered near the doorway all evening. When midnight came, Theodore woke up and went to bed, and Isaac locked the door, slamming home each bolt with venomous satisfaction.

Let her climb over the wall.

PART THREE

ISAAC,
ELEANOR,
MOSHE

11

The hundredth day came and went uncelebrated except
by Isaac. Theodore renewed the contract; he had
nothing to complain of now. The summer's heat cur-
tailed all extra-mural activity and no one ventured out of
the houses in the light of the savage star that threatened
to burn them off the face of her planet. Errands were
run in the early morning or at evening when Mnemosyne
ebbed towards Lambda.

Eleanor never left the house at all, save as the tail of
the small procession that crept out to the church and
back on the tenth day. She began working at dawn and
hammered until noon; rested during the worst of the heat
and started again when evening approached, just as
Theodore and Isaac were preparing to relax after a day's
work.

Moshe almost vanished from their lives. They saw him
in church and Isaac sometimes caught sight of him
irrigating Cameron's lawns with a bucket, but Moshe no
longer strayed from his terraces. Gregor too stayed at
home and any messages were delivered by his underlings.
Eleanor had never gone again to Cameron's after that
one nocturnal visit, and Isaac did not care to risk
questioning her about it. He presumed that Gregor had
taken the situation in hand and could only feel relieved,
although he did wonder why no account had been
rendered.

Eleanor managed without friends, after all. Instead,
old adversaries kept her company by night, and soon

Isaac knew them too. By paying careful attention to her raving dreams he at last satisfied his curiosity about life on Euterpe, although he thought he probably knew more about death on Euterpe. He was eavesdropping on a survivor's conscience. If Eleanor went back, he knew what she would be going back to and in his own alcove he shuddered and drew closer to himself.

Theodore believed himself to suffer from insomnia and took tablets. He heard nothing, although on the rare occasions that he came face to face with Eleanor, he remarked afterwards that she looked unhealthy. Fear of infection provoked his interest, for the nearest doctor was at Omega, and overworked.

The block was a block no longer. It had become a form, a thing, though it was no thing that looked familiar to Isaac. Towards the house it fell away in a series of stepped masses, while at the other end remained a huge, hunched shoulder, still of the original height.

'If she'd used those power tools you got her,' said Theodore, one morning, 'this much could have been done in a week.' He went in to his breakfast, leaving Isaac to reflect that Eleanor had used her hundred days well.

Maybe she had been counting after all.

The clay had finally arrived from Clio. It was, of course, too late to be of any use to Eleanor, or so she said, but in the last day or so she had stopped carving and now sat in the brief shade of the block with a bowl of water and a body of the plastic earth that had so puzzled Isaac, until he saw it.

It was red and her hands seemed bloody to the wrists as she worked it. Half a dozen maquettes stood round her as though she were creating her own audience, but these lumpen spectators crumbled as they stood and the figure that she moulded turned to earthenware in her hands.

'What are they meant to be?' said Isaac.

'Ideas,' said Eleanor. She swatted the maquettes, one after the other, and they were dust.

'You should try plates,' said Isaac. 'You'd make a fortune.'

'It's not my craft,' said Eleanor, blotting her forehead with her arm and leaving a clayey smear that was lighter than her skin.

The ladies of Epsilon took care to preserve a pale complexion as a sign of gentility. Eleanor had boiled, blistered, peeled and finally kippered to a parched, porous consistency. Her hair was crowned by a blonde chaplet where the sun had bleached it.

'Not good ideas?' said Isaac, as the last figure went down. The shadow was moving away from him and he followed it.

'Can't think. Brains burning.'

'The heat won't last much longer. Can you see the study door curtain?'

'It's moving.' She turned her head slowly in case her shirt caused friction burns.

'Wind,' said Isaac. 'Not much, but a good sign. You can't feel it down here, but if you go up on top you might.'

Eleanor dealt the *coup de grâce* to her latest model and climbed onto the stone. Proceeding upwards by way of the steps, each knee-high, she went in search of the promised wind.

'It's a hot wind.'

'Not for long. It'll change in the next few days.'

'Will it rain?'

'No, not till spring.'

She stood above him, peering at the horizon through eyelids that were permanently gathered against the glare. Then she looked down at the road.

'Here's Moshe.'

Isaac was suddenly discomforted. Moshe had felt the wind too, and was on the move again. Their isolation was about to end.

Eleanor was already climbing down from the stone, not hurrying, but with some constraint. Moshe rang the bell in the porch and then came to them through the loggia without waiting to be answered, his boots skidding on the marble floor.

'What do you want?' said Isaac ungraciously. Moshe had a small cut on his chin, recently shaved.

'A note from Cameron,' said Moshe. 'Will you give it to Theodore? There's no reply needed.'

'Then there's no need to stay, is there?' said Isaac, taking the note. He moved towards the door, indicating that Moshe should follow. Moshe stepped round him with an air of decision that was so out of character that Isaac let him get past. He went over to Eleanor, who was sitting on the end of the block, watching him.

'You don't look well,' said Moshe, gazing at her anxiously. 'You stay too long in the sun.'

'She doesn't spend any longer in the sun than you do. If she covered her head she wouldn't be in that state.'

'What have you done to your hands?' said Moshe.

'It's clay,' said Eleanor. 'Red clay.'

'Oh yes, you told me,' said Moshe. 'I didn't think it would look so much like bleeding.'

'I never told you.' Eleanor's voice was sharp and Moshe faltered.

'No, you didn't,' he said. 'Someone else must have . . . must have . . .' By his foot stood one surviving maquette, abraded by passing kicks. He picked it up. 'Did you make this?'

182

'I did.' She reached out for the maquette and Isaac thought she was going to smash it, but she allowed Moshe to look.

'It's like a man.'

'It might have been,' she said, and broke it against the stone. 'It didn't come to anything.'

'A golem,' said Moshe, and bent to examine the lump of soft clay that she had been working from, impressing it with his fingertips. 'Eleanor, make me a golem.'

'What's that?'

'That,' said Moshe, 'would do my work while I sat under my tree.' He laughed.

'A robot?' said Isaac. He had forgotten the tree.

'No. For a robot you need electricity, wires,' said Moshe, vaguely. 'To make the golem work you must write on its forehead the Name ...'

'Moshe,' said Eleanor, warningly. 'Grow the tree first.'

'Whose name?' said Isaac.

'It is more than a thousand years since the golem was made.' Moshe sat down and drew up his feet under him so that he was crosslegged. His quiet voice became persuasive. 'In Prague,' he said. 'It was a very bad time, worse than this –'

'Moshe!'

'– and Rabbi Loew made one night the golem out of clay.'

'Who?'

'Moshe, shut up.'

'It served the Rabbi and protected the ghetto.'

'What's this Prague? What – ?'

'And it was good – good that he made it – but it was still only a golem. It could not think. It could only do what it was made to do.'

183

'Ghetto? Look, Mo, are you trying to tell us a joke?' said Isaac. Moshe was not known around the town for his sense of humour, and if he was making a joke it was having an adverse effect on him. He looked from one to the other out of his long eyes.

'You wanted to know what the golem was,' he said.

'Not now,' Eleanor shouted. 'Not now.'

'I think you've gone mad,' said Isaac. They each took Moshe by the shoulder and shook him, aware that they had jumped on him for different reasons.

'Don't do that,' he said.

'It's the wrong time and the wrong place,' said Eleanor.

'What's this on *your* forehead?' said Moshe. 'The mark of Cain?'

'Clay,' said Eleanor. Moshe raised his hand and rubbed the smudge away with his thumb. Eleanor shivered.

'What did you say?' said Isaac. 'Mark of who?'

'Why should I tell you?' said Moshe, with a rare show of ill-temper. 'What will you do if I tell you? Kick my teeth in?'

'You said Cain,' Isaac cried. 'It's important. Who was Cain?'

'Don't try to tell him,' said Eleanor. 'You'll tie yourself in such knots . . .'

'He was the son of Adam,' said Moshe. 'Who was the first man who ever lived.'

'Adam,' said Isaac. 'No, it wasn't Adam.'

'It was,' said Moshe, getting to his feet. 'What the hell do you know about it?'

'There was another name, not Adam.'

'Abel?'

'That's it, Abel.' He was balanced on the edge of a freight truck, while old Mr Peasmarsh sat wheezing below him. 'Moshe, what did Cain say when the Boss asked him where Abel had gone?'

'The Boss?' said Moshe, coldly. 'The Boss?'

'I was told to ask you – years ago. I'd forgotten. What did he say?'

'He said, Am I my brother's keeper?'

'What does that mean?' Isaac thought he had waited a long time for nothing.

'What can it mean but what it means?' Moshe, still sore from his last attempt at story-telling, was not eager to try again. 'The Boss, that you called him, said, Where is Abel thy brother? And Cain said, I know not: Am I my brother's keeper? Do you want to know the rest?' he said, overcome by his natural urge to ameliorate.

'No,' said Isaac. 'Not now. Tell me some other time.' He sat down where Moshe had sat and tried to find some sense in Mr Peasmarsh's riddle. Am I my brother's keeper? There was sense there all right. But.

'Why don't you go home?' he said.

'I've not said what I came to say,' said Moshe.

'I think you've said far too much,' Eleanor snapped.

'I wanted your help; about the garden.'

'Garden? Our garden?' said Isaac, quickly. Gardens was a safe topic.

'My garden,' said Moshe. 'You wouldn't know it, Eleanor, but this year's been hotter than usual. Everything's drying up. We're almost out of water.'

'You're not having any of ours,' said Isaac.

'Cameron's going off grass. I can't get enough water to it. I told him we'd planted too much, but he wouldn't listen, and now it's all dying. He wants something new. I had an idea.'

'Oh yes? Very likely,' Isaac jeered.

'Do you know what a rockery is?'

'Epsilon's a rockery,' said Eleanor.

'It's a kind of garden. You put rocks in the earth and plant flowers round them. It looks nice.'

'All you need is earth, then,' said Eleanor. Unsteadily, they were reassembling themselves.

'We've got that. I thought I could take away some of your stone – the big lumps. That would save you having to clear it away.'

'We've been slinging it over the mountain,' said Eleanor. 'I put it in a tarpaulin and then we haul it up to the top and let go. It was meant to save the lawn. I suppose we could get it back.'

'It didn't save the lawn,' said Isaac, who was not at all pleased to hear that Cameron was going off grass.

'I'll help you re-seed it when you've finished,' said Moshe. 'You needn't get any back. I'll take the biggest bits from now on and cart them up on the trolley.'

'There won't be any big bits from now on,' Isaac interrupted. 'She's finished cutting big bits, at least I hope you have,' he said, turning on Eleanor. 'Theodore's getting very tired of that lump out there, if you ask me. He wants to see some real carving.'

'He'll see it. I'll be ready to start in a day or so.'

'See, no more big bits.'

'There'll be a few big bits,' said Eleanor, tiredly. 'I'll cut them for you.'

Moshe nodded and went away then, reduced to silence as he had so often been in the old days.

'Look here,' said Isaac, when he had gone. 'You were right. Epsilon's a rockery. He could find all the rocks he wants two metres from his own back door.'

'Perhaps he likes this better. It's a different colour, different stone.'

'Like hell he does. He can't tell stone from cake. That's not what he wants.'

*

186

The real carving began and ended two days later. Isaac was in the kitchen, preparing a cold lunch for Theodore before he went to the city, and listening to the new sound from the garden; a steady, refined tapping instead of the old percussion. Suddenly the tapping stopped on a bum note and there was silence. Then Eleanor calling:

'Isaac! Isaac!'

He was so startled by the sound of her voice and his name that he dropped the rice bin on the floor and ran out to the garden. Eleanor was crouched on the end of the block nearest the house, head bent, nursing her left arm against her chest.

'What have you done?'

'I smashed my hand.' She seemed incredulous that she could have done anything so careless. As far as Isaac was concerned it was only the latest in a long series of grazes, gashes and contusions, all shrugged off unnoticed.

'You're always smashing something.'

'I can't move my fingers. Is it broken?'

He took her hand and worked the fingers up and down, rotating the wrist. 'I can't hear anything. Wouldn't the bones grate if it were broken?' he asked chattily. 'You really aren't safe with a hammer.'

'I don't know how I did it. The chisel slipped. Isaac, can't you do something?'

'What?'

'Isaac, please.'

'Wait there. I'll get some water.'

'And a bandage?'

'All right, a bandage.' He went indoors and fetched cold water in a bucket from the sink, and looked round for something he could use as a dressing. In the end he tore a length from an old towel that looked as if it might soon fall to pieces, and went back to the garden, taking care as he crossed the hall not to spill any water on the

187

newly swept tiles. At the end of the stone he found
Eleanor and with her, Moshe.

'You again.'

Moshe was kneeling and Eleanor leaned against him,
eyes closed. His arm was round her shoulder.

Moshe looked up. 'I came for the stone.'

'Oh did you?' said Isaac, and emptied the bucket over
his head.

'You won't be able to use your hand for a bit. You'll
have to rest it,' said Isaac, trying to make amends.
Eleanor sat against the kitchen wall and stared at him,
speechless. Her hand was bruised, not broken, she knew
that much. Whatever troubled her now was more than
the fear that she would be unable to work. Something
had come between Eleanor and the stone and turned her
own hand against her.

'Do you want to go and lie down?' He tried to catch
her eye. 'You can't stay here, I've got to go out. What do
you want to do?'

In the ugly scene that had followed his performance
with the bucket, no one had said anything that could be
interpreted as words. Moshe had fetched more water and
bound up the hand himself. Then he had gone, without
speaking to either of them, as though Eleanor too had
been at fault. Eleanor had merely sat green and
shaking until he left, and then crawled indoors.

At last she said, 'Why did you do it?'

'I don't know,' said Isaac. He didn't know. He tried
to recapture the rage that had attacked him as he
rounded the block and saw them together. Eleanor
hadn't done anything wrong. Moshe had only done what
he should have done himself; one friend comforting
another in distress. But Isaac and Eleanor were not
friends, and Isaac had not put his arm round her

shoulder. He had not even bandaged her hand. Isaac had poured a bucket of cold water over Moshe's head and now he was wondering why she was angry.

'I don't know,' he said. 'I don't know.'

And at that moment, he did know. He saw all the interest from his investment disappearing into the wrong pocket. Through the lethargic months of summer he had forgotten his original designs in his relief that she was obeying the rules and offending no one. Now it was time to revive the old Isaac.

'Would you like to come for a ride in my train?' he asked.

'No, I don't think I would,' said Eleanor. At least she was answering him.

'We could go to the city. You've never been there.'

'I don't want to go there. I've seen the terminal, that was enough.'

'There are shops.' He had an idea. 'Look, Eleanor, you may not believe this –'

'I won't.'

' – but it will be winter soon. Autumn, anyway. Already the wind is cooler, and you don't know how cold it can get. You must have some more clothes. If you came with me today you could buy some. You might as well. You can't carve with your hand like that. I shan't be going again till next week, and it might be better by then and you won't want to come.'

'I don't want to come now.'

'And it will be colder by next week, I know that for certain. I live here, remember. Please come. I'm sorry. I didn't mean to throw that water at Moshe.'

'No,' said Eleanor, getting up. 'You meant to throw it at me.'

*

'Here we are,' said Isaac, posing beside the three freight trucks with unwise pride.

'Is this it?'

'It used to serve the mine. Now if you don't like it you can run along behind.'

Eleanor climbed into the front truck, favouring her injured hand. 'Why don't you use the carrier?'

'Because I have this. The Government owns the carrier and it only calls three times a day. This belongs to Theodore and I can use it when I like. Hold on.'

He started the motor. As they moved out into the valley Eleanor stood facing the way they had come and getting her first sight of Epsilon at a distance.

'How little it is.'

'That's how it will stay,' said Isaac. 'Epsilon's just about full up. Theodore won't part with any more land. Other places are different. I'm told Iota doubles its size every year. Delta's not fussy.'

'Perhaps we should be in Delta.'

'That's enough of that.'

There was no wind in the city. They reached it in the quivering heat of noon that flared at them from every reflecting surface. Isaac applied the brake with his usual panache, expecting to see Eleanor go flying; but somehow forewarned about his horrendous braking system she was already on the floor, braced against the side of the truck. He climbed out and made for the noisome mouth of his subway.

'Are we going down there? I said it was all under ground.' Eleanor looked over the edge of the truck and seemed prepared to stay there.

'Only the terminal, which is where we're going. You can't see the city from here, it's on the other side of the slope. Now stop fooling around and get out.'

He went into the dark without looking back to see if she

190

were following, although after a moment the thumps and curses told him that she was having as much trouble negotiating the tunnel as Moshe did.

'We didn't come this way before,' said Eleanor, unexpectedly close to his ear. 'I remember, there were pipes on the ceiling.'

'And here they are,' said Isaac, cleverly, as they rounded a corner and came out into the corridor that led to the main concourse. 'We went that way last time,' he said, pointing to the right. 'We're going up to the grain terminal now.'

They went from bay to bay, ordering and rejecting. Isaac pointed out the Intergalactic concerns and sketched in a short history of the company to which Eleanor listened although without any obvious interest. He had always intended to do this, to introduce her to his circle, to make her, in fact, one of the Intergalactic concerns herself. Instead he had turned his back on her and she had concerned herself elsewhere.

'Wensley should be about here, somewhere.'

'Who's he?'

'A friend of mine – a business partner.' He stopped a passing porter. 'Wensley around?'

The porter ducked past them and hurried on.

Isaac felt prickly alarm all down his back. He went to find one of the Intergalactic clerks, an acquaintance of some years, who sometimes brought messages out to the house. 'What's happened to Wensley?'

'Don't ask.' The clerk made throat-slitting motions with his stylus. 'I haven't seen him lately.'

'He was here last week.'

'Later than that. Two days ago.'

'Well, where's he gone then?'

'Back where he came from, I should think,' said the clerk. 'He's been asking for it for years. But you and me

191

are still here, so why worry? He wasn't particularly a friend of yours, was he?'

'No,' said Isaac. 'Not particularly. N-n-n-not a friend.' He rejoined Eleanor who was waiting where he had parked her on a sack of lentils.

'Found your business partner?' The owner of the lentils came up to retrieve his property and Eleanor moved off.

'He wasn't there.' Here was a chance to enlarge upon Aumer's dicta on the perils of self-determination, but he hadn't the heart to do it. 'Come on, I'll show you where you can buy your clothes.'

The street leading from the terminal was as alien to Isaac as it was to Eleanor. He trod with painful unfamiliarity on the paved roadway between the buildings; tall buildings that had been built, unlike the squat domiciles of Epsilon that were cloven from the rock on which they stood. The third-class eating house patronized by diggers and, on occasions, by Gregor, was on a corner opposite the clothing store.

'I'll wait in here for you.' Isaac was not anxious to sit among diggers, but even less anxious to enter the store in Eleanor's company.

'What do I do?'

'You've been into a shop before, haven't you? Or don't they have any on Euterpe? Perhaps you all steal each other's belongings. Just go in and tell them you want a dress and they'll sell you one.'

'How much will a dress cost? I don't want a dress.'

'You need one. It'll be about sixty dinars – miners' prices. They don't have cheap things, but you can afford it by now.'

'I haven't got sixty dinars,' said Eleanor, aghast. 'I haven't got thirty.'

It was Isaac's turn to be aghast. 'Where's it all gone

192

then? You told me you were getting fifty a month. You haven't been anywhere, done anything. Where has it gone?'

Eleanor turned on him. 'Where do you think it's gone? Where does everybody's money go?'

'Gregor?'

'He's not the only one. You told me yourself that everybody does it. You also told me that I couldn't. You said I didn't have anything that anyone needed. You were right on all counts.'

'But what are you paying them for?' A dinar here, a dinar there, naturally, but he had never conceived of extortion on that scale. He calculated that she must have parted with three-quarters of her salary over the last few months.

'For god's sake, what are you doing? Nothing's worth that much.'

'I'll get what I can for thirty,' said Eleanor, making no attempt to answer him. 'After that I shall have nothing. Tell them, I shall have nothing.' She turned and crossed the street. Isaac watched her go and felt the hair rise at the back of his neck. Something wrong, something unnatural, not nice, was at work here. Who was she paying, and why? He saw in his mind's eye his colleagues lined up, claws extended. Gregor obviously, but who else? Barnet? Sean? Sachiko? Paying them not to tell, but whom were they not to tell? Theodore? Loukides? Himself? And what? Nothing's worth that much.

A woman on the other side of the street was eyeing him speculatively. Unable to deal with this he went into the eating house, where three diggers wearing the Rho insignia on their overalls were playing cards in the far corner. Isaac looked away, out of the dirty window, which being glazed instead of shuttered was enough to interest him by itself, but his mind was ever distracted by other thoughts. Who is she paying, and why? And how? She never went out of the house.

Across the street the blind in front of the store's doorway was pushed aside and Eleanor stepped out, frowning in the light. She was carrying a bag under one arm and a man pushing past knocked it out of her grip. The wrapping tore and she stood on one foot with the parcel balanced on her thigh, readjusting the contents. Isaac took a long look at her. It was something he was always enjoining her to do, yet never did himself, if he could help it. He saw her often enough; he never looked.

Did she ever wonder what he thought of her? Didn't she care, or had he made it clear enough? He had never told her that he had taken her for a man the first time he saw her and if this had been the first time he would have done it again. Flat chested, well-muscled, she was as tall as any of the men who passed by. No wonder Theodore never looked at her either.

Oh what a mess, said Isaac. What a mess she is. What a mess I'm in. And what sort of a mess is she in, come to that?

Who is she paying and why?

Nothing's worth that much.

Eleanor began to cross the street. Several people stared, taking her for a quarryman or a porter, and then looking again, uncertain. Superimposed on the staring faces he saw another face that stared as hard and liked what it saw. He can stare as much as he likes, thought Isaac. He'll get nothing. It's not allowed and he wouldn't break the law. He does what he's told. He was even angry about my grass seed.

It occurred to him that Moshe might not equate breaking a Government embargo with falling in love, but the law was the law. Cameron was the law. Loukides was the law. Let him stare.

Him and his golems: First he wants to be seen, now he wants to be heard. He's going off his head. Yet Eleanor's frantic efforts to silence him had risen from a very tangible fear of what he might say next, almost as though she had known what he might say next. How could she? They hadn't met in the last three months. Do they write to each other? Is someone carrying letters? Is that illegal or isn't it, and even if it isn't, what will it lead to?

No wonder they want to keep it quiet – but, all that money. Nothing's worth that much.

She paused in the middle of the street to let a string of wagons go by; slumping round-shouldered and scuffing one foot against the other. How unhappy she looks, thought Isaac. Unaware that he was watching her, her normal expression of arrogant dislike had relaxed into a look of abysmal misery. Whatever they've been doing, it hasn't cheered them up any. The last of the wagons rolled on and she moved towards him again.

What's been going on? He knew that whatever had been going on, he should have known about it.

He slipped through the curtains and met her outside the door.

'What did you get?'

'Not a lot. New trousers; another shirt.'

'That won't be much good to you when it gets cold,' he began, and then stopped. She hadn't really much choice in the matter, and he suspected that had he not caught her at a weak moment, she would never have consented to spend the last of her money on clothes. Almost, he thought, as though she had not dared to refuse.

'Let's get back to the terminal.'

Conversation was impossible on the way home. The

train racketed through the cuttings with dreadful clangour to leave Isaac wondering uncomfortably how much longer the track would hold together. Each journey seemed noisier than the last, the trucks rocked more violently, the couplings shrieked with greater reluctance. Eleanor lay on the floor of the truck, using the parcel of clothes as a pillow, her bandaged hand propped above her head. He would have guessed that she was asleep except that he doubted if it were possible to sleep down there, so close to the wheels. The trucks clanked over the rails towards Epsilon, but when they were in sight of Lambda Crag he halted the train. Eleanor sat up.

'Get out,' said Isaac, dropping to the ground.

Eleanor's head appeared atop the truck. 'You want to show me something?'

'Yes. Come down.'

'I'm not sure I want to see it.' She came down anyway and he started off up the disused track to the canyon. It was more than two years since he had last walked between these rails, below the crag, bracing himself to report the death of Mr Peasmarsh to Loukides, having discovered that Mr Peasmarsh's sculptor, Eleanor Ashe the dream girl, was safe on board the ship and bound for Erato.

Mr Peasmarsh had willed that he be buried in front of his cabin but the authorities had come out from the city and put him away tidily in an approved place. It was one occasion when Epsilon had been glad to abdicate its municipal responsibilities in favour of the Government.

In the absence of heirs the land had reverted to the Government and they had begun to quarry the stone as they had originally intended, shifting it in Intergalactic freighters supplied by Theodore. The new workings were beyond the canyon and the little shack stood undisturbed as Isaac had last seen it, windows gaping and the door hanging open.

Here was the rock where Mr Peasmarsh had sat. *What did Cain say when the Boss asked him where Abel had gone?*

Am I my brother's keeper?

Ask Moshe.

He doesn't know anything. That had been a mistake. Moshe knew a great deal; too much for his own good. Isaac had no intention of asking him for any more information. He was too confused by the implications of what he knew already.

Am I my brother's keeper?

One thing was certain; he would not tell Theodore.

He sat down on the rock by the door of the shack and let Eleanor catch up with him. She first sat, then lay full-length in the dust, chin on fist.

'Why have we come to this place?'

'Because this is where you should have come. This is where you would have worked.'

'Here?' She looked all round. 'But there's nothing here.'

'There would have been,' said Isaac. 'If Mr Peasmarsh had lived there would have been a house by now and you would have been working on it. He died very suddenly; I haven't been here since.'

'But why are we here now?'

'I thought you should see it. I wanted to – to remind. To remind you of what ... You're forgetting everything I told you,' he burst out. 'I don't know what you've been doing, but it can't be good. I went to s-s-s-so much trouble to get you here and look what's happened.'

'Nothing's happened to you,' said Eleanor, thoughtfully.

'Not yet. But it was me who brought you here, and

if you start making trouble again, someone's going to remember that. It was me that persuaded Th-th-th-theodore to take over your contract.'

'I know. I can't think why you did it.'

Isaac groaned quietly. He, personally, had trouble working out why he had done it, and he had always to remind himself that no one, least of all Eleanor, knew how he had done it. Hearing the first stub of his stammer he knew he must take care of what he said. He started again.

'Don't imagine you are safe,' he said. 'Even now. You could still go back. Is that what you want? Don't you care?'

'Do you care what happens to me – except insofar as it affects you?' said Eleanor. 'Have you any idea what it's like, back home?'

'I hadn't,' said Isaac. 'No one speaks of it, I could only guess. I know now, though. You talk in your sleep.'

If he had intended to surprise her he had succeeded admirably, and he only wished he were in the mood to enjoy his victory. She sat up with her back to him and he observed a dark blush spreading over her neck. She's been cutting her hair again, he thought inconsequentially. And I told her to grow it.

At last she asked, 'What do I say?'

'You don't say, you scream. What shall I tell you? What would you like to hear? About the last great riot before you left, that lasted three days and trapped you on the wrong side of the barricade; when all the tenements in your street were burned and the factories bombed. Do you remember the massacre at the Technical Institute when the troops broke in? Do you remember the man who died in your room? Vladimir, wasn't it?' He catalogued incidents to watch her reactions. 'Nine died trying to break the barricade, and you were stabbed in

198

the back, but not killed. Well no, of course you weren't killed. You were a street fighter, weren't you, no better than the rest. Those tools you take such care of have all been weapons; that's why you kept them so sharp. I know what you've done with those hammers, and yet today when you hit yourself with one you nearly fainted. Worse things have happened to you, I know. Something else frightens you now. What is it?'

'It hurt. It's a terrible bruise.'

'Hurt? More than a knife in the back?'

'Is that all? Is that all I say?'

'You mean there's more?' He had the impression that she was more relieved than embarrassed by his revelations.

'No names?'

'Plenty of names. No one I know.' He was right: she was relieved. Her frightful dreams must conceal something even more disturbing.

'I suppose I keep you awake?'

'Not any more. You're at the other end of the hall, after all, and I'm used to it now.'

'You don't listen, then?'

'Ehhhh, not really,' said Isaac, mendaciously. 'But that's still not all, is it?'

'What do you mean?' She gave up all pretence of calm and came closer.

'Whatever it is you're doing, there's more to it than just talking in your sleep. All that money, for a start. Where's it gone?'

'It doesn't matter. I don't need it.'

'Don't talk nonsense. You'll need it all right when winter comes. You may have been roasting all summer, but you're going to freeze, I promise you. What's been going on? If you were in trouble you should have told me.'

199

'I'm not in trouble. I couldn't have told you.' It was Eleanor now who stammered. 'What do you know, stuck away up in your citadel?'

'What do you know? You're stuck in it too. You never leave it.'

'Down in that town they prey on each other. You're out of it, you don't know.'

'I do know.'

'Not what I know. You say, do I want to go back? People will do anything rather than go back, pay anything. Anything. Look at Moshe.'

'Ah.'

'He's even afraid of you. How can someone like you have any hold over Moshe? And yet he's afraid of you; of what you might do to him. He should have beaten the daylights out of you when you slung that water at him, but he did nothing. He's afraid of you. How's it done?'

'He needn't be,' said Isaac, backing away. 'I wouldn't do anything to Moshe.'

'Make him believe it, then. Make me believe it.'

'Why should I do anything to Moshe?' Then he realized that unless common sense prevailed he would have to do something. 'Eleanor, I know what he wants. You surely aren't trying to keep that a secret from me. I can see it. Anyone could. But if you're planning anything –'

'Planning?' said Eleanor. 'Planning?' She was walking away from him, back to the train, stumbling over the dislocated rails. He ran after her.

'Now what?'

'If you're not planning, what are you paying for?'

'Great godalmighty,' Eleanor shouted. 'What do you think I'm paying for?'

They did not speak again, all the way back to Epsilon, and when he stopped the train she climbed out and went away without waiting for him. Isaac loaded up the trolley and began his ascent of the hill. Usually he found some-one to help him, but when he saw Moshe approaching from the other direction he could not look at him. At last he raised his eyes, but Moshe had turned aside and taken a different way.

He can't be afraid of me, thought Isaac. I don't believe it. But he did not believe his disbelief and Moshe's sad eyes seemed to watch him all evening and all night, fear-ing him; while at the other end of the hall Eleanor sat rigidly upright in the darkness, nursing her inflamed hand and fearing sleep.

12

If Isaac still woke sweating each morning it was not because of the heat. At dawn a small wind sprang up, flickering about the hillsides until noon. The days were warm but the wind kept the heat moving. Eleanor recovered the use of her hand and she went back to the block. Suddenly the carving took on a new shape as she cut into the stone where before she had cut round.

'It begins to be very pleasing,' said Theodore, running his uninformed hand over the surface, and Isaac rested easy for a few days.

'The steps have gone,' he said one morning when he went to climb them and found instead a diagonal slope.

'They never were steps,' said Eleanor.

No one came to the house, except to deliver messages; and no one asked to see Eleanor. Even Moshe stayed away and Eleanor did not go down to the town. She was too much occupied with the stone. As Mnemosyne's days grew shorter her own lengthened and she worked from first light until last, speaking to no one but Isaac, and then only when he brought her food.

He knew she was glad of the excuse for her seclusion. He also knew that even when she had finished work for the day, no matter how exhausted, she would not go to bed until after he had gone, and wouldn't sleep until he slept. There were no more voyages to Euterpe. Night after night he saw her sitting alone on the shoulder of the carving, knocking one hand against the other to keep awake. One morning he found her asleep on it, a precarious bed; an unconscious move would have sent her over the edge, down to the rock-strewn lawn.

Some awakening, thought Isaac, and woke her himself. Eleanor whimpered and pushed her head against the stone as if into a pillow. She flung an arm against him and said indistinctly, 'Moshele?'

'What? Moshe what?' demanded Isaac, shaking her. He took her by the hair and banged her head on the stone.

'Wake up. Wake up. You can't stay here.'

'It's cold,' said Eleanor, sitting up. She had the hung-over look of someone who had slept badly and there was a dark swollen line under each eye.

'What do you expect? Have you been here all night? You'd better come in and I'll get you something hot.'

He waited for her usual response of 'I don't want it', but she got up and followed him inside.

'Sit by the stove,' said Isaac, putting a bowl of beans on the chopping block. 'I told you it would get cold and you wouldn't take any notice. I wish I'd never told you that you talk in your sleep. I don't repeat it.'

Eleanor sat rubbing her fingers together. 'Can you lend me some money?'

'I thought that would come, sooner or later,' said Isaac. 'I don't know. How much do you need?'

'Twenty dinars.'

Here we go again, thought Isaac. 'You get paid next week, don't you? That'll be nearly half your salary gone, all at once. What do you want it for?'

'I need it,' said Eleanor, examining her thumbnails with minute attention. 'I must have it.'

'Why should I bail you out? I'm sure you've got a better friend than me,' said Isaac, maliciously.

Who is she paying and why?

He went along to Cameron's house, hoping for a quiet word with Gregor, if such a thing were possible, but before he arrived he could see that complications might arise. Gregor was on the flight of steps that led up to the middle terrace, talking to Moshe.

Moshe had his back to Isaac. When he heard feet coming up the steps behind him he turned, and seeing who it was abruptly walked off, leaving Gregor still talking and grinning.

'That boy's getting so nervous,' he observed to Isaac. Then he yelled after Moshe, 'That's right, isn't it, Mo? You're getting nervous.'

Moshe stooped and picked up a rake. Isaac thought he was going to come charging back and smite them where they stood.

He could kill us. He'd love to, and he could do it, easily.

'Not like the dear old Mo we used to know,' said Gregor, softly. 'What do you suppose is upsetting him, Isaac?'

Moshe bent to scrape at a flower bed with great deliberation.

A golem would do my work while I sat under my tree.

First he wants to be seen, now he wants to be heard.

You talk too much. I couldn't have said that once, could I? Who's being influenced?

Eleanor, what have you been doing? And how, and when?

'And what do you want?' said Gregor, beaming at him.

'I wanted to ask you something,' said Isaac, looking away from Moshe. 'About some money.'

'Yes?'

'Eleanor's money. What is she paying you for?'

204

'I can't tell you that, can I?' said Gregor. 'She's paying me not to tell.'

'It's not only you. Half the town's involved, it seems to me.'

'That's a lot of people to be keeping a secret.'

'Who are they?'

'Look, Isaac, that's your affair, not mine. I have enough to do, taking care of this lot.' He made a large gesture encompassing the whole property, terraces and house, where several smirking heads were watching them from the back premises. 'Why don't you try asking some of these others? They may be less scrupulous than I am.'

Isaac doubted that it was possible to be less scrupulous than Gregor. Wensley had tried. Where was Wensley?

'How much would you take to tell me?'

Gregor sat down on the steps and made a tally of his fingers. 'I don't think you could afford it,' he said. 'After all, she's paying us everything she's got, very nearly. Could you match that?'

Isaac shook his head.

'Information's expensive,' said Gregor. 'But ignorance costs more in the long run. Why don't you ask Barnet? He's usually willing to bargain. Or Moshe.' A crevasse opened between moustache and chin. Gregor was laughing. 'Moshe knows.'

Barnet opened the door, took one look at Isaac and began to slam it. Isaac had his shoulder in the aperture before Barnet knew what was happening, and forced it open again.

'What are you playing at, Barnet?' said Isaac, catching him by the collar. Barnet folded under his grasp and Isaac shoved him up against the wall, holding him there at arm's length.

'Don't hit me,' said Barnet. Isaac had had no intention of hitting him, and he was amazed that Barnet thought he might until he noticed that Barnet was much smaller than he was. He had thought of himself as a runt too long; it was no longer true. He worked his thumb under Barnet's ear. Barnet went limp and swore at him.

'Lunatic,' he said at last, when he had run out of ideas. 'What's got into you, Isaac, attacking a fellow steward? That's an indictable offence.'

'Are you going to report me?' said Isaac. I should have done this before. I shall never have to do it again. Then he remembered Moshe, gentle Moshe, gripping the rake and looking murder.

Don't let her be an influence.

'What's Eleanor paying you for?'

'Why pick on me – I'm not the only one.'

'What for?'

'I don't know. Gregor said there was money to be had there, so I said, Three dinars to say nothing.'

'When did you?' said Isaac, squeezing. 'You've only met her once.'

'Not her – Isaac, let go – Moshe.'

'Moshe?'

'She doesn't pay, he does.'

'She gives him the money?'

Barnet tried to nod, and choked.

'He gives it to us. So we won't tell –'

'Tell who? What?'

'I don't know – for god's sake, Isaac – I don't know. I never asked.'

'That won't do,' said Isaac. 'Don't tell me he pays just because you say so.'

'He's got to, hasn't he?' said Barnet, looking crafty even in his extremity. Isaac dropped him in disgust.

'Not any more,' he said. 'Leave them alone, Barnet,

or I'll break your bloody neck.' Barnet's astounded eyes followed him as he walked out of the door. He didn't slam it.

In the road he had to stop and lean for support on Ansell's mural. He drew long breaths and stared at his hands, mottled from the late pressure on Barnet's throat. *Don't let her be an influence.* If I'd had a rake back there I'd have opened his head.

She doesn't influence me. I've always loathed Barnet. But Moshe . . .

He looked up and there was Moshe, regarding him solemnly.

'I thought you'd been taken ill,' he said.

Isaac wanted to throw his arms round him. Gentle Moshe, dangerous Moshe, angry and afraid, but unable to pass by on the other side.

'Did you follow me?' he said.

'I have some plants; for Heinrich,' said Moshe. He held a bundle of roots in his hand. 'They won't grow, but Evans will have them.'

'Moshe, what are you doing? Tell me.'

'Taking these roots to Heinrich,' said Moshe.

'That's not what I meant. I don't think you know what you're doing yourself.'

Moshe's dark lashes closed over his darker eyes. He swung his head unhappily and walked on. Isaac called after him.

'Moshe, don't. They won't let you.'

Moshe turned in at the open door and closed it quietly behind him. Isaac went home, clinging to false comforts.

It's impossible. It's impossible. It's impossible.

'Have you been out without your coat?' Theodore asked him from the doorway of the study. 'It's better you do wear it,' he went on, reprovingly. 'It looks better. Still, you'll be needing your cloak soon, won't you? You

207

might look out the winter curtains in a day or two, this warmth won't last, I think.' He backed into the study and Isaac heard him hectoring the secretary.

Isaac kept his money in the drawer under his divan. He went to it and took out a five-dinar note and fifteen singles from the heap that he had amassed over the months, only some of it his wages. He folded the notes inside a scrap of paper and tried to compose a suitable message to go on the outside.

Information is expensive, but ignorance costs more in the long run. No; she wasn't buying information.

You can't afford to go on like this. She knew that well enough.

He wrote bluntly, *Stop it*. And put the bundle on Eleanor's pillow.

Isaac had not listened to one of Aumer's sermons for years. Once he had known all twelve by heart, but hearing them in rotation, week after week, had only served to help him forget the words, although Aumer's extravagant inflexions could have prompted him to join in at any moment.

The atmosphere in the church was as unwholesome as ever, but Isaac was sitting near the window and the chill wind stroked his hair in front of his eyes. Beside him, Eleanor fidgeted in her new shirt, plucking at stray threads and running her finger round the stiff though collarless opening at the neck. Her hair had been washed. She looked very clean, like a recently completed building, a fact loudly remarked upon by Gregor as they entered the church.

Gregor was several rows in front of them, with the rest of the Cameron household. In between were the Osinga servants, sharing a bench with Barnet's mob. In spite of the closeness of the air Barnet was wearing a scarf round his neck. Isaac glanced down at the long hard fingers locked in his lap, ashamed and gleeful. Next to Barnet sat Sachiko, easily known from behind by her hairstyle, an engineering miracle held up by a fabulous cantilever of hairpins.

Eleanor sighed between exhortations and scraped at her own hair which, since the last trim, was much the same length all round. She could only see her way about by pushing it back behind the ears, and being straight it soon dropped forward again. She might do it ten times in five minutes and the continuous motion of scrape and flop had annoyed Isaac to the extent of wanting to tear the lot out by the roots, but he was growing used to it.

You can get used to anything, thought Isaac, half asleep. That's the trouble with us, I suppose. We've all got used to Epsilon. Except Eleanor. That thought woke him up again.

She had thanked Isaac awkwardly for the money without mentioning his injunction on the wrapper. Instead she had retreated into tighter silence as she cut further into the block. She seldom left it, even at night, although it was now so cold after sunset that Isaac had begun to put up the shutters along the loggia. He had suggested that she come indoors before he did this; he should have insisted, but he left a small gap at the kitchen end, so that she could get in again. Once that week he had woken early and seen her uncurtained alcove in the thin light; and told himself that she had slept with the stone.

'LUSSSSSST!' Aumer shouted, and the word zipped through Isaac's thoughts like a meteor. He knew at once, by the mention of lust, that Aumer was giving them one of his rare sermons on population control – as opposed to immigration control which came round regularly every month. It was delivered only once or twice a year, in response to a particular situation.

'Friends, we have all seen the result of licence, the fruit of unrestrained desire. It has driven us from one world to another and from that world to this. Shall we see evil reproduce itself a thousandfold before our eyes and lift not a finger to stop it?

'Friends, it is happening in Delta. I say this unto you: it shall not happen here. We swore among ourselves to preserve this planet and preserve it we shall. Here in Epsilon the serpent is raising his head, and where he strikes once he may strike a hundred times. Let the fornicator be warned, that he put aside his sin, lest he be sent out from among us.'

Isaac, like everyone else, cast about covertly for the said fornicator. Don't be seen not wondering. No name was ever mentioned on such occasions; the threat was enough. Whoever the message was for knew that it was for him.

The money had run out.

Who is she paying and why?

She's paying us everything she's got, very nearly. Could you match that?

Nothing's worth that much.

Ask Moshe. Moshe knows.

Eleanor was not even pretending to wonder. She was gazing ahead and sideways and he followed her eyes. The Cameron servants were too numerous to get onto one bench and two or three of them had overspilled to the other side of the aisle. On the end sat Madam's hairdresser and beside her, Margaret the dressmaker. For a hopeful moment Isaac thought that Eleanor was admiring the hairdresser's coiffure of brazen sausages: then he saw Moshe's rough head.

Moshe was wearing a hat. No one wore a hat indoors, never in church. Sachiko yawned and shifted on her foundations, obscuring Isaac's view. He waited until she

210

moved her swaying superstructure and looked again.

It was a very small hat, a round cap on the back of his head, but as outrageous as a gold crown.

'What is he doing in that?' Isaac hissed under his breath. 'Does he think no one will notice?'

'I don't know what he thinks,' said Eleanor, desperately. Isaac began to feel sick. He guessed that the little cap had more significance than the fact that it was an item of clothing. He had never seen such a thing worn, or on sale in a shop. Clearly it was a private possession, a relic, and not designed to keep Moshe's head warm. It was a declaration. Here I am. This is me. Now what are you going to do about it?

A challenge. Gregor was looking too, and Barnet, and Casimir.

The noose tightens, thought Isaac. Eleanor clawed at her hair again and he brought his fist down across her arm.

'Stop it!'

It was only a cap – but – the noose tightens the noose tightens the noose tightens –

'And so, friends,' bawled Aumer, a universe away at the front of the church, 'beware of the man who walks by himself, the man who turns aside from his fellows and takes his own way.

'Beware the man who declares himself apart, who walks at night –'

At night.

'– and turns his back on the law and the people; who says, I will do as I please.'

The challenge had been taken up.

'This man is an infection, for where there is one such there will be another and another!'

Moshe stood up and stepped over the four knees between his seat and the aisle. Aumer's sermon dribbled into silence and every miner's head in the front rows turned to see what was happening, while Moshe paused in the middle of the aisle to put on his coat and settle the cap more firmly among his curls.

'Where are you going?' said Aumer, in the small voice of an ordinary man.

Moshe turned and nodded to him, quite civilly. 'I'm going home,' he said. 'I've listened long enough to your filthy sermon.'

Cameron rose up and reached out an authoritative hand.

'Sit down, you.'

'To your tents, O Israel,' said Moshe, and walked out of the church.

13

'Barnet's got a sore throat,' said Gregor. 'How did he get a sore throat, I wonder?'

'There's always something the matter with Barnet,' said Isaac. 'I've got a letter here, from Theodore. Will you give it to Cameron and let me have the answer at once?'

'It's a very bad sore throat. He can hardly speak.'

'He gets everything badly. I remember he nearly died of steerage fever. No one's ever done that before.'

'My goodness, here's a quarter-dinar rolling around loose and nowhere to go. Would you like to tell me what's in the letter?'

'No,' said Isaac. 'Just deliver it and give me the answer.'

'Money's short in your house, I hear,' said Gregor.

'The letter.'

Gregor took it, laughed, and went out, leaving Isaac to pass time in the servants' hall. It was a large room, as it needed to be to contain all the people who serviced the Camerons. Margaret, Madam's dressmaker, was sewing at a table in the corner. Isaac thought she looked friendly enough and perched on the table.

'Mind the pins,' said Margaret.

'Where's Moshe?' said Isaac, directly.

'He's not here.'

'I can see that. Where is he?'

'I don't know.' Margaret looked continually at the door through which Gregor had left.

'How much did he give you?' said Isaac. Margaret refused to look at him. 'He gave you something, then. Didn't you know what you were doing to him?'

'Everyone was doing it.'

'Every time?'

'Every time he went out at night. Gregor would tell us. "It's up to you, now," he'd say.'

'So who took his money and told?'

'I don't know,' said Margaret. 'It could have been anyone. He had no more money.'

Isaac leaned over the table and looked at her. She had come to Erato on the same day as Eleanor. How quickly she had learned her way about.

Gregor returned, sized up the situation wrongly on purpose and covered his eyes with ghastly discretion.

'Making hay, Isaac?'

'Conversation.'

'They all say that. Here's your answer. Now, how's little Nell?'

Most of Gregor's Old World sayings were lost on Isaac, but he appreciated this one.

'You saw her this morning, in church,' he said carefully. 'How did you think she looked?'

'As usual,' said Gregor. 'Dead and dug up again. And talking of little Nell, what about little Mo. How do you think he looked?'

'Maybe it was the heat,' said Isaac. 'It gets bad in there. I've often wanted to go out.'

'So've we all wanted to go out,' said Gregor. 'And not because of the heat. Nobody does, though.'

'It's not against the law, is it?'

'Only because no one's ever done it. It'll be against the law by tomorrow morning. No, his real mistake was being so rude.'

'What will happen to him?'

'For being rude? I say, he was rude, wasn't he? If he wanted to get out he could at least have done the decent thing and pretended to have a fit – which is what Cameron is having, by the way. But not our Mo. Oh no. To your tents, O Israel, and out he goes. An old Earth saying, perhaps.

'Then there's the other matter, of course.' Gregor began to squint. 'A very substantial fine, I should imagine, which could be embarrassing because he can't possibly pay it, as don't we know?'

Isaac looked miserably at him. In spite of the horrible moustache, Gregor was a kindly looking man, a jovial architect of gibbets and guillotines.

'Why did you let him out?' he said.

'Because he wanted to go,' said Gregor. 'More's to the point, why did you let him in?'

'I didn't,' said Isaac. 'I didn't even know he was there.'

'You didn't know that they – you mean you didn't know? Anything?'

'He never came in. She went out,' said Isaac. 'And I didn't even know that.'

'Ah no. I forgot that you leave your arcade open in summer. Moonlight trysts on that lump of rock, no doubt. I had nothing against Moshe, Isaac. Nothing at all. He was an instrument, no more. Cast your mind back to a day in early summer ... a crowded terminal ... the back seat in the second-class section ...'

'All for her?' said Isaac. 'All for that?'

'It was just hard luck on Moshe that he happened to get in the way. Now, to use yet another old Earth saying, he appears to have gone off his rocker. Don't blame me for that.'

Little whirlwinds of cold air escorted Isaac up the hill; vanguards of the hurricanes that would follow them in the coming weeks, to take up the summer's dust and bear it away, leaving Epsilon dry and echoing, naked; the white rocks turning yellow under a whiter frost.

Once home, he gave Cameron's reply to Theodore and went back to his half-completed task of hanging the winter curtains. The worst of the work, involving the great drapes in the loggia, was already done. The smaller curtains were stacked in the linen room, the door propped open by a stepladder. He went in and knelt among the curtains, sorting them into piles, room by room.

'Four in the dining hall, six for the study, two for the kitchen – old ones, one for the study doorway, one for –'

Theodore stood by the ladder, holding Cameron's note in his hand. 'Aren't we a little late with this?'

'Late?'

'We usually have the curtains up before we feel the cold.'

'The weather's been so uncertain,' said Isaac, sulkily.

'Has it?' Theodore crimped the paper between his fingers. 'Don't let yourself be distracted, Isaac.'

'I don't understand.'

'Your duty is to this household, not to Master Cameron's. Keep our house in order, if you please. I'd prefer it if, in future, you closed all the shutters at night.'

'Eleanor works late,' said Isaac, aware that this sounded like the lie it was. Who but Casimir worked by moonlight?

'Is this place run for a sculptor's convenience?' Theodore said, coolly. 'Anyway, Master Cameron will be visiting us this evening. You had better look out some good wine.'

I suppose that means we'll have Gregor as well, thought Isaac, appalled. He went out to the stone, a curtain slung over his shoulder.

'If you don't stay in tonight you'll be locked out. Theodore's complaining.'

'What's it to Theodore if I stay out late?' Using a claw bit Eleanor cut a chequered curve into the stone below the shoulder of the block so that an arm seemed to grow from it.

'He expects the shutters to be shut at night. They're his shutters, after all,' he said. 'You shouldn't be carving today.'

'You're hanging curtains.'

'That has to be done. Anyway, you don't stay out late, half the time. You stay out all night. And he knows why you stay out all night.'

'How?' Eleanor swung the hammer and cracked off a piece that by its size was surely accidental.

'Didn't you hear Aumer this morning?'

'He didn't mention us.'

'He didn't need to. Listen Eleanor, not only was he talking about you, everyone knew he was talking about you. You gave everything you had to buy a secret. There's no secret. If there ever was, how could there be a secret after what happened in church? He turned his back on Aumer, on Cameron, and walked out. He's wearing the hat. Do you call that secretive? Put that hammer down before you hit yourself again.'

'He may wear a hat if he wants,' said Eleanor, shelving the hammer on a ledge of rock.

'Not that hat. Is he wearing it for you?'

'No. For himself.'

'Really? He cut off his hair and shaved his face for you. You call him Moshele, don't you? Did he ask you to? No one else does. We call him Mo for short.'

'I know. He doesn't like it.'

'Damn him then,' said Isaac. 'Damn what he likes and what he doesn't like. You won't be staying out here tonight because he won't be coming, will he? Will he? God knows what will happen now.'

'Would you care what happens?' said Eleanor. 'Yes, of course you would. Trouble for me is trouble for you. I'd forgotten that.'

'Don't you care?'

'It can't be helped,' she said. 'We can't pay any more. There's nothing left.'

'Let him look out for himself, then,' said Isaac. 'If he wants to cut his throat, there's no need to hold the knife for him.'

Eleanor said, 'If he wanted me to hold the knife I would hold it. If I could do nothing else for him, I would do that.'

The doorbell rang across the cold tiles of the hall. Isaac, stirring soup in the kitchen, dithered with the ladle.

'It'll burn if I leave it. Can you answer the door?' he asked Eleanor.

'Who will it be?'

'Cameron, I expect. And probably Gregor.'

'I'll stir the soup,' she said, taking the ladle, and Isaac hurried to open the door. Moshe was in the porch.

'You are mad,' said Isaac with conviction. 'You are mad. You are raving mad.'

'No,' said Moshe calmly. 'Gregor sent me with a message. Can't I come in?'

'Gregor sent you?'

'It's cold out here.'

'You should have put on your cloak. Come on, then.' Moshe stepped into the hall and Isaac closed the door.

'Gregor and Cameron are busy. I had to come.' His eyes were wide and glistening, like black stones under water. Isaac looked towards the kitchen, but in hanging the new curtain he had forgotten to loop it back. No one moved it.

'Don't you want it?' Moshe was smiling, his eyes unfocussed, straight at Isaac and out the other side.

'What?'

'The message. Don't you want the message?'

'What does it say?'

'I don't know. I never read messages.'

'I'm well aware of that,' said Isaac. 'Look, you grinning idiot, just at the moment you can't afford not to read them.'

'I can't read them at all. Not now, not ever,' said Moshe. He sat on the steps and began to laugh.

'You can't read?'

'Not from left to right.' He put his head down and laughed soundlessly until his hair brushed the floor.

'I don't think it's very funny. Your hat's falling off,' said Isaac, repressing an urge to clip him round the ear.

'Yarmulka.'

'The hat.'

Moshe sat up, clutching it. 'It's a yarmulka. It's mine.'

'I know it's yours. Don't start again. I don't understand a word you're saying.'

'I have never learned to read English, or write it. They taught me to write my name, that's all. So I could sign forms.'

'Everyone knows English,' said Isaac.

'Not everyone. And nobody expects a gardener to write anything.'

'Is that why you never read messages?' Moshe did stop laughing.

'I wouldn't have read them anyway. I don't buy and sell secrets.'

'Much good that's done you,' said Isaac. 'Prig.' He held up the note to the light. It was written on thin paper but well sealed, and the writing was Gregor's scrawl. 'I can't read it either. There's a name here, Ben somebody. And another, two a's together, like mine. It's not Isaac. I don't know anyone called Ben, do you? I'd better open it.'

'Isaac! Who is it?' Theodore was bleating in the study.

'Wait a minute and I'll tell you the rest,' said Isaac, carrying the letter to the study. 'Any answer?' he asked, as Theodore scanned the few lines of writing.

'No, no answer,' said Theodore, and crunched the paper under his hand. 'Can I smell something burning?'

'Soup!' Isaac scrambled into the kitchen.

Moshe was there before him. He was standing beside Eleanor at the stove; two hands linked behind them, two hands linked over the hot iron handle of the soup pan; under a canopy of steam.

'You couldn't have taken it off the heat, could you?' said Isaac, looking angrily at the glutinous slurry at the bottom of the pan.

Moshe looked up, Eleanor looked down, not at Isaac.

'Why don't you find someone your own size?' he said to Eleanor, wrenching the pan handle away, so that the clasped hands dropped onto the hot stove. No one seemed to feel it.

'And you,' he said, elbowing Moshe out of the way, 'if you want a woman you can go to the city like anyone else.'

'Like you?' said Eleanor, offensively. He scraped the remains of the soup into the sink, where it formed globules and quivered like some rare form of algoid growth, hitherto unclassified.

'Won't you go away?' said Moshe. 'Please go away.'

'Get out,' said Eleanor.

Isaac hefted the soup pan. 'If anyone gets out, he does,' he said, poking Moshe with the handle. 'Right now he gets out. Don't you know a warning when you hear one? We've never had the Squad here and we aren't starting now.' He couldn't forgive them for having deceived him so long, when no one else was deceived. 'The party,' he said, 'is over.'

'The party's definitely over,' said Moshe. 'We were saying good-bye.'

'You'd better be. Five minutes.' Isaac put the pan on the table and went into the hall, where he stood with arms folded, squaring up to the clock. He thought he heard voices on the road outside, but there came no knock at the door and his ears were strained towards the kitchen.

'One ... two ... three ... four ... five ... and one for good measure, don't let's be harsh.' Behind him, Moshe came out of the kitchen and let fall the curtain.

'Go home now Mo – Moshe – Moshele,' said Isaac. 'And don't come here again.'

'I won't come here again.' Moshe started to laugh once more and then buried his face in his hands.

'Learn to read English,' said Isaac. 'You might know what's going on, another time.'

'There will be no other time.'

Isaac caught his hands and pulled them away. Moshe was crying as silently as he had laughed. They drew together until for a moment their faces touched.

'Itzhak, don't be a golem. On your forehead is nothing written.'

He took back his hands and walked to the door. Isaac saw the night and the sky and the dull unfriendly eye of Euterpe, glaring in. He stayed where Moshe had left him, watching the door swing shut, then open, as the wind struck it.

Voices.

He ran up the steps and through the porch to stand in the road where a single figure should have walked downhill, away and alone.

Instead he saw a small group hurrying, close together,

like revellers leaving a party; or six men, dragging a
seventh.

The implacable call of duty hauled him inside again.
'Isaaaaac!'

He was restrained, as though a thread were tautening
between him and somewhere else, but he answered the
summons to the study.

'Clear this away, will you?' said Theodore, indicating
a moraine of crumpled paper on the desk. 'Burn it.'

It was an open invitation to pry and they both knew
it. Somewhere in that heap was Gregor's letter. Isaac
swept the scraps into a rubbish bin and took them into
the back hall where he sat on the divan in his alcove
and sorted through them.

. . . considering his request . . . await further notification. F.B.

*. . . Inspector Agnolo . . . no suggestion of any . . . returned
to . . . refunded . . .*

. . . seven thousand tonnes Grade D @ 9 dinars . . .

*At least 15% has had to be destroyed owing to deterioration
in transit. Unless some kind . . .*

*To Master Theodore Swenson. Sir, Master Cameron instructs
me to inform you that no action will be taken against your em-
ployee, Eleanor Ashe, at the present time. Moshe Ben-Yaakov
will be arrested within the hour. Master Cameron trusts that
this will solve the problem. Gregor Evgeniev.*

'Eleanor Ashe, Moshe Ben-Yaakov, Gregor Evgeniev;
suddenly we have names. What can mine be?' said Isaac,
reading aloud from the paper on which the names were
written.

Moshe Ben-Yaakov. *There's a name here. Ben somebody.
I don't know anyone called Ben, do you?*

If I'd known what his name was, I might have warned

222

him. He must have guessed, though, as soon as I'd said it. That's why he wanted to say good-bye.

He can't have told her. Perhaps he hoped he was wrong.

Why didn't he run away?

Voices.

Isaac had the answer then. Moshe might have run away, only Gregor had sent him to the one place where he could be sure Moshe would go.

Then Casimir had convened the Squad and outside they had waited, while Gregor no doubt related his latest joke. That Moshe himself had carried the information to Theodore, unable to read it; stupid, upright Moshe, too honest to ask for a translation.

I can't read from left to right.

Ben somebody.

Ben-Yaakov.

Moshe.

14

After a while he got up and went into the hall, leaving the papers scattered about the floor, except for one which he held in his cold hand.

The clock told him that an hour had passed since he last stood there, counting off the six ungenerous minutes that he had allowed Moshe to say good-bye to Eleanor; and to Epsilon. He tried not to think what might have happened to Moshe in that hour. *Master Cameron trusts that this will solve the problem.* The problem had not been Moshe, or even Eleanor, but the two of them together. One of them had to go, and Moshe had wanted it over quickly, on his own terms.

This man is an infection.

I've listened long enough to your filthy sermon.

So he put on his hat and went to war, said Isaac. What a small war. What a huge defeat.

His own problem remained. He knew what had happened, Eleanor didn't. That expert at hand-to-hand combat with hammers would never sit quietly in the kitchen while her lover was beaten unconscious.

'Well now,' said Theodore, coming out of the study. 'Isn't it time we had dinner?' Isaac faced him.

'Why?' he said. 'What harm could he do? Either of them? Both of them?'

'Work it out for yourself,' said Theodore testily. 'Why do you imagine we are safe here? Why don't we fear attack, or robbery or murder? What happens to potential criminals, hmmm? What does everyone fear more; even, dare I say it, Gregor?'

'Being sent back to Euterpe,' said Isaac.

'Is that what you fear most?'

'Would it be Euterpe?' Isaac's old nightmare stood at his shoulder.

'We wouldn't be so inhuman as to send you back to Orpheus,' said Theodore. 'Anyway, you know what I mean. Now Moshe had ceased to fear it. He simply didn't care what we did to him, so he had to go. What could we do?'

'Why not Eleanor?' While safeguarding her future for so long, and thereby his own, he had never considered that anyone else's might be at stake.

'Because I want that thing in the garden finished,' said Theodore. 'It's good work and there's no one else here who could do it. Besides, we don't want to have to import another sculptor and start all over again.'

'She always said you would keep her for her work's sake. She thought she was too good to lose.'

'She was right, for once. On the other hand, any fool can grow a lawn, even you. Now justice has been done, and will have been seen to be done, which is more to the point. He did us a favour, making himself so conspicuous. Without one, the other really is harmless. Go and get the dinner.'

Isaac looked towards the kitchen.

'She's in there,' he said. 'She didn't know what happened. She doesn't know.'

'Then you'd better go and tell her yourself. I'm sure you can get her to understand the situation. Life should be simpler for us all, from now on. Dinner.'

Isaac went slowly to the kitchen. Eleanor was at the table, sketching patterns with rice grains and crumbs.

He approached the table and stood looking down at her.

He didn't tell her, thought Isaac. She thinks he has gone home and she's wondering how they will manage in future. Let this grain be Moshe and let this grain be me, and all the others are between us; what shall we do?

'Eleanor, what did he say to you?'

'Say? He didn't say anything.'

No. Under the circumstances there wasn't much he could have said. Why waste your last six minutes in talking?

'He didn't tell you where he was going?' Well, he wasn't certain himself, then. He couldn't know what Gregor had done. Let Gregor tell her now.

Isaac opened his hand and spilled the letter onto the table.

He said, 'I didn't do it. It wasn't my doing.'

'Is this from Moshe?'

'Could you read it if it were? I thought he could only write his name in English.'

'And mine.' She unfolded the letter and began to read it.

'It wasn't me,' said Isaac. 'I didn't do it.'

'Arrested?' said Eleanor. 'Arrested within the hour? Where will they take him?'

'He is already taken.'

'What will they do to him?'

'They have already done it.' He realized that still she did not understand. 'Eleanor, what did you think would happen? You said yourself the end had come.'

She said stupidly, 'But it has come. It's all over. Why has he been arrested?'

'Because that is the end,' Isaac shouted. 'It had to be one of you. Before you came, Moshe was like a stone. He never spoke, he never laughed, he never did anything and we all kicked him. It was his own fault. He didn't have to be at the bottom of the heap, he put himself there. As soon as he saw you he started to change. He told me to be careful: he told you to be careful, but he couldn't be careful himself. You did that. He's been arrested, he'll be deported. They've taken him and they should have taken you!'

She stood up. He thought, she's going to faint. He had once seen a woman faint in the terminal. She had dropped to her knees, swaying, and raising her hands she had slid to the ground as if lowered on an invisible rope. He didn't suppose that Eleanor would do anything so graceful and stood back, but she stayed on her feet and began to move round the table, very cautiously, eyeing the door.

'You can't go after him,' said Isaac. 'You can't get him back. No, Eleanor, it's too late. You can't!'

She made a sudden dive past him. Isaac put out his foot as she went by and they staggered against the table, ankles entangled. The table reared up on one end and shed its load of food; all Isaac's preparations for dinner, meat, peas, rice, carrots, bread and a miner's ransom in crockery hit the floor with a crash that made the wine goblets ring on their shelves.

Eleanor came down on top of the avalanche and Isaac last of all, skating out of control on the split peas and treacherously varnished carrots. A little tin bowl bounced clear of the debris and rolled into the hall. He heard it meander across the marble tiles and spin round and round on its rim wyang-wyang-wyang until it settled.

Eleanor sat up and looked round.

'Did we do all that?'

'Theodore's dinner,' said Isaac gloomily. The curtain was flung aside and Theodore himself stood there, gaping at them. 'Your dinner, Theodore. On the floor.'

'Did she attack you?' said Theodore. He was holding an iron stool before him, legs out-thrust like three bayonets. Eleanor struggled upright and leaned on the upended table for support. Theodore turned the stool in her direction and made a threatening motion, but she did no more than look at him.

'Why not both of us?' she said.

This was an aspect that had not occurred to Isaac, that one should have wanted to go with the other, no matter where. It occurred to Theodore at the same time.

'First Isaac, then you,' he said. 'Suddenly everyone wants to go to Euterpe. I was always under the impression that it was the one place nobody wanted to go.'

'He did no harm.'

'So Isaac tells me. Neither of you did much harm, as you put it, but we are concerned for the future, not the past. You've always been a nuisance, but we can deal with your kind of nuisance easily enough. You wouldn't have lasted a month if it hadn't been for Moshe, and he was another matter entirely. You set him off, you know, and once he was set off there was no telling where he would go. First he started leaving his house at night; harmless, you may say, but forbidden none the less. We sleep soundly here because we know that no one walks at night. Then that hat –'

'Yarmulka,' said Isaac.

'Is that what he called it? Well, it never was just a hat, was it? He wore it with a difference and he walked out of church. Next week, someone else may walk out of church. Most of us would like to. Do you see what I mean?

'And then that other affair.' He smiled at her until she looked at the floor. 'Affair's the right word, isn't it?' His voice altered very suddenly. 'Only certain people

228

are allowed to have children here, and you certainly aren't one of them. Nor was Moshe.'

'Children? Children? We weren't thinking of children.'

'Maybe not. But there would have been a child sooner or later. Or hadn't that struck you?'

Isaac could only feel amazed that it should have struck Theodore. This was not the dimwit he had grown up with and he suddenly saw himself during the last three years, descending a smooth and fatal slope from one disastrous error of judgement to the next and, drawn helplessly in his wake, Eleanor and Moshe.

I did this. Not her, not him. I did it.

'I believe the two of you had some idea of going to Delta,' Theodore went on, blandly. Eleanor rounded on Isaac, fist raised, and he got up quickly. 'No, Isaac didn't tell me. Moshe was always followed when he went out at night, and you were overheard, every time, so don't waste more time by denying it. Delta is a permanent temptation to people like you. It's like a fruit, fresh fruit of course, good to look at and rotten on the inside. A lot of the dried fruit used to be of very poor quality too, until Intergalactic set up its own standards of selection.

'Delta prides itself on its liberal traditions. If you lose your job there, they give you six weeks to find another one. There's a Government centre where the unemployed can get food. No one is ever turned away, people breed there. What's Delta going to look like by the time they've made room for all the people, people like you and Moshe who don't do any harm? They're all like you, harmless. We tried to leave Euterpe behind but it forces up everywhere, unless we crush it, and we shall. Even at Delta, one day. They think the Government will save them, but the Government will be glad to look away when that day comes. Oh no, Eleanor, you are not going to Delta. You are not going to Euterpe, even. You are going to stay here and finish my sculpture.'

'I shall not finish it,' said Eleanor, and Isaac saw that she had a weapon in her hand after all. 'I shall never touch it again.'

'You will finish it,' said Theodore. 'When it is done you will go back too, make no mistake about that. But for now you will stay here and finish it.'

'How will you make me finish it?' said Eleanor. 'And what will you do to me if I don't?'

Theodore had overreached himself. Isaac understood at once the simple implication of her refusal. There was only one deterrent on Erato and Theodore had used it.

'Fines?' said Eleanor. 'Flogging? Thumbscrews?'

'We shall send you back,' said Theodore, trying to regain his ascendancy. 'We shall send you back as we sent the other fellow and many more like him.'

'Ansell?'

'Who was he? Has everyone gone mad tonight?'

'Then send me back,' said Eleanor. 'Send me now. Don't spend any time trying to persuade me. Don't keep me out of kindness; it wouldn't be kind. If I am to go, I want to go at once. I will swear it if you like. I shall never work for you again.'

Theodore began to sidle back into the hall, stool at the ready. He kicked the tin bowl and it struck the iron shutters with a final dolorous clang.

'You spent your entire income trying to buy connivance,' he said. 'Are you forgetting that?'

'I didn't buy, I hired,' said Eleanor. 'Now I have nothing. Hasn't it come home to you yet that some people might prefer to die on Euterpe than live on Erato? Moshe was one; I'm another.'

'Who's talking of dying?' said Theodore. 'We have

no capital punishment here. Deportation is the humane alternative.'

'Deportation is no alternative,' said Eleanor. 'No one survives going back. They vanish. You have taken Moshe and killed him. He will be two years dying, but he will die. Let me go too.'

Theodore put down the stool and sat on it.

'You could be another year on that carving. Are you proposing to throw away the remainder of your life for that deranged lout?' he said, and so vicious was his tone that it took Isaac some seconds to realize that he was talking about Moshe. Eleanor was not so slow.

'That deranged lout was all that kept me here. Isaac, open the shutters.'

He went into the loggia and she followed him with the old, uncouth stride that he had first seen in the city terminal, as she bore down on him, an unarguable fact out of the mists of his imagination. He drew the bolts and lifted a shutter to one side. Over the garden the frantic moon hurtled in its groove about the planet and shed a hasty light upon the block of stone.

'What do you see?' said Eleanor. 'What have I made?'

Theodore answered, 'We can't tell yet,' and Isaac was about to agree, but he looked again. The thing that lay by the wall in the moonlight was a human figure, cast down upon its face: the high plateau that he had always thought of as a shoulder was truly a shoulder and below it the head hung defeated, to rest on folded arms. Theodore saw it too.

'Your monument to a great man,' said Eleanor. 'Given time I would have cut fetters and chains. This person would like to stand up, but he never will. May I go now?'

*

231

'Yes,' said Theodore, finally. 'I think you may. Isaac, Sergeant Loukides is still at the police station, I believe. Go down and tell him to re-form the Squad, first thing in the morning, and then you'd better go to Master Cameron and request him to be ready for an emergency sitting. These things are best done at night, but we can't very well wait until tomorrow evening.'

'Why at night?' said Eleanor. 'Why do you do it at night?'

'You don't want to be taken through the town with everyone watching, do you?' said Theodore. 'We have our decencies.'

'Would anyone watch? Does anyone know?'

'Not till afterwards. That's the object of the exercise.'

'There's no need for the Squad,' she said. 'I go willing.'

'No one goes willing when the moment comes, do they, Isaac?'

'No,' said Isaac, recalling the massed boots of the men upon the hill, and the other man fallen on his knees among them.

'They won't tap on the door and say "Please come with us". They'll come up here and tie your hands and drag you through the streets.' Theodore was riled and showed it. 'See how willing you feel in the morning. Now, you can't stay here. You'd better wait in the linen room.'

'The linen room?' said Isaac. 'She can't wait in there. It has no windows.'

'She definitely isn't going to wait anywhere else. We shall be alone in the house while you're gone,' said Theodore. 'Do you think I'm going to risk my safety on your judgement of character?'

'Oh Eleanor,' said Isaac. 'He thought he could walk away too, and you should have seen him go.'

232

'The linen room,' said Theodore. 'Either open it your-self or give me the key.'

Isaac crossed the hall and opened the door. Eleanor followed him, losing impetus with every step, until she stopped in the doorway.

'Go on,' said Theodore, advancing suddenly.

She turned then and retreated backwards into the linen room; one hand raised, palm up, in an instinctive plea for mercy, the other trailing across the surface of the door as if to delay her imprisonment by even a little; and Isaac saw that she finally understood the nature of the machine that she had set in motion. Theodore jerked the door out of his grasp and slammed it in her face.

'Lock it,' he said.

'It locks itself,' said Isaac. 'There's no handle on the inside.'

'Nor there is,' said Theodore, with plump com-placency. 'That was never built to be a store room.' He reached up and placed his thumb over the light switch by the door.

'Don't leave her in the dark.'

'Why not? She's going into the dark; she might as well get used to it.' Theodore was paying himself back for all the years of grinding monotony endured as an upright citizen of Epsilon. The memory of this small unkindness might last him for as many years ahead. Isaac was glad, on the whole, that Theodore lacked the imagination to conceive of a really monstrous cruelty which would sustain him for the rest of his life.

'It's a useful little room,' said Theodore. 'My father always called it the cooler. He guessed it might be useful some day, I expect. He was full of devices. You are rather like him, in an unsuccessful way.'

Now we're coming to it, thought Isaac. Why tonight?

He must be feeling sure of himself with two victims under his belt. He's waiting for me to ask him what he means. From the overcrowded recesses of his memory he drew his reply.

'Am I my brother's keeper?'

'No, I am,' said Theodore, beaming. 'I always thought you must know, but you never said anything. Who told you, Peasmarsh?'

'He died before he could tell me,' said Isaac. 'But he left me enough to go on. Half-brother, I take it.'

'Certainly half,' said Theodore, firmly. 'We can't discuss it now. You'd better get down to Loukides before he shuts up shop. There will be plenty of time to talk when you get back, and we really must talk,' he said. 'I wanted to make the position clear because I think the situation has been allowed to coast long enough. This house must be run properly in future, you understand me?'

'Perfectly,' said Isaac. 'I'm sure we understand each other perfectly.'

A third voice broke in on them, he thought. *Itzhak, don't be a golem.*

He walked up the hill from the police station and wished that he might never have to walk there again. Behind him, Loukides and Casimir gloated against the morning; on his right the moon bowled down towards Lambda and the furred pallor in the sky beyond it, where the restless city turned in its sleep; on his left the white wall of the house rose up to contain Theodore basking at his desk, and Eleanor as she waited in the black room behind the door with only one handle.

Theodore heard him come in and craned his neck round the curtain as he approached the study.

'All arranged?'

'At first light. I didn't have to go up to Cameron's; Casimir said he'd see to that.' This favour had cost him three dinars. He reached for his bunch of keys. 'I'll let her out now.'

'Not yet,' said Theodore. 'We have one or two things to discuss first.' On the desk stood an empty bottle and a half-empty bottle of red wine. Isaac planted his hands between them and looked down at him; Brother Theodore. Half-brother Theodore. They were not alike.

'Did you know my mother?' said Isaac. He didn't care whether Theodore had known his mother or not, but the conversation needed careful delivery if it were not to come out stillborn.

'Good lord, no,' said Theodore. 'Father had all sorts of little indiscretions. You were one of them. When the news about Orpheus came through he couldn't get out there fast enough to see what was left. He came back with you. He never actually explained who you were, but it wasn't very difficult to work out. He wasn't ashamed of you.'

'I'm glad to hear it,' said Isaac.

'I was,' said Theodore, candidly. 'But he said you were sure to improve. I didn't believe it myself. After all, everyone else on Orpheus was dead; there didn't seem to be any good reason why you shouldn't die too. You always appeared to be on the verge of it. I couldn't credit it when he told me he'd acknowledged you in his will and left half of everything to you – the house, the land Epsilon stands on, the Intergalactic, everything. I made up my mind to lose that will when the time came, but when he died I couldn't find it. No one knew where he had deposited it, so I said nothing and hoped that it would never turn up. It didn't, by the way.'

'Really?' said Isaac, very courteous. Theodore was obviously drunk and he wondered how much information he was going to get before the effects of the wine wore off. He let the keys drop.

'Isaac, what could I do?' said Theodore, with dreadful, wheedling reasonableness. 'It was more than seven years ago. You were very nearly an idiot seven years ago. How could I tell the miners that you were going to grow up to be their landlord? What would that have made of me, and of the company? I wanted to get rid of you, I'll admit, but I daren't. I was always afraid that someone would find the will. We take desperate measures sometimes, Isaac, but to have it known that you had deported your own brother? Oh no. So I said nothing and kept you here. I did my best for you, let you have the train and the run of the house; let you call yourself steward and never engaged any other servants. I knew you couldn't cope with them. I was your keeper, all right. Well, that's all over now. We can't go on like this.'

'Thank you so much for letting me have the train,' said Isaac. He could not trust himself to say anything else and he was pressing so hard upon the marble surface that he expected to see dints appear round his hands.

'You've grown up,' said Theodore, with maudlin regret. 'Though it doesn't seem to have made much difference. I've arranged with Evans and Barnet to hire Heinrich during the winter months. He'll help you straighten the garden.'

'Moshe was going to do that,' said Isaac.

'Well, he can't, can he,' said Theodore. 'Are those power tools still in the shed?'

'I haven't sold them, if that's what you mean,' said Isaac.

'Right then.' Theodore got to his feet, apparently having trouble finding enough floor to stand on. 'In the morning the two of you can get to work on that abortion

236

in the garden. I want it completely destroyed and taken away. Nothing is to remain. Then, I think, we'll have another lawn.'

Wiped out. They are to be utterly wiped out, eclipsed, swept away for ever. And yet I'm still here. Isaac turned away from the desk, found the linen room key again and fitted it into the lock. On the point of turning it he paused.

'Tell me one thing,' he said. 'Why didn't you kill me? It would have been so much easier.'

'Murder? To have had that on my conscience for the rest of my life? What are you saying?'

'Won't you have anything else on your conscience?' said Isaac.

'I told you, you were a sickly child,' said Theodore. 'I never thought you'd live to be a man, coming as you did from Orpheus. You know you'll die young, don't you?'

'Yes,' said Isaac. 'And so will Eleanor, and so will Moshe, although they didn't come from Orpheus. That may not be on your conscience, Theodore, but it's still murder.'

'Suicide!' Theodore shouted across the corridor. 'Suicide! She demanded to go back. You heard her.'

'Only to be with Moshe,' said Isaac. 'Didn't you realize that? She wants to go with him. They will have two years before Euterpe gets them.'

'She did it to spite me. Revenge,' said Theodore.

'No. Only to be with him,' said Isaac.

'Don't open that door!' said Theodore. 'Give me the keys.'

'Why?'

'You are not to let her out.'

'Why not?'

'She isn't safe. Give them to me, now!'

Isaac slowly drew the key from the lock, unbuckled

237

his belt, and slid the heavy ring into Theodore's waiting hand; a hand he could no longer trust to keep him. And, he argued with himself, having nothing to lose she might add violence to her wretched list of misdemeanours; but he thought it unlikely.

'Are you afraid she'll run away? To Delta?'

'No,' said Theodore. 'She'd never get that far. Even if she did, they would turn her over to Loukides. They aren't fussy in Delta, but with the Government presence they've got, they don't take in fugitives; not fugitives with Intergalactic behind them.'

'Then let her out.' He could no longer contrive, only plead. 'Don't keep her in there all night. Tomorrow will be bad enough.'

'Tomorrow,' said Theodore. 'Tomorrow, I assure you, will be worse than anything she expected. She is going to get exactly what she asked for, and more.'

15

'We will come at first light,' Casimir had said, as though promising him a treat. Without doubt, it was going to be a treat for Casimir; two arrests between one sunset and one sunrise.

Isaac lay on his divan, dressed, awake, dreaming, the curtains pulled apart so that when first light came he would be the first to see it.

'She will get exactly what she asked for, and more,' Theodore had said. Couldn't he understand that all she had asked for was Moshe, and that anything they did to her in the next few hours would be a small price to pay.

'Don't be a golem,' Moshe had said. 'To make the golem work you write on its forehead the Name.' From right to left, presumably. So much he would never find out now. Moshe had been a well he should have gone to more often. 'On your forehead is nothing written.'

He slept a little and Casimir came down with a list to enrol his Deportation Squad.

'Me first,' said Casimir, through pink teeth, like pieces of Thalian core stone. He called out the list of names. One of them was Isaac.

Isaac ran to join the others and they all had EUTERPE written above the eyebrows. He looked in the mirror, the big concave one from the dining hall which someone had thoughtfully hung in the sky for him, and on his forehead nothing was written.

He half-woke, shivering. It wasn't impossible that

Casimir would conscript him in the morning. Then what do I do, join in?

Even if he doesn't, I shall be there. What do I do? Help, applaud?

The water rose above his waist to his shoulders, to his chin. His feet left the ground and he swam in the water that stretched greyly away to unseen horizons. He held up Gregor's letter to the sun and read the words with ease: Delta Reservoir.

'It's bigger than I thought,' said Moshe. 'No wonder they can grow trees.'

Trees sprang up like mushrooms all round them. Moshe dived to the bottom of the reservoir and Isaac could see him rooting about in the mud.

'What are you doing?'

'Picking flowers,' said Moshe, and drifted up towards him with his arms full of lettuces. 'I want you to have these, to remember me by,' he said earnestly.

'But they won't keep,' said Isaac.

'Then you won't remember me for long, will you?' said Moshe. He seemed to find this terribly funny and he began to laugh, his head tipped back. The water rushed into his open mouth and he drowned.

I would have expected it to take longer, thought Isaac, watching his dead friend slip away from him under the water. It can take years to drown. The light in the window at the end of the hall was no longer moonlight. Behind the autumn clouds Mnemosyne was crawling towards the horizon.

Isaac rolled off the divan and stood up. It was still too dark to see the floor, but he fumbled for his boots and pulled them on, sure that down in Epsilon other men were already putting on their boots.

In the kitchen he picked his way through the wreckage of the dinner and unbolted the window shutter to look down the hillside to the plain, where Omega grew in outline against the sky. Then he went to the loggia and began to remove the shutters there, noiselessly easing the bolts. It was a mad hour to be opening the house at this time of year. The wind was in the north so the arcade sheltered him, but it was a cold, insistent wind and the bolts were like ice in his fingers. Through the winnowed dust he saw the sculpture, less of a man in this light, but unmistakably a man. He walked the length of it, wondering how he could have lived by it for so long, without knowing what it was.

'I never saw a man carved in stone,' he said aloud, by way of excuse. How far would she have got with the chains and the fetters before everyone noticed?

As soon as Moshe saw that clay model he knew what it was. I thought he was joking.

I knew Moshe for years before I knew him.

And Theodore.

This stone thing is all my mistakes. I know nothing.

The light was climbing the clouds, hauling Mnemosyne behind it. At any moment might come a knocking at the door that even Eleanor would hear in the deafening linen room. If she had cried out in her sleep last night no one had heard her, if she had slept. He wished he could open the door now and rob Loukides of his thunder, but he no longer had the keys. All he had retained was his own key; the key of the train. He was so accustomed to the hanging weight at his side that he felt as if he might float without it. He climbed onto the block, onto the man, and stood on his back to look over the wall; searching the hazy road for a more purposeful dust.

'Going away?'

Theodore stood by the knee, looking up at him. It was three hours before his usual rising time, but some kind of excitement had roused him early. Theodore, the limp nonentity with iron insertions, his brother's keeper.

I tried not to know that.

'Come down,' said Theodore. 'Comb your hair and wash your face. Look like a steward if you can't be one.'

Isaac walked over the hip and down the thigh past Theodore, and jumped to the ground from the ankle. When the worst was over, Heinrich would come and together they would take the man apart and lose him, like the evidence of a guilty secret.

As he entered the hall the floor shook under his feet. Loukides was beating on the door, with a stone.

Loukides was in an evil mood, so early in the morning. His breakfast rollicked inside him, providing an irreverent descant to the day's baser dealings.

'Why have the shutters been removed?' he complained. 'It only makes things more difficult for us. They always think they can get away.'

'Oh,' said Isaac. He had wanted Eleanor to have a last sight of her creature as she went. Now he doubted if she would have the chance to look. Round the linen room door stood six strangers in black uniform coats and visored caps, but when he looked more closely he saw that only three of them were strangers. From under their visors Casimir, Gregor and Sean stared back at him. Sean rubbed his hands expectantly. Perhaps he had been a long time on the waiting list.

Casimir had his hands clasped behind his back, holding what Isaac took to be a pair of pastry cutters, and he toyed queasily with the thought of Casimir taking up cookery.

'Well, let's have her out,' said Loukides impatiently, and Theodore turned the key. Something on hands and knees behind the door shrank away from the light.

Casimir stepped forwards and pulled her out till she stood swaying in the doorway.

'Eleanor Ashe,' said Loukides, emphasizing that a name in the file at the police station was not obsolete after all. 'Eleanor Ashe, known as Eleanor-at-Swenson's, you will be taken from here and brought before the magistrate to answer the charges laid against you. You will then be conveyed to the city and placed upon a ship returning to Euterpe. I must warn you that nothing you say will make the slightest difference.'

Casimir, almost frisky, positively rosy, jangled his pastry cutters. They were handcuffs. Eleanor looked through him, as Moshe had looked through Isaac, and held out her hands.

'Just a moment,' said Theodore. 'Which ship?'

'Does it matter?' said Loukides, surging tidally from one flat foot to the other.

'Since it is certain to be one of my ships, yes it does,' said Theodore. 'Isaac, where are the schedules?'

'I know them by heart,' said Isaac, who had almost forgotten that he was there. 'There are two ships in orbit right now.'

'I thought so.'

'There's an empty freighter going by way of Clio to pick up wheat; and an oil tanker calling at Calliope that leaves at noon.'

'We put Ben-Yaakov on that one last night,' said Loukides. 'They might as well go together. Get on with it, do.'

Isaac smiled in spite of himself and Eleanor's stiff fingers relaxed a little although Casimir was just then clamping the second cylinder round her wrist.

'No,' said Theodore. 'I don't think that's a very good idea. Let her go on the freighter.'

'Not together?' said Loukides. 'I see. Fair enough.'

'But they won't even get back together,' Isaac cried out, and saw that he had underestimated Theodore yet again.

'No they won't,' said Theodore. 'Because the Clio run takes approximately six months longer, doesn't it, Isaac, and the chances of one surviving to meet the other are remote, to say the least of it. Or so I gathered, from what you said,' he remarked to Eleanor with an apologetic lift of the eyebrow.

Casimir's head was in the way and she didn't see. Casimir was grinning, very close; too close. She brought up her hands smartly and her wrist, in its heavy steel bracelet, caught him under the chin. Isaac watched in stunned admiration.

I would never have thought of that.

Casimir had not thought of it either. As he dropped, Gregor closed in eagerly, but she clobbered him over the head with her crossed hands and he fell, felling Loukides as he went.

Eleanor ran. The door was shut, the loggia was open. She ran for the stone, swarming up the side of it by a route she must have plotted in that frozen second after Theodore said 'No'. The Deportation Squad, the remains of the Deportation Squad, started after her as they saw her hesitate half-way up. She had come upon the hammer that she had left there the day before. As the first man reached the foot of the stone, she turned and hurled it downward. It missed its target and scattered the others, impacting into the marble tiles and skidding away among splinters. Then she was gone, over the wall, and the Squad followed in disarray.

'Very foolish,' said Theodore, stepping over Casimir and ignoring Loukides' efforts to rise. 'What can she gain from this? I told her no one went willing when the time came.'

'She was willing. She was willing,' Isaac yelled at his indifferent back. 'Don't you know what you've done?'

'What I've done? She did it herself. Why should she expect any favours from me?' said Theodore. He opened the front door and went through, into the road. 'Now, what on Earth is all this?'

Isaac followed him, not knowing what he would see and prepared for a repetition of his last view from the porch. The quarry, however, had vanished; the hunters were dispersed about the hillside and the road, searching blindly in the furious dust. Sean followed his squint, wildly off course.

'She'll get away,' said Isaac.

'You'd like that, wouldn't you?' said Theodore. 'Consider it; if they don't get her before she leaves the town she'll go into the hills. She has no money, no food, no coat – and in this weather. She's handcuffed. How long do you think she'll last, assuming that she doesn't break her back in the next ten minutes?' He paused and pointed towards the church. 'But she won't get away, not now.'

She had climbed onto the flat roof of the police station, and from there jumped the intervening gap between it and the church which had a defensive parapet all round it. A cry echoed across the valley and the township, from one end of Epsilon to the other.

'LOOK!'

'What does she think she's doing up there?' Theodore murmured, as if the whole business had been set up to help him pass a dull morning.

Eleanor stood up, on the parapet, and raised her

manacled hands above her head, shouting, 'Look! Look at me! Look!'

In every house on the hillside the sleepy inhabitants, masters and servants, came to their doors and windows and gazed at the maniac on the roof.

'This is what is done in your name in the dark. Look at me. Look!'

'Does she really think they don't know?' said Theodore. 'Deportations are carried out in secret for the sake of the prisoner, not the populace. Now we shall see a holiday.'

Isaac stood at his side and watched the people of Epsilon making up their blunted minds. Then they began to move, and Eleanor, from her vantage point, saw her error. Her call for humanity had brought the whole town out against her, and while six would have beaten her up, three hundred would tear her apart.

'They do hate an outsider,' said Theodore.

Gregor came out of the porch, unsteady but determined to do his duty, and made his way down towards the police station where the Squad was regrouping. Above them, Eleanor crouched on the parapet of the church, waiting for them to make a move, and always watching the hillside where the submerged citizens were coming to the surface: people she had never seen or known, people Isaac had never seen or known, except as stupefied faces in church, rallying to a common victim.

One of the faces split open in an overwrought squawk and as if at a signal, someone threw a rock. It was a long shot but it struck Eleanor on the shoulder and sent her sprawling backwards, onto the roof, which was obscured by the dust that boiled up as the Squad spread out round the church. When the haze cleared the roof was empty. Isaac guessed that she had jumped and feared that she had fallen, until a helpful observer pointing and hullooing on Cameron's top terrace put him right again. She was running once more, driven uphill by a salvo of stones from the creeping figures that turned after her, gathering speed as she scrambled across the flinty track to the da Vincis' house, and was lost among the boulders that broke the skyline.

The houses below were emptied as the whole population drained unnaturally upwards, armed with a variety of unlikely weapons; shovels, rakes, brooms, fencing posts. Isaac recognized Sachiko's huge bobbing head, barbed with loose hairpins, and saw the meat knife that she carried.

'Theodore, stop it,' he said. 'You can't allow it.'

'I can't stop it,' said Theodore. 'She would have it she knew best. Now she knows everything.'

'Now I know everything,' said Isaac.

'It's about time,' said Theodore. He nodded humorously at Isaac and went indoors. Isaac did not move. Cheerful hoots and ululations drifted towards him over the roof, mixed with a deep-chested baying that did not sound like people.

They are going to kill her. *They are going to kill her.*

If she kept running in that direction she would be driven into the unsheltering desert, but someone in fear of her life, with any wits at all remaining, might find her way among the rocks, might lose her pursuers, might cut back across the hill behind the house, down the sheer slope on the other side, to the railway.

Isaac began to run too. There was no one to see him as he took the lower road, past the police station, past Ansell's mural. The train was waiting for him, fuelled and ready. He uncoupled the two rear trucks, started the motor and drove out a little way, until he had a clear view of the town spread upon its hill; and anyone running down that hill had a clear view of him.

247

There he sat, waiting, watching the rampart of boulders where she would surely appear; if she were still running. The sounds of the hunt were carried away from him by the wind, and he had no means of telling what was happening out of sight. His own home lay palely peaceful in a ray of light that slid between the clouds. Theodore was probably there now, waiting for him to come and get the breakfast. How long could it be before he realized that whoever got the breakfast in future, it wouldn't be Isaac.

When she came, it was from the other direction on the hill path, the narrow gully that ran headlong down, and she came headlong down it, not running but rolling, over and over and over.

Either she had lost her footing or she had decided that it was the fastest way to the bottom, for he could hear close footsteps behind. He dared not leave the train but stood up and called.

'Eleanor! ELEANOR!'

She heard him, saw him, picked herself up and began to run the last hundred metres to the waiting truck. As she drew alongside him the pursuers burst out of the culvert and seeing the two stationary trucks failed to notice, in the thrill of the chase, that the operative one was not attached to them. Isaac released the brake and as the train began to roll, he reached over the side, caught her by the chain between the handcuffs and pulled her up. She fell to the bottom of the truck and had nothing to say, for once.

Isaac looked back. The hunting party had left off whanging the sides of the abandoned trucks with their staves and started to come after him. Black uniforms were beginning to show among the civilian clothes and the men in them were soon ahead of the others. Isaac could make out Gregor's face very plainly, but although the train was not fast, it was still moving faster than any of them could run. He took time to wave as the truck clattered sedately round the curve and into the hills.

'I think we have an hour before they come after us,' he said. 'I don't know what we can do in an hour.' There was no answer. He left the train to pilot itself, since his intervention was a mere formality, and slid down into the truck. Eleanor's eyes opened stickily. Her head was bleeding and there were streaks as red as clay on her face and down the front of her shirt.

'You would fall,' he said irritably.

'I couldn't help it.' Her voice had gone and he had to lean very close to hear what she said. 'Are we going to the terminal?'

'No. What good would that do?'

'I thought perhaps ... the oil tanker.'

'That's the first place they'd think of.'

'Delta?'

'That's the second. Anyway, Delta's no good to us now. I said I knew the schedules by heart. There's an Intergalactic carrier due in at Epsilon within an hour. Cameron will commandeer it and they'll follow us. This isn't an escape, Eleanor. I've gained you an extra hour, that's all. No more.'

'Why?'

'He told me not to be a golem.'

She answered in a voice as wretched as his, 'Is this your idea of not being a golem?'

'There was nothing else I could do, but stand and watch. That would have been as bad as joining in.'

'I'm glad I'm still of some use to you, even in this state.' She seemed to grow stronger with anger.

'Still of use?'

'As a way of easing your conscience.'

249

'You were never of use.'

'I was meant to be.'

'No.'

'Yes. Sure you'd have felt bad if I'd been torn to pieces before your very eyes, but if it had happened out of sight, while you were in bed, you'd have turned over and gone to sleep again. I didn't turn out to be what you expected, did I? So you let me go to the devil.'

'No.'

'The trouble is, I didn't go alone.'

That silenced them both. Isaac stood and leaned on the edge of the truck, watching the mountains slide by. After a little while, they began to look at each other again. Eleanor held up her hands.

'I suppose you can't do anything about this?'

'I'm sorry,' said Isaac. 'There was a tool kit in the rear truck. We know what's happened to that.'

'Only,' said Eleanor, 'I don't think I can sit here for an hour and wait to be caught. Can't I get out and walk?'

'Walk? Walk where?'

'Anywhere. It would take them longer to find me.'

The mountains were strangers to him. He could give her no directions and to let her make her own way would be no kindness. He put on the brake, surprised to find that it could be done gently.

'Can you get out by yourself?' He had to steady her, half lift her, take her weight until her feet touched the ground. She sat down by the track and looked up at him.

'Off you go, back to your mates.'

Isaac started the engine again, opened the throttle and jumped clear. The truck took itself away into the shadows. They could hear it fumbling over the tracks long after it was out of sight.

'They may follow it,' said Isaac. 'We'd better be moving.'

'You're coming with me?'

'I can't go back,' he said. 'I'm a criminal now. Everyone saw what I did, I can't go back.' The enormity of his action dawned on him. 'I've given up everything.'

'You hadn't much to give up.'

'I had a living.'

'That was living?'

'You may not have thought so,' said Isaac. 'But it was all I knew. From what I remember, we're about ten kilometres from the old Gamma mine. Could you get that far?'

'I don't know. What's at Gamma?'

'Nothing, probably. It was one of the first to close down. But who knows, there may be another Mr Peasmarsh hanging out, nearby.'

'And maybe not,' said Eleanor. 'Help me up.'

'I'm sorry about your hands,' he said.

'I might strangle you if I had the use of them,' said Eleanor. 'Which way do we go?'

'I don't think it matters,' said Isaac. 'We may as well go straight ahead. It will mean a long climb, but when we get to the top of the canyon we'll be able to see where we are.'

They walked very slowly across the rocks, away from the tracks. The cliff face came closer, darker.

Eleanor, already out of breath, began to slip and stagger at the smallest obstacle.

'Sit,' said Isaac. 'You'll never get up there like this. Rest.'

'It's cold,' said Eleanor.

'I should have brought my cloak,' he said. 'I didn't stop to think of that. I just ran for the train.'

Eleanor leaned against a boulder and looked back along the track. 'You called me a street fighter. I only fought to get away. I'm always running from something. I only wanted to work. I knew I was good. I might have been so nice, too . . .'

Beware of the cold, thought Isaac. 'Not you,' he said, rudely. 'You could never have been nice, under any circumstances.'

'I wish I could have seen him once more, to say good-bye. Last night I didn't know. I thought . . . I thought . . .'

'He's better off without us,' said Isaac. He intended to sting, but he suspected that he was probably right.

'He's alone.'

'He isn't alone,' said Isaac. 'He has something with him, always. He knows who he is.'

'He told me.'

'He told us all. To your tents, O Israel. Isn't that a country? An Old Country?'

'A people.'

'That's it. People,' cried Isaac. 'Wherever he goes, millions of people. Right back to the first man who ever lived. We never had that.'

He saw that he had warmed her, if only with a memory. She rose stiffly, and looked towards the top of the cliff.

'Moshe's people,' she said. 'Now there's a story. He told me. I'll tell you, if you like, as we go up.'

Isaac's chest was hurting.

'I don't think I could hear it.'

'If I can tell it, you can listen. We can both cry for him. I'm sure he cried for us.'

'He did,' said Isaac.

They began to climb.

Jan Mark comes from a London family, although she was born and spent her first ten days in Welwyn Garden City where the City of London Maternity hospital was evacuated during the Second World War. She was educated at Ashford Grammar School and Canterbury College of Art. She began writing at an early age, winning second prize in a *Daily Mirror* short story competition at fifteen, and while teaching art at Gravesend she wrote plays – 'comedies with lots of fights'.

She now lives with her husband and two children in the Norfolk village of Ingham. Since their home is on the flight path of an RAF air base, she has become accustomed to aircraft spotting and this subject formed the background to her first book, *Thunder and Lightnings*, which won the Penguin/*Guardian* Award for an outstanding first novel. (It is now published in Puffins). It was subsequently awarded the Library Association's 1976 Carnegie Medal, and was runner-up for the *Guardian* Award for Children's Fiction.

Under the Autumn Garden, *Hairs in the Palm of the Hand* and *Nothing to be Afraid Of* are also available in Puffins.

More Puffins for Older Readers

MISCHLING, SECOND DEGREE
Ilse Koehn

Ilse was a 'Mischling', a child of mixed race, a dangerous birthright in Nazi Germany. The perils of an outsider in the Hitler Youth and in military girls' camps make this a vivid and fascinating true story.

SURVIVAL
Russell Evans

The high tension adventure of a Russian political prisoner on the run in the midst of an Arctic winter.

THE WONDERFUL STORY OF HENRY SUGAR AND SIX MORE
Roald Dahl

Often macabre, always unexpected, this dazzling selection contains the true story of how Roald Dahl himself became a writer.

ONE MORE RIVER
Lynne Reid Banks

The conflict of personal and political loyalties explored through the friendship of a Jewish girl with an Arab boy.

THE TWELFTH DAY OF JULY
ACROSS THE BARRICADES
INTO EXILE
A PROPER PLACE
HOSTAGES TO FORTUNE
Joan Lingard

A series of novels about modern Belfast which highlight the problems there, in the story of Protestant Sadie and Catholic Kevin which even an 'escape' to England fails to solve.

THE KING OF THE BARBAREENS
Janet Hitchman

The true story of an orphan, a plain, intelligent girl who is passed from one foster-home to another. She longs for love but ruins her chances by her defiant attitude.

THE HOUSE ON THE BRINK
John Gordon

An eerie story which shows the author's ability both to portray delicate relationships and also to evoke a chilling sense of the unknown.

THE ENDLESS STEPPE
Esther Hautzig

The exile of a young child and her family to Siberia, and their subsequent life there. A magnificent and moving book which will long live in the memory of any reader.